UP THE RIVER

UP THE RIVER

and

82 Short Stories

WAYNE PAGE

MILL CITY PRESS

Mill City Press, Inc.
2301 Lucien Way #415
Maitland, FL 32751
407.339.4217
www.millcitypress.net

Paperback ISBN-13: 978-1-6628-3796-8
Hard Cover ISBN-13: 978-1-6628-3797-5

ALSO BY WAYNE PAGE

NOVEL
Barnstorm – A Novel

NOVELLA
Up the River

SCREENPLAYS
Barnstorm
The Ghosts of Serpent Mound
Up the River
Lady
Cabin Fever
Stuck

MUSICALS
The Woodsman and His Backpack
Bury Old Man Gruff

TEN-MINUTE DRAMAS
Stuck
Woody

FOREWORD

Retired 2011. Final lifetime move—really?—to Cincinnati. To maintain marital sanity and keep me busy, I took pen in hand, or more correctly, fired up my laptop. After cranking out *Barnstorm A Novel* and adapting it into the *Barnstorm* screenplay, which earned quarter-finalist status in the 2018 Los Angeles International Screenplay Awards, I focused on four more screenplays. My novella, *Up the River* snagged quarter-finalist placement in The ScreenCraft 2017 Cinematic Short Story Contest. Ah shucks, might as well adapt it to a screenplay: *Up the River* then earned quarter-finalist in The 2018 Los Angeles International Screenplay Awards, out of 2,500 entries. In 2021, my *Lady* script earned quarter-finalist status in The Atlanta Screenplay Awards, out of 1,000 entries. Enough about screenplays.

I was introduced to the short story genre by Barry Raut and George Weber; excellent facilitators and mentors in their University of Cincinnati OLLI creative writing classes. We were all super-challenged when introduced to "flash" stories— shorter than short—no more than 300 words. Each word had to matter. I enjoy leading UC OLLI creative writing classes— *Curing the Blank Page*—and appreciate the input and support of fellow writers.

In 2016, I was fortunate to participate in the University of Cincinnati CCM inaugural Playwrights Conference. Thirteen writer participants "workshopped" 10-Minute Plays with a talented cast of CCM Acting students (most were headed for Broadway and/or Hollywood). We spent a week "creating, honing, editing, refining, and sweating" our dramas. I workshopped *Stuck*. It was a thrill working with CCM talent and fellow writers: culminating in a production Showcase of our creations. *Stuck* is included in this collection you now hold in your hands.

To this day, I still subject my stories to the valued input and tender critique of fellow writers in a challenging writing group: *Legendary Writers*. Hats off to founder Harriet, and Vicky, Carol, Jan, Juris, and Dan. Every story in this anthology has been through their eagle eyes. If you think you've found a grammatical error, nope. As the group says about my fragments and choppy sentences: "That's just Wayne." However, I've yet to use a semi-colon correctly.

And finally, thanks to my family that has endured life with me and provided much of the fodder for the stories in the last section: Non-Fiction (True). This anthology would not be possible without my spouse of 51 years and lifelong best friend, Laura, and daughters Miranda and Allison.

Wayne Page

PURE FICTION

AGAIN?

Note: This story was inspired by a prompt based on Norman Rockwell's painting "Shiner" or "Outside the Principal's Office."

* * *

The admitting doctor was clear and concise.
"Yes, Mrs. Baker, his nose is broken." Clipboard cocked against his hip, Doc Smith waited patiently for a chance to get a word in edgewise. As his livelihood did require a keen sense of hearing, he held the iPhone a good six inches from his ear. The stethoscope was bought and paid for, might as well use it again someday.

"I haven't looked at the X-rays yet, ma'am. An arm hanging like that from the shoulder, generally isn't a good sign." Tapping his foot, he once again gave Mrs. Baker an opportunity to blow off some steam.

"Yes, we did check his testicles. The swelling should subside in a day or two. I wouldn't worry too much about that." That last medical opinion was probably communicated a bit prematurely. Young doctors sometimes learn the hard way. The practice of medicine does involve some practice.

"Mrs. Baker, let's wait for the swelling to go down. I'm frankly more concerned about the ruptured spleen. Pardon me? No, I don't make attorney recommendations. You might want to confirm all the facts with Principal Gardner before you decide to sue Mayor Jenkins."

Every ear within fifty feet of the ER heard Mrs. Baker's hang-up "click" thunder from Doc Smith's cell phone.

"That went well," he muttered as he returned to the ER.

Mrs. Baker wasn't done burning up the phone lines. The school secretary interrupted school principal Gardner with the news that Mrs. Baker was on the phone.

"Thanks, Martha," Principal Gardner offered as he wiped his brow. "Tell her I'll be right there."

As Sally Brown, the sixth-grade teacher was still at his elbow, Mr. Gardner didn't cast his usual eye toward Martha's dancing hams as she porked her way from his office.

"Are you sure that's the way it happened, Miss Brown?"

"Pretty much, sir," Miss Brown tried to choke back a grin.

"She kicked him, there? Crunch!" Mr. Gardner flicked a finger toward an eye that offered a sympathetic tear toward his own manhood.

"Had a self-defense class at my college sorority, sir. Wanna take a guy down fast. Go for the..."

"I get the picture Miss Brown. That will be all. I better get to Mrs. Baker."

As teacher Brown exited Principal Gardner's office, she coughed that fake cough one coughs when one tries to avoid something with a nervous, fake cough. Eye contact with the bleeding urchin seated on the hallway bench would be a fatal mistake. Miss Brown closed the Principal's door behind her and scurried off to her classroom.

Mr. Gardner straightened his tie, stiffened his spine, and cleared his throat. His hand quivered, only slightly, as he raised the telephone to his ear. "Principal Gardner," he started. "Are you at the hospital, Mrs. Baker?"

He listened to the expected harangue, and finally interrupted, "Well, let's start with the obvious. Gonna pinch a little girl on the tuchus? Pick someone other than Emily Jenkins. Secondly, please tell Coach Baker that he's suspended, pending probable dismissal by the School Board. Good day, Mrs. Baker."

Principal Gardner opened his hallway door, restrained a needful chuckle, and looked at the triumphant future President of the United States seated on the hallway bench. "Miss Jenkins, let's have a little talk."

* * *

THE LAST LAUGH

Robert Temple knew everyone in Charles County by their first name—he could whip off the middle name of most. As the funeral director in a small farming community, he knew all the secrets. Grieving families found comfort in knowing their final journey from this life would be in trusted hands with the Temple family.

Robert turned in the tree-lined lane leading to the Grayson spread with a heavy heart. Best friend Jake neared the end of his month-long homebound hospice ordeal. Procrastinator Jake had settled on his final arrangements and wanted to confirm that Robert would make good on every detail.

Minister, organist, soloist, scripture—all the usual—agreed. Most expensive solid steel casket surprised Robert a bit, but the Graysons could afford it, having scored millions from the family asphalt and concrete business.

Five of the pallbearers were as expected. High school skinny dippin' buddies, hooligan land-rich farmers all, each with a long history of practical jokes and streakin' escapades that would make a mule blush. The sixth nominee shocked Robert.

"Frank Wilson? You can't stand Wilson."

A weakened Jake implored, "I want Frank Wilson as a pallbearer."

"That curmudgeon has been a thorn in your side ever since he became a County Commissioner," Robert overemphasized the obvious.

"Let's call it making amends. Entire county will see I've taken the high road."

"Anything else?" Robert asked.

The dying Jake motioned for Robert to lean in closer and whispered one last instruction.

Suppressing a smile that resulted in a twisted grin, Robert whispered back, "You are an asshole, you know."

Jake enjoyed a belly laugh that initiated a coughing frenzy that almost did him in.

The funeral hit all the right chords. As the organist concluded with *Just A Closer Walk With Thee*, Robert whispered a final goodbye to his best friend and closed the casket lid. Six pallbearers struggled with their burden of an extra 400 pounds of poured concrete from the Grayson Construction Company. The five buddies were in on the prank. Frank Wilson sweat bullets and cursed under his breath.

Robert grinned and murmured, "He who laughs last, laughs best."

* * *

JB's Wool Scarf

Pickett's Charge was a one-year memory. Soldiers wrote "death letters" to loved ones in advance of important battles. Sarah Benton received her husband's blood-soaked last words from Gettysburg two months before Lincoln's prayerful address. Josiah Benton's words to his wife and teenage son might not have been as eloquent as Lincoln's, but Sarah treasured her husband's grammar errors. She struggled as she read a father's lament to a son who would be forced to grow up before his time.

Lieutenant Benton answered the Union call in 1861 and wrote to Sarah weekly, until that fateful July 3, 1863. His Pennsylvania Company B held the Union line that repelled Pickett's Rebels. JB, as known to his hometown troops, was cut down by a Confederate sniper.

Her hand shook as she read JB's letter to son Jacob. She knew in her heart how "Little JB" would react—no seventeen-year-old young man liked being called "Little JB"—but she knew her wishes would not prevail. Sarah began knitting the blue wool scarf the day Jacob started target practice at Confederate squirrels in the woods behind the barn.

Sarah dropped the "Little" and Jacob became JB as the wool scarf lengthened. JB knew his mother objected to his enlistment, but he knew she understood. The bond between father and son was stronger even than Lincoln's call to action. Shared words were few as mother and son went about their preparations. Words couldn't express what love and respect conveyed.

Horse saddled, fall leaves scattered from the apple orchard, JB was ready. Sarah was not. A mother's love for an only son sealed her breaking heart as she draped the completed blue-wool scarf around her son's neck. She tousled his coal-black hair. JB dabbed his mother's tears with the JB initials embedded in a scarf he vowed to always wear.

Sarah didn't watch JB gallop out of view; she didn't want her last image to be that of departure. With closed eyes, she begged to remember the warm touch of wool against her cheek. Letters were few, but young JB did write that he received medical training as a medic. Sarah found comfort in his role that healed rather than one that shouldered a carbine.

Sarah's stomach knotted at the thought of a medic rushing to the front lines. The months without a JB letter seemed an eternity. At least her husband's blood letter remained the only "death letter" she suffered. She lost herself in the fall harvest. Neighbors lent extra hands and mules. Sarah was not alone in her grief and concern about her absent son. Pennsylvania welcomed many a coffin and one-legged farm boy back from a war that had no end. Sarah read her Bible and rocked near the window overlooking the apple orchard.

It was a Tuesday afternoon when a dozen too many Old Testament begats lured Sarah into a much-needed nap. Her rocker stopped. The afternoon sun arched across the sky, warming her shoulder. Sarah jerked awake as the Bible slipped off her lap onto the floor. She leaned forward and thumbed to the New Testament; maybe The Beatitudes would be a welcomed respite from Old Testament blood and guts. Blessed are the peacemakers.

Comforted, she gazed through lace curtains to the orchard. Her pulse quickened. She saw him. Tattered and bedraggled, he stood balanced, one foot on the split-rail fence to reach an over-ripe forgotten apple. Tears pooled as she saw his wounded left arm nestled in a sling, a blue wool scarf sling with blood-stained JB initials in shreds.

His uniform was soiled and torn beyond recognition, looking as though he had wallowed through a newly plowed field. He sat and devoured the rotting apple. As his half-starved body rejected the vinegary fruit, he lurched forward in a dry heave, losing his cap. The afternoon sun glistened on his oiled red hair.

Red hair? On further examination, Sarah realized the dried mud was masking a grey uniform. Johnny Reb was in her orchard, a Confederate soldier with JB's bloodied wool scarf.

Sarah gasped as the young enemy limped toward her front porch. The Bible crashed to the floor, begats be damned, as she rushed to retrieve the rifle from above the mantle. She closed the distance to the front door with focused determination. With her marksmanship, she could dispatch this killer of her beloved "Little JB" with her eyes closed.

The front door flung open so fast that Johnny Reb stumbled off the porch step onto his backside as his one good arm reached skyward.

"Don't shoot," he cried.

Blessed are the peacemakers; for they shall be called the children of God.

Damn. Why couldn't the last Bible verse she'd read involve some deserved massacre of Philistines? Sarah had a child of God in her sights. A child. This red-headed Johnny Reb was barely fifteen-years-old. She lowered the rifle; *I can't do to another mother what this ugly war has done to me.*

Sarah collapsed on her front porch step and sobbed. Old tears for her Pickett's Charge hero husband. New tears for her "Little JB".

Johnny Reb summoned his courage as he scooted closer to Sarah. He reached in his pocket, retrieving a letter that he stretched to offer this grieving woman who still had a rifle at her side.

Sarah accepted a soiled envelope that had a rudimentary map to her farm scrawled on the back.

"What's this?" she whispered.

"It's from your son, JB."

"Oh, no!" Sarah wailed. "Another death letter," as she crushed it in her hands.

Johnny Reb was emphatic as he knelt, "No, no! He's coming home."

"How did you get that scarf?" Sarah demanded.

"Your son saved my life."

Wincing in pain, Johnny Reb freed the sling loop from around his neck. Sarah rose and readjusted the sling. She retreated to the porch step and opened a joyful letter from her son.

Blessed are the peacemakers; for they shall be called the children of God.

* * *

THE FORGETFUL PRIEST

To say that Father Murphy was "old" doesn't do that word justice. This fossil of a shriveled shell of a man was born old. Birth wrinkles in his lush baby face never faded. They merely dried into creases of knowledge that foretold his eighty-plus years. Marketers of Dead Sea skin care products paid him royalties to use his face in the "before" photos popular in TV infomercials. Every time he approached life's finish line, he pulled through. Kept circling the drain, so to speak.

Father Murphy had been semi-retired longer than any local parishioner could remember. In the Chester Heights community of Philadelphia, he was revered and loved for the one assignment he was permitted to continue – hearing confessions. It was widely acknowledged that Father Murphy had a terrible memory. When asked to reminisce, he usually forgot the question before he could form an answer. Things remembered from yesterday were few. This made him Chester Heights' most sought-after confession priest. More popular than the free-giveaway Godiva Chocolatier at a compulsive eater's convention. The most heinous sins received a few Hail Marys and Our Fathers and be forever forgotten. One hundred percent confidentiality.

Fourteen-year-old Bobby Flannigan took notice. He observed the steady stream of frustrated housewives, ashamed teenage girls, and repentant hookers lined up outside Father Murphy's confessional. One of the few unmolested altar boys in Philadelphia, he was tired of virginity. He thought about it day and night. He could almost hear his eager sexual organ whimper,

"Come on coach, put me in." The unlit wick of his Yankee candle longed for action.

That's when his plan blossomed. He had a robust collection of videos he had taken with his GoPro. His tiny, hi-tech camera had perched astride his ski helmet on Utah's best North Face black diamonds, balanced atop his Nikes up the Rocky steps at the Philadelphia Art Museum, and spied on Francine, the pretty waitress at the Bourbon Street Grill. His GoPro was now nestled in an upper corner of Father Murphy's confessional.

It only took a week. It came to pass that the pretty waitress Francine was married. And a confessed nymphomaniac. She was so ashamed. And so susceptible to extortion. Bobby Flannigan was ecstatic. Bobby Flannigan discovered the cure for virginity.

* * *

THE EULOGY

E ulogies are nothing new to me. When asked to say a few words about my neighbor, Farmer Smith, I was gracious in my acceptance. We had been inseparable forever and I had more than enough anecdotes to pepper and enliven my remarks.

The small country church, filled to the rafters, fell in rapt silence as I exited my pew and walked to the pulpit. I pulled a few note cards from my breast pocket and surveyed the room of lifelong friends. Then it struck me, while I had given many eulogies, this was my first with an open casket.

Previous successes had been closed caskets, memorial services, or cremation urns nestled amongst Easter lilies. From my lofty pulpit perch, when I looked at my notes I could see Brother Smith, peeking at me through his cheap, drugstore glasses. Why morticians perch glasses atop a corpse's nose bridge escapes me, but that's a story for another day.

To cut to the chase, I got flustered. I may have failed to mention a critical detail that further explains my sudden bout of stage fright: Farmer Smith was my identical twin brother. Sorry about that oversight. As twins are wont to do, my brother and I often dressed exactly alike, without consultation. Today was no exception, gray flannel slacks, white starched shirt, blue wool blazer and tightly-knotted red bow ties.

Previous public speaking coaching kicked in as I walked it off; I paced back-and-forth behind the rostrum until my nerves settled. Thinking I had gathered myself, I once again referred to my notes. All I saw was those damned drugstore glasses. I took one step to my right and caught my toe under a loose seam in the old church's carpet. Olympic gymnastics judges would have awarded my twisting, acrobatic flip a perfect ten, with a few landing deductions as I flopped face-down into my brother's coffin.

The balance of this miserable tale is a blend of personal recollection with dashes of first-hand witness commentary. The force of my landing atop the main event caused the casket lid to slam closed. I heard the latches lock tight as it all went dark. I heard only muffled sounds. I grew faint from the lack of oxygen and overwhelmed at the smell of dime-store makeup and formaldehyde.

I kicked and rocked back-and-forth, causing the casket to tumble from its wheelie bier. As the casket hit the floor, the lid flopped open, rolling Farmer Smith and me toward the first pew, just as the paramedics arrived.

The last thing I remember before passing out was the EMS team splitting into two groups: one attacked me, the other started working on my brother. Fat women fainted. Slender women squealed. Curvaceous proportioned women squealed and then fainted. Everyone became a supervisor: yelling instructions, tugging, pulling. It was mayhem.

"You're working on the wrong Smith!"

"This one's turning pale!"

"This one's cold and gray!"

"I knew we should have cremated him!"

"CLEAR!"

"Who said that?" I heard myself murmur. *Oh God, they're trying to revive my brother*, I thought, through a brain foggier than a cemetery movie set on Halloween.

"Stand back... CLEAR!"

I must have passed out; that's the last I remember from the church scene.

Later that evening I awoke in my hospital bed. A nurse was taking my blood pressure. She rubbed my forehead and said, "Sir, looks like you're gonna make it, just fine."

Being a small country hospital with no private rooms, she motioned to my roommate who was tubed in ICU paraphernalia from head to toe, "Looks like your friend might not be so lucky."

My brother's drugstore glasses lay on the end table between our beds.

* * *

THE CELL PHONE CALL

The sliver of a new Afghanistan moon offered only a modest challenge to the billions of stars begging to touch the hot desert sand. Framed against the arid foothills thundered the silhouette of a 130J-Hercules turboprop with its precious cargo of two dozen Marines.

As two rows of paratroopers faced each other, each Marine escaped into his own private thoughts. Squad Leader Murphy and his crack team waited to be dropped into Taliban-infested territory. A red light turned to green. It was time. Murphy's unit rose as one, shuffled to the door. No words were needed: hand signals, looks of confidence and resolve were enough. Sgt. Murphy flashed a crooked little grin; this leader could be followed to hell and back.

The engine roar that conjured up memories of a Harley-Davidson rumble was replaced with the peaceful rush of wind as parachutes burst open. Sgt. Murphy's green, night-vision goggle view of Afghanistan faded into childhood memories of dare devil jumps from a swing lashed in the front-yard tree of his Ohio farm home. The little boy left the wooden swing seat at its peak. In slow motion, he flew through the air, cape fluttering behind him. He arched his back, nailed an Olympic ten-pointer as his sneakers hit lush, green grass in the shadow of the mighty oak. He shot a silly, crooked grin to his adoring parents.

Twenty-three other daydreams abruptly ended as boots hit rocky, Afghanistan soil. Sunrise over the devil foothills created long shadows as the newly inserted Marines met their Humvee rendezvous. Sgt. Murphy pounded each hood, assuring each Marine buddy with a thumbs up, and that crooked little grin.

Sunrise signaled the start of another routine day for an insignificant teenage Taliban recruit. His perch on the cliff overlooking the valley below provided the necessary vantage point to complete his cell phone call. Dirty, crusted fingers touched a keypad built in China. Software developed in the Silicon Valley encoded the communication to the IED hand-crafted in Iran that it was time for a Navy Chaplain to pay a visit to the parents of Sgt. Murphy in Ohio.

* * *

FINDERS KEEPERS

July was hot at the beach, so hot that swimsuit cover-ups disappeared. Bikini bottoms got smaller—kinda thong-like, if you get my drift—with top straps un-did. Jesse Joe Bob and me, bein' all of twelve-years-old and startin' to experience that magical tinglin' and stirin' in our nether region, would fill our water pistols with ice water. A well-placed squirt in the small of a nubile gal's back would produce a yelp and an ill-planned rollover, revealin' one of God's better creations.

I was what's known as a beach town "Sand Crab." A local, year-rounder who would see the tourists come-and-go. We'd clean the cottages, deliver the bike rentals. Realtors need an odd job performed? Call a Sand Crab. We got the crustacean nickname based on our scavenging of the beach. Tourists would lose watches, rings, money clips. Sand Crabs would find 'em, hock 'em, make some pocket change. Sheriff Foster would demand we turn over our loot to his office. The stuff was ours if nobody claimed it in 30 days.

Only one thing had been claimed the summer of 1998: a Rolex watch. I swore that I'd never turn anything valuable over to Sheriff Foster again. I was lollygaggin' on the beach after the July 4th weekend, nursing a chocolate double-dipper when I found it. An ivory-cream pearl ring. Then I saw Sheriff Foster comin' my way. My Speedo had no pockets, neither did my T-shirt. Bein' 'bove average in quick thinkin', I jammed the pearl ring an inch deep into my ice cream cone.

"How ya been, Jimmy?"

"Just fine, Sheriff," as I licked my cone.

17

"Find anything this weekend?"

"Nope," I lied as I licked. The sun was hotter than blazes.

"Ya wouldn't feed me a line, would ya, Jimmy?"

"Oh, no sir." I was sweating bullets. Catching a glance at my cone, I saw that my pearl treasure was making an appearance. I took a big bite of ice cream... and swallowed.

"Well, say hi to your folks," the unsuspecting constable said.

A fleeting stop by the pharmacy, Ex-Lax in hand, I rushed home. While I knew it would forever ruin spaghetti night, I scurried upstairs with Mom's colander sieve and swallowed six tablets. I regretted the half-dozen ears of sweet corn ravished for supper the previous night.

This too shall pass.

* * *

LOVE ON THE ROCKS

Traces of ozone remained from the previous night's electrical storm. Nestled securely in a crevice on an Appalachian Trail rock outcropping, the inseparable romantics had weathered another blast from Mother Nature. Soggy, yet refreshed by the morning sunrise over the Shenandoah Valley, another day gazing on God's splendor had dawned.

Stretching her arms toward the sun, Fern gave thanks for her full-time job gauging the perfect balance between oxygen and carbon dioxide. "Gonna be a glorious day, Douglas," she announced.

A little slower to shake off the night's dew, Doug agreed, "Scientists and botanists might be paid more than us, but we got a cool volunteer gig up here."

Looking up at Doug's taller stature, Fern had once been green with envy. She had learned to accept her role and let the breeze brush her gently against her companion's strength. "I do love you, Doug," she whispered.

"And I love you," Doug barked, as he reached for the sky.

* * *

COLD JUSTICE

"How is he doing today?" Father Whitaker asked the attending nurse.

"No change," came the cold, clinical response, as Nurse Foster fluffed a pillow and adjusted the wool blanket over the gray fingers that hadn't twitched in twenty-two months. Grace Foster had a routine and she barely glanced at her aged charge as she re-positioned tubes, noted gauges, and checked the hi-tech medical equipment that surrounded the hospital bed. "He never changes, no response." The ever-so professional nurse warmed a gentle smile toward the priest as she whispered, "It's so nice of you to visit every day."

"Lifelong friend of the family," Father Whitaker said, as he rose and placed a hand on the old man's forehead. "Roommates at Yale. Thought we would go to law school together. I had a change of heart," he paused at his choice of words. "Literally, my heart took me to divinity school."

"Well," Nurse Foster interjected, "the country's better off that he went to law school. Oh, nothing personal, you're a great priest, but, where would we be without...?" Her voice trailed off as the lump in her throat betrayed her feelings for the old man at her side. With a gentle touch, she adjusted an oxygen mask that needed no attention.

"Twenty-two months," Nurse Foster continued. "Comas are the worst."

"I know one that lasted ten years."

"Oh, dear God," she exclaimed. "Pardon my bluntness, but I'm askin' for an explanation of that when I get to the pearly gates."

"Nurse, you may be confused as to who will be asking the questions at heaven's gate."

With a bit of a stammer, her fumble of a verbal recovery was interrupted by a shared laugh. "You, you know what I mean."

"We all have questions. Doubts. I'm challenging celibacy. Ole Jake's stroke would have killed most anyone else. Yet, here he is. It'll be two years next January. Tell you what, if I get there before you, I'll ask St. Peter myself."

Nurse Foster patted Father Whitaker on the shoulder as she made her way to exit the hospice room. "Thanks for being here," she smiled. "Justice Baker knows you care. I do wonder, however, why that massive stroke didn't take him."

The Secret Service agent rose from his hallway chair as Nurse Foster opened the door and left. Father Whitaker confirmed that the door closed securely. He sighed as he surveyed the room. The constant whirl of the life support equipment created a haunting, eerie white noise, providing a rhythmic rise and fall of the Associate Justice's chest.

The good Padre eased his chair close to his old friend's bedside and prayed. He leaned forward and whispered, "I remember our pact." He looked around to confirm they were alone as he continued, "We won, Jake. A new President will nominate your replacement." He uncoupled one simple connection. He rested his head on the chest of his best friend and cried. He could no longer hear the electrically-induced heartbeat as he whimpered, "Goodbye, Jake." Father Whitaker heard a long, diminished exhale as a hand caressed his head.

Long live the Republic.

* * *

THE TRIAL OF BOBBY JOE HENRY

Note: Many writing groups use prompts, a suggested theme to jump-start the writing process. I think it's fun to include ALL of the prompts. This story is based on Elvis songs. Can you find them?

* * *

Bobby Joe Henry sat at the defendant's table in the Eastern Kentucky court house, head bowed as the jury door opened. His exposed red neck muting to a cinnamon-brown tan as it hadn't seen the sun since the judge denied him bail three months ago, he passed a smooth, jailhouse rock between his weathered hands. A previous prisoner had left the rock on his cramped cell windowsill. Denied smokes, Bobby Joe fingered the rock to dissipate nervous energy.

Blue Suede Shoemaker, Bobby Joe's flamboyant attorney, leaned to his client and whispered, "Sit up straight, show the jury some respect. If we get to a penalty phase, you're going to need one of these folks to like you."

Bobby Joe grunted as he raised his head and acknowledged the jury as they took their seats. His gaze turned to the window behind the jury box, half-clouded by the morning's gentle Kentucky rain. He mused, *where had he gone wrong? How had Peggy Sue discovered Mary Beth?* There had been no love letters. Even though he married Peggy Sue with honest intentions, he couldn't stop seeing Mary Beth. He had been discreet; at the county fair, Mary Beth was just another stranger in the crowd.

Paths might cross at Wal-Mart. A rendezvous at the next county's Hideaway Motel for a few hours seemed safe enough. Even the most suspicious minds couldn't connect his adulterous dots.

Or so he thought. As the judge took his seat and gaveled the courtroom to session, Bobby Joe reflected on the day that Mary Beth moved to Bobby Joe's neck of the woods, as the locals might say. He again bowed his head as he remembered thinking, *my wish came true.* Mary Beth's new job at their local Holiday Inn Express gave them easy undercover opportunities.

The Holiday Inn Express was just off the main highway, near the abandoned Vegas coal mine. Black coal dust still permeated everything, even though it had gone bankrupt in 2009. The nearby combination package store / fireworks emporium / watering hole sported a flickering neon sign that barely communicated *"Viva Las Vegas."* For some reason, all of the vowels had died, leaving an incoherent swagger of consonants: *"V v L s V g s."* The entire area, save the struggling Holiday Inn Express, looked depressed, like it belonged in the ghetto of Detroit.

Peggy Sue discovered the philandering with an accidental observation of geology. All the country roads around her neighborhood were gravel with a heavy slather of red clay. Bobby Joe's pick'em-up truck was never clean. Though pearl-white off the dealer's lot, the Ford F-150 became a constant burnt orange, except on those days when Bobby Joe lied about stoppin' in at the Dew Drop Inn for a beer. Peggy Sue surmised that he might be droppin' in somewhere, but he was leavin' somethin' behind other than dew. Three months ago, she figured out the difference between red-clay burnt orange and coal black. It didn't take long to stake out the Vegas coal mine district and find Bobby Joe's coal-dusted truck parked in front of room 107 at the Holiday Inn Express.

Turns out that Peggy Sue was a better detective than truck dodger as Bobby Joe ran her down and crushed her skull against the steel pole supporting the "V v L s V g s" neon sign. The vowels flickered for a moment but again expired, along with Peggy Sue.

Bobby Joe blinked, shook his head, and muttered, "What?"

"Stand up and face the judge," Blue Suede repeated.

Bobby Joe couldn't remember the jury foreman say *guilty*. The following week of penalty phase was all a blur. He did recall asking about the damage to his truck, but Blue Suede got that lack of sensitivity omitted from the record.

Bobby Joe and Blue Suede rose and faced the bench. The judge's words were chilling. "I sentence you to hang by the neck until dead. Ashes to ashes, dust to dust. Bobby Joe Henry, may God have mercy on your soul as you are returned to the earth, boy."

* * *

WORSE THAN GLOBAL WARMING

Global warming may be real, but there's another crisis to keep the world tossing and turning – or more correct – more tossing, less turning. Wobble here. Loss of gravity there. This is real. Yep. Global slowing.

The earth is wobbling off its axis. It's not fracking. The increase in earthquakes is caused by plate realignment. We are spinning less, more plate friction. More heat, ouch. Rotate on that one. Global slowing.

How, you ask? Wind turbines, that's how. Yeah, sure, you know all about the dead birds strewn about the bases of thousands of whirling wind towers. Horse feathers. And those moose antlers ripped off the heads of Canadian Bullwinkles; we'll pause for a second as reader tears are shed and dried.

The truth? The wind blows, the wind turbine wings/blades spin, and pressure is applied to the wind tower. Torque transmitted to the wind tower is transferred into a concrete base. Push. Push. The earth resists – pushes back. The rotation of the earth whimpers, slow, slower… multiplied by tens-of-thousands of worldwide wind turbines, this big blue marble we call home is screeching to a halt.

No political spin. Join the fight. Stop global slowing.

Support sarcasm.

* * *

CEMETERY HILL

It had been Jake's idea. Biggest train robbery of the 1870's. The loot buried in a shallow "non grave" in the southeast corner of Cemetery Hill marked with the headstone of Zeke Collier. They made up the name; held a fake funeral. Bought the cheapest pine box the local mortician offered. They said goodbye to their pretend-friend Zeke and didn't take a dime. Nothing. The plan was to lay low for five years and dig up ole Zeke under the darkened cover of a new crescent moon.

Jake died first. Poker game gone bad. Jake was known to cheat now and then. Mostly now. When the pot hit $400, his self-dealt draw to an inside straight was a bit much for the out-of-town stranger who held three queens. With a bullet in his chest, Jake's dying breath was misinterpreted as, "Bury me next to Zeke Collier." So, they did.

Bubba Hopkins died second. The town hanged Bubba – strung up for the attempted rape of schoolmarm Harriet Fingernut. An open and shut case. Picnic gone bad. It started out as an innocent Sunday afternoon picnic under an apple tree. Blanket. Wicker basket. Potato salad. Fried chicken. When Bubba reached for a thigh, Harriet took umbrage and kicked him where it hurt. The back of his hand was enough to snap the petite educator's neck. Bubba could have explained it all as an accidental fall were it not for young Jeremy Wilson's perch, high in the apple tree. Sex education, peeping-Tom style. The jury believed Pastor Wilson's son's story. Harriet recovered, but still has bad headaches.

And then there was one. He tossed and turned every night wondering whether to wait the full five years. The last partner couldn't decide whether to cash in early. Jake and Bubba were dead. Buried at Cemetery Hill. Zeke Collier wasn't six feet under. As the local mortician, Floyd Haskins was able to coordinate the two-foot shallow grave for Zeke. The actual robbery had been pulled off by Jake and Bubba. They had brought in Floyd as a silent partner, thinking that the mortician would keep his mouth shut. Use of Cemetery Hill as their temporary cash hiding place also seemed safe. Now it was just Floyd, the mortician.

Floyd held the final secret. He decided. Why wait? The next new moon and he would retire. Move to San Francisco and explore the new West.

Digging was more difficult than he had anticipated. Floyd always hired grave diggers. His usual job was to wear a dark suit, stand with his hands cupped, and nod assurances that everything would be fine. His public persona was one of reverence and comfort. After an hour of digging in the rock-hard dirt of Cemetery Hill, the pine box with no Zeke Collier in residence was finally reached. On hands and knees, an exhausted Floyd opened the coffin lid and beheld glory. Lifting the five sacks of cash graveside was easy.

The new crescent moon cast no shadows. Floyd's huffing and puffing muffled all but the rustle of the breeze through the nearby trees. He didn't hear it. He didn't see it. He probably didn't feel it when the shovel crushed his skull. Another ten minutes and Zeke Collier's headstone once again stood guard over a miss-marked grave.

The small-town gossip mill was torrid. Where were they? Three at once? Had they run off separately or together? The local school board started to interview for a new schoolmarm.

And Pastor Wilson prayed for the safe return of his son Jeremy. The saloon keeper assumed future burial needs as Floyd had also vamoosed.

* * *

CHEF DOM PIERRE

The key to Uncle Herbert's Vail ski chalet was precisely where he had instructed. Dusting the foot-high snow from the jumbo pine cone at the northeast corner of the stacked firewood was not as intimidating as originally thought. Having a rich, Wall Street uncle with estates in St. John, Tuscany, and Vail certainly had its advantages. The fact that he and Aunt Laura produced no cousins, while disappointing to some, had other long-term advantages not lost on lone nephew Peter.

Peter slid the key in the lock and presto, the ski-in, ski-out chalet opened its arms to greet the family of five. Three raucous teenagers plopped their luggage in a haphazard fumble of chaos as they explored the rambling five-bedroom, mountaintop retreat that would host their Christmas-week adventures.

Warming her hands at the already blazing, two-story stone fireplace, Peter's wife Suzanne said, "Nice touch. How'd Uncle Herb know when we'd arrive?"

"Probably his secretary," Peter guessed. "She manages all of his details."

"And all this is ours, yours someday?" Suzanne asked.

"I'm it," Peter beamed. "Only heir."

Their warm embrace was rudely interrupted as two rambunctious sons and an athletic daughter clamored down the rough-hewn stairway. Skis, poles, and boots clipped banister, lamps, and anything else in their path. "They fit!" Came the excited chorus.

"That's some secretary," Mom Suzanne admitted.

As dusk chased the Colorado Rockies' long shadows into the night, the travel-weary family retired early. The chalet's perch near Vail's Pepi's Face black diamond run assured an early start to tomorrow's skiing.

It wasn't a morning rooster's reveille. The sunrise through ice-crystalled windowpanes overlooking snow-laden aspens didn't waken anyone. The crackle from the ceiling-tall stone fireplace provided some sound, and warmth enough to disperse a morning blue haze in the peak of the vaulted ceiling. But not enough to stir the sleeping family. It was the coffee and hot chocolate. What was that cinnamon, vanilla smell wafting, ricocheting off the cathedral-beamed ceiling? Bacon was easy to identify. No real smell to hollandaise sauce.

Like a first Christmas, toddlers in sleep sacks and footed jammies, the entire family emerged, expecting to catch a glimpse of Santa's boots dangling from the fireplace. Instead, they found a bearded, white-aproned, rotund of a man sashaying around the kitchen like a Swan Lake ballerina teasing her pursuing cob. Meet Dom Pierre.

Eyeing the full breakfast spread already being destroyed by his famished teenagers, Peter inquired, "And, you are?"

"Mademoiselle, Monsieur, excusez-moi. I am your chef for the week. Dom Pierre."

"Uncle Herb thought of everything!" Susanne exclaimed.

"Our chef?" Peter asked.

"Oui, Monsieur."

"What's for dinner?" The youngest rudely asked.

"That's up to you, juene homme," Dom Pierre responded as he poached the last of the dozen eggs.

And so, it went. Breakfasts for kings. Dinners for queens. The ski slopes took the pounds off – Dom Pierre put them back on. It became clear that Uncle Herb's secretary's task was not that difficult. Arranging Dom Pierre resulted in great food, ski boots that fit, and blazing fires.

"How we gonna keep 'em down on the farm?" Susanne asked.

"Yeah, after they've met Dom Pierre," Peter agreed.

After dinner on the last night, the phone rang. It was Uncle Herb. Just a few questions and an assurance that the key would be returned to the pine cone near the wood pile.

"I'm glad you enjoyed it," the rich uncle said. "Next year, how about joining us in Tuscany?"

"Perfect," Peter answered. "I suppose you have an Italian chef too?"

"Only the best," Uncle Herb said, matter-of-factly.

"We've certainly appreciated Dom Pierre this week."

"Excuse me," came the puzzled reply.

"Your Vail Chef. Dom Pierre."

"He died three years ago," Uncle Herb said angrily, a hint of disgust in his voice.

"What?"

"I fired him. Poisoned my dog when I 'over-instructed' him on a soufflé recipe."

"Poisoned?" Peter gasped as the indigestion that would keep him up all night rumbled through his lower tract.

"Out of spite, hanged himself from the main crossbeam in the vaulted great room."

* * *

OAK CREEK

I t would be a good day at Oak Creek.

To call Oak Creek a halfway house is misleading as the residents had already accomplished ninety-five percent of their journey and promised release. Each woman had a specialty. Democracy, good humor, and mutual respect resulted in Margaret owning the kitchen. Frankly, Margaret was just a better cook than the others.

"Mary Alice, you handle the window treatments," they all agreed. "You've got the decorator's touch."

"I'll drive the old upright piano," Mrs. Jones volunteered.

The six ladies had come from similar backgrounds. They had all witnessed sickness, death, family turmoil, inner city strife, prison, and the worst that this life had conjured. Each had joys, triumphs, and moments when she touched the face of God.

Today was like any other day at Oak Creek. They rose at dawn – breakfast wasn't much, just coffee, toast or maybe a muffin, if Margaret had been baking. They read, sewed, laughed, and became more serious when they thought about their futures and freedom after Oak Creek.

Dinner would be the highlight; all that the day revealed would be shared. Tonight's dinner was a mixed blessing. Because Margaret had completed the last five percent of her journey earlier that morning and her release was complete, the smells from the kitchen were not quite up to par. Biscuits, just a bit flat.

The five ladies joined their weathered hands in thanks for their many blessings. Each hand told a different, but similar story of service to a family, a community, and many churches.

Widows all, they had followed their minister husbands through many moves and new adventures. While they understood that Margaret was still with them, they each prayed that they too would be blessed to walk that final five percent.

It had been a good day at Oak Creek.

* * *

HOPE SPRINGS ETERNAL

"Look how the morning dew..."

"Give it up, Bud," the realist of the bunch implored.

"I can dream, can't I?" Bud insisted.

"She's way out of your league."

"There, she's doin' it again. Swaying in the breeze. She looked at me. Me, directly at me. She's blushing, look how red she is. Man, I'd like to flower her with..."

"Come on, look around the park. Look at the competition. You think she singled you out?"

"You're yellow with jealousy. Oh, to be a butterfly. I'd flutter over and land on her..."

"Stay, man. You ain't fluttering' anywhere. Remember yourself. Why set yourself up for disappointment?"

"Disappointment? I'm already rooted in disappointment. Embedded in misery. Stuck next to you, all this bull shit, how much worse can it get?"

"What if? No, when... when she says no. Then what? Imagine the pain. Wilting in shame, falling to the ground, spent."

"Thanks for your vote of encouragement," Bud smirked.

"Take a baby step. Send her a message."

"A note, like an eighth-grader in study hall?" Bud scoffed.

"Sunday, Central Park. Here comes a skateboarder. How 'bout one of these hot shots on a bicycle? One close brush with them and the pollen would fly."

"But she's all the way over there," Bud lamented, bending a glance across the cinder pathway.

"Befriend a bird."

"Remember? I tried that last week. Hummingbird poked and tickled me 'til I sneezed."

Thus, the banter continued. Spring, summer, autumn. The first hint of frost triggered Central Park's landscape team to trim, prune, and dig up all the beds. Bud developed a plan; he would lay low and somehow cross the sidewalk, the path that separated him from his true love. He wasn't sure it would work, but he hoped, and prayed.

The bushel baskets were labeled. Worker shovels dug, bulbs were sorted, baskets filled. Bud leaned left, then right. He twisted and ducked. He eluded capture—his moment came—his buddies squeezed to provide one more space in his intended basket, Basket Yellow #17B. Bud seized the moment, surrendered to the spade, and landed atop Basket Yellow #17B.

Baskets were hoisted onto a flatbed truck for the short trip to the Central Park greenhouse. Basket Yellow #17B was nestled next to Basket Red #14C. Bud clung precariously to his lofty perch and waited for the pothole he had eyed all summer. The truck tire sank only an inch or two. Basket Yellow #17B jostled. Bud quivered, rolled, and bounced into the adjoining basket, Basket Red #14C. He would hibernate all winter, dreaming of the love of his life. Two lips would meet. Pollination would be so sweet.

Hope springs eternal.

* * *

GYPSY LADY

S he lived deep in an unkempt woods that none of my teenage buddies could describe. They pretended to know but lacked the cojones to round the last vine-ensnarled bend toward her shack. Older, high school wannabe men wouldn't share what they knew—or bragged knowing. Rumors abounded: fortune teller, wish granter, prostitute, woods nymph? Woods nymph was my favorite; cheaper than a hooker, wrapping wish granter and fortune teller into a perfect package.

I was thirteen, about to burst. The last weekend before my first day in the eighth grade. I had to know. Pocket full of summer lawn mowing cash tucked in my Levi's and too much of my older brother's English Leather splashed behind my ears, I hid my Schwinn behind a hickory tree halfway back Gypsy Lady's lane. Short breaths would be called rapid pants were I a dog. More than wadded up cash bulged in my Levi's. Oh, sweet anticipation. Sweat stung my eyes reminiscent of saltwater squirt gun battles. At the final trail bend, I parted the grape vines. Before me nestled a paint-neglected shack with a moss-covered shake roof that seemed alive in the full moon. A curl of smoke danced above a chimney. Calico tatters draped the mildewed windows, blocking all but a flicker of light from the shack.

I took a tentative step toward her cabin. Only four more steps and I'd have to summon the courage to knock on a door I had dreamt about for years. A twig snapped beneath my tentative sneaker, scattering goosebumps that begged to explode. There would be no courage summoned this night. No door knock. A dog barked, announcing my arrival. I pivoted; my foot tangled in ankle-deep creepy vines that sucked me to the ground like a boa constrictor caressing a rabbit. It was destiny; decisions were being made for me. The door creaked open. Chimney smoke, reinvigorated by the open-door draft, tumbled down the shack roof, masking my hostess as she balanced a coal-oil lamp and clutched the collar of her mutt companion.

In a full-fledged panic and fighting the vines that encircled my legs, I gazed at the woman in the doorway. Gold necklaces, midnight-black hair, ivory dangles from earlobes that failed to match, floor-length fabric twisted in an early evening breeze. A slight bend in the waist, she held the lamp to explore the shaken creature at her doorstep. My heart quickened as the lamp and moonlight shadows teased her welcoming cleavage. Was this happening? To me? Oh, please be a woods nymph.

As she straightened, retreating into her lair, she glanced over her shoulder and challenged, "Are you coming in, or not?"

Not sure if it was the loose porch board or my knocking knees that caused me to tumble into the shack, flat on my back. Introduced to a menagerie of stuffed crows, hawks, foxes, and other critters ready to pounce from the rafters; my brain added taxidermist to fortune teller, wish granter, prostitute, and woods nymph.

My hoped-for temptress knelt at my side, "You alright, lad?"

Nodding affirmative, now half-sitting and half-squatting on the rough-hewn floor, it was my budding manhood that was hurt. I wobbled to my feet as I surveyed the dim shack interior. Though eerie, taxidermy wasn't the most unique feature. Gypsy Lady must be a direct descendent of Jackson Pollock. Easels, canvasses in various stages of mind-bending confusion, and art supplies cluttered every nook, every cranny. The smell of paint and alcohol threatened to waft into the fireplace and consume Gypsy Lady's art studio.

Gypsy Lady straddled a kitchen chair like riding a mule, arms draped over the back. She surveyed the solitary one-room shack, as if to confirm we were alone, and asked, "What do you want?"

Still seated on the floor, I unbuckled my knees from my chin, straightened my shins from their fetal position and stammered, "I-I...'

"I-I... what?"

Gutless. Wimp. I'd come all this way only to be tongue-tied. I rocked. I swayed. *Oh, Lord, give me wings.*

"You couldn't fly, even if you had wings," she laughed.

Shocked, I looked up and stared deep into Gypsy Lady's eyes. "What?!"

"Fortune teller? Granter of wishes? Ha. I've heard them all. Tell all yer little friends to add mind reader to the list."

She rose and closed the short distance to me. Extending her hands, every bone-twisted finger bejeweled, Gypsy Lady pulled me to my feet. She dusted off my shoulders, cupped her hands around my cheeks and kissed me on the forehead.

I was speechless. Anything I thought worthy of expressing... I swallowed.

Gypsy Lady released my shoulders and purposed her way through her maze of easels and paint supplies. She selected a small canvas and wrapped it in brown craft paper. Secured by string, she placed the package in a bag. Handing me the gift, she smiled, "Dream of this, young man. Your every wish will be granted."

It was a painting of a chicken, laying an egg. Took me five more years to get laid. The chicken painting hangs on the wall in my rectory.

* * *

Prince Albert in a Can

I was twelve—the summer of '42—brave, fearless, and stupid. Best friend Ken Worthington was my equal in every way, except he really was stupid. *Hey, Ken, how deep is that quarry?* He'd dive in head first, return to the surface with stalactites of snot hanging from his nose with the answer. Loyal to a fault, ya had to be careful with idle ponderings or musings 'cause he'd squat over a land mine at the least provocation. This be the facts 'bout how two stupid kids got rich.

We ruled the roost in Possum Holler, South Carolina, not that there was much roost to rule. Back woods gnat of a crossroads that couldn't weasel a stop sign out of the County Commissioners. Ken and I fixed that oversight when we stole two stop signs from next county over and planted them in front of our Possum Holler General Store. Village got all proud and puff-chested until the sheriff started askin' questions. Seems a Fuller Brush drummer lost his rear bumper to an eighteen-wheeler at the newly-neglected intersection. Ken and I played dumb – came kinda natural to us. Kept our stop signs, and whenever that traveling salesman stopped at our little burg, we'd sneak up behind his car, jump on his rear bumper and make a noise like a semi-truck.

Ken and I bonded for life in that summer of '42. Hitler was causing mayhem in Europe which depleted the adult supervision in Possum Holler. Hell, guys only a few years older than me lied 'bout their age and joined up. Bein' the South and all, every able-bodied soul donned a uniform and left town. Ken and I had free rein that summer.

Yer probably thinkin' we rode our bikes all over the South Carolina country roads causin' our own mayhem. Mayhem? Yes. But wrong as frog lips 'bout the bikes. We fixed up a 1933 Ford pick-up truck and collected scrap iron and tires to support our boys overseas. In '42, the sheriff had better things to do than chase a couple of pre-teen hooligans drivin' without a license.

One hot July afternoon, it was my turn drivin' and I turned down old wider Soames dirt lane.

"Where da hell ya think yer goin'?" Ken screamed.

"Shut up."

"Gonna git us kilt," Ken insisted.

"She's been dead 15 years," I said with all the confidence of a coroner.

"Her ghost surely be alive," Ken shivered as he fought me for the steering wheel.

Truck ditched one bend shy of wider Soames shack, we argued 'bout the circumstances of her demise. Bein' a loner—recluse bein' the growed-up word—her dead body wasn't discovered 'til the month of August had roasted her near buzzard ripe. Rumor is the coroner took 'er out in pieces. Two or three sections per burlap bag. County seat mortician refused to take her, so the half-dozen or so burlap bags were dumped in a hole at the edge of the potter's section of the village cemetery.

"It's haunted," Ken repeated as we approached the stone cottage.

We hadn't been back this lane for five, maybe six years. No longer scared rabbits, we didn't run, but we didn't recognize the place. Kudzu had taken over. What previously had looked like a run-down version of the Seven Dwarf's house was now totally obscured. As we hacked our way to the front door with our under-sized pocket knives, the cottage emitted a damp, musty fog that cooled the mid-afternoon scorch. The rusted hinges gave way under our shouldered assault as the oaken door creaked and collapsed into the house.

Rats scurried, birds exploded from the safety of the rafters and escaped through the porous shake roof. I ducked as a white barn owl swooped at my head and out through the now-open door. To this day, though it changed our lives, I can't recall why I turned down that abandoned dirt lane.

Ken had fallen head-over-heels into the solitary one-room cottage. His right leg was wedged to the kneecap through a rotted floorboard. Yelping in pain, he was like a flailing octopus sinking in quicksand. The more he wiggled and squirmed, the worse his predicament became.

"Relax," I yelled.

"Now who's the moron?" Ken pronounced.

I stomped on floorboards surrounding Ken's trapped leg, freeing him from his prison. That's when we found it. I reached under the floor and retrieved a Prince Albert tobacco can. Squatting beside Ken, we rubbed away decades of dirt. I shook the can—metal on metal—Ken ripped Prince Albert from my grip and pried open the lid. A single key tumbled to the floor.

"Anything else?" I asked.

Ken handed me a folded sheet of letterhead. "What's it say? What's it say?" He screamed.

"First National Bank of Charleston."

* * *

DOPPELGÄNGER?

"Members of the jury, have you reached a verdict?" Judge Carson asked.

"We have your honor," came the much-anticipated reply as the jury foreman rose to deliver my fate.

"Will the defendant and counsel please rise?" the Judge instructed.

I was weary, yet defiant after my three-month ordeal in orange jump suits. Twenty pounds thinner blamed on stress or credited to county jailhouse cuisine, I rose and faced the jury.

Judge Carson's baritone order to announce the verdict echoed off the marble and arched courtroom ceiling that had witnessed my unwavering plea of innocence.

I begged eye contact with the jury foreman as he unfolded a scrap of paper and announced, "On the sole count of murder in the first degree, we find the defendant..."

The trial had ripped out my soul. My best friend and business partner was dead. My wife was in her third round of chemotherapy; words like "stage four" and "metastasized" shadowed my being from early waking to middle-of-night insomnia.

I didn't do it. My attorney did his best with what he had. But even he winced when I first said "doppelgänger".

"Doublewhater?" he quizzed. "You mean like the mysterious one-armed Hollywood stranger in *The Fugitive*?"

"You could have at least feigned belief in the innocence of your client once during this trial," I scolded.

"You expect me to stand in front of a jury and convince them there is an exact body double of you wandering around

Cleveland who snuck into your offices at 2 am and bludgeoned your business partner to death? All caught on the security cameras your partner secretly had installed? Why did your partner install those cameras? Sure as hell looked like you."

"Of course, it looked like me."

"With no motive. Stole nothing. Left no fingerprints."

"Yes."

"And under terms of your partnership agreement, upon death of either partner, the multi-million-dollar business reverts to the surviving partner?"

"It's legal. And common."

"And you are the sole beneficiary of a $4 million life insurance policy on your now deceased business partner?"

"As he is on my policy."

"Except he is dead," the inpatient counsel observed.

The verdict was read in a nanosecond but echoed in my ears for an eternity. "On the sole count of murder in the first degree, we find the defendant..."

* * *

Madame Lucille

The summer storm was turning the cow pasture at the edge of town into a mud fest of tents, banners, and goopy stables. Blip. Blip. Drip. Plop. Rhythmic, yet random. Earthy, musty. The rain echoed off the rotting canvas tent allocated Madame Lucille by the grotesque carnival owner Leon. While the tent mostly accomplished its intended purpose, huge drops of rain succeeded in annoying the gathered menagerie. A nasty drop of rain chilled Florence, the tattoo lady, as it exploded on her bald head, then trickled down her spine.

"Next time, I'm throwing a camel turd at the jerk," Rosie the gypsy midget promised. "The things they say. I'm people too."

"And what good would that do?" Lucille scolded. "Times are tough. At least you've got a job. It's 1932, most of these folks haven't worked in years."

"Bottom of the barrel job," Swazi the Nepali rubber boy contorted. Swazi was no longer a boy. That would be stretching it. The ten-by-ten canvas poster flapping in the storm outside depicted a teenager, legs wrapped around his neck, arms bound in a knot. That was forty years ago. He could still elicit an "ooo" when he stretched his lower lip over his eye brows.

"Find a more subtle way of returning the insult," Lucille advised. "They've paid their dime. They deserve a show. Swazi's got it figured out."

Lucille didn't like these little pep talks before show time, but she had to keep the troupe focused. It was expected that the freaks be a little crude. This low-brow blend of vaudeville and burlesque required that. However, cross the line? Local sheriff might shut her down.

The downtrodden were trudging their way through the mud to take their seats on the bales of straw arrayed in front of the foot-high performance platform. A full house would be twenty-five. The rain held the first show to only a dozen or so; dirty, bedraggled, unshaven drunks who had invested ten cents to abuse their fellow man. The kids huddled in the front row even looked bedraggled and unshaven.

The insults of "ugly bitch," "hey midget breath, you stink," and "lemme see ya stretch yer private parts rubber man" were somewhat dampened by the leaking canvas tent. Lucille was proud that her gang of entertainers were keeping their cool so well. It was now her turn. As she larded her way onto the stage, the hoots and the hollers could be heard halfway across the midway. Six-hundred pounds of porcine rolls and wrinkle-folds oinked her way through her routine of sword swallowing and belly dancing. The Richter scale was off the chart.

Lucille ended each show with a sit-down chat with the crowd. The abuse was horrid. Her retorts were hilarious. She'd wave off the worst of the insults with a flick of her handkerchief.

"Hell, my old mule wouldn't mount you," an old man bellowed.

"Yer so fat, how do you wipe yerself?" another quizzed.

"She don't, that's why she smells like an August-baked outhouse," a grungy woman shot.

Lucille took it all in stride, until a chubby little girl in the front row raised her hand. "My daddy made me come 'cuz I been bad. He sez I'za gonna look like you some day."

The hoots and the hollers ceased. The rain challenged the canvas show tent. Blip. Blip. Drip. Plop. A drop of rain violated the canvas, piercing Lucille's soul. She gently dried her cheek with her handkerchief.

* * *

I MISS YOU

My Dear Departed Brother:
I miss you.

We were inseparable. You were the right to my left, the ying to my yang. You always had my back. Brothers are naturally close, but our closeness was unique. Living so remote, out on the farm, we had nothing. We had to make it on our own, invent our own games. Swing a stick at a rock. Someday, they'll call it stick ball. Run, kick a bag of sheep hide stuffed with straw. They'll call it soccer. I'm so isolated, so alone. I've experienced so little, like a new born lamb sucking at it knows not what. Metaphors fail me because I have no life experiences. Comparisons work only when one understands both ends of the "if this, then that". No traditions, no heritage. I feel so lost. Alone.

A small family. No aunts. No uncles. No cousins. Other than our sisters, and our dog Yazi, we had no playmates. No friends. Throw the stick. Bring it back, Yazi. Let's call it fetch.

It's been years since your death. I think of you every day. I sit on the rocky hill, watching the sunrise over my new spring field of wheat. I feel your presence, the warmth of the sunrise. But you cast no shadow. You are gone. I ponder what, if anything follows death. Your death ripped our family apart. Father has yet to recover; he may never. I miss him too. We haven't spoken in years.

I still marvel at your farming prowess, the quality of your flocks. Decades from now, maybe even centuries, your breeding techniques, the quality of your wool will be legendary. You were truly honored. I'm sorry if I reacted poorly to your success. I've come to manage my jealousy better as the years have passed.

Our sister Awan and I have remained close. The remoteness and your untimely death brought us closer together. Our family bond has grown in unexpected and unique ways. I wish you were here to share in my joy. We married and have children. Our son Enoch favors you in many ways, broad of shoulder and strong of will, so able.

At sunset, on the eve preceding the anniversary of your death, I burn golden shocks of barley and wheat as a reminder that your memory continues to burn in my heart. It's a small sacrifice. A dam of rocks and cedar timbers creates a pool of brook water that reminds me of the sparkle in your eyes. As long as I am able, I will remember you every year on the sad anniversary of your death with another letter. I miss you.

I remain your humble and remorseful brother,

Cain

* * *

LAYERS

T he sweat carried rivulets of dirt from the old professor's brow and stained his rumpled silk shirt. Dr. Drake's pulse quickened. Trespasser? Fool? The toil of historical research— not his strong suit—perched him on the precipice of success. He thought he had set up his scientific equipment in the right place. Had he dialed in the right time?

The months, years of testing in his Ohio laboratory proved his theories correct. He had listened in as his great-great-grandfather proposed to his sweetheart on the farmhouse Victorian front porch. He replayed a newborn's wail dozens of times as the midwife slapped his bottom at his own birth. Would his universal truths, algorithms, time warp extrapolations work in the November afternoon chill on this Pennsylvania pasture?

Dr. Drake's theory was simple. Complex. Ludicrous. Radio telescopes employ this concept as they scan the heavens for radio, television, radar, any kind of transmission from little green men from Mars and beyond. He had proven that once a sound wave is created, it exists into eternity. Just find it and listen in on history across millennia.

Dr. Drake limited his research to his modest farmhouse laboratory where he thought he understood and could limit the extraneous inputs. On Dr. Drake's front porch, every word ever spoken, from the carpenters' blabber as the porch was built to a young couple pitching woo, lingered. Electric energy, sound waves, all jumbled together in a mishmash of confusion. Dr. Drake discovered how to unmash the mish. All the energy, created in layers, had to be un-layered. Slice, dice, dissect. Great-great-grandma said, *yes*. The midwife announced, *it's a boy*.

Ears pinched in the headset; Dr. Drake adjusted his invention based on the results of his historical research. Static. Garbage. Frustration held at bay, he accessed his computer and made minute adjustments. Squinting, focused, his frown evaporated into hope. A haunting, high-pitched, almost shrill voice broke snippets through the static:

... cannot... dedicate... we... consecrate...

Dr. Drake bent over his equipment, stroked, almost caressed his invention, coaxing cooperation. He was so focused he didn't notice the newly arrived shadow that enveloped him. The low-flung, setting sun further lengthened the elongated darkness. Dr. Drake peered over his shoulder and collapsed at the sight of the stovepipe hat.

Professor Drake's hospitalization was brief as Park Service Ranger re-enactors are trained in CPR.

* * *

NATIVITY SCENE

Christmas is great. Presents. Family. Presents. Food. Did I mention presents? But the best part? The Christmas Eve service at church. Singing. Costumes. All those kids crammed full of cookies, candy, and sugar. Nothing better than a hundred, up-past-their-bedtime urchins loaded with sugar.

Best Christmas pageant ever was in 1959. Danny Murphy and I were two-thirds of the wise men—better known in perpetuity as "wise guys"—Levi Abramowitz was the other third. That was okay since he had a better bass voice—important when singing *We Three Kings of Orient*—and there were probably a few Jewish people wandering around on that first Christmas, census and all. And Levi wasn't otherwise busy on Christmas Eve. Where was I?

Oh, yeah. We three wise guys had finished our rendition about the Orient, so we moved over by the shepherds. They sorta smelled bad because they had been hanging around the sheep on loan from Farmer Jones all day; plus, they were young teenagers who hadn't developed consistent deodorant hygiene habits. That's when Danny and I implemented Phase II of our plan. Danny knelt down beside the loaner sheep, eased his pocket knife out from the twine-rope sash around his regal-purple bath robe, and cut the sheep loose from its tether. We predicted an appropriate level of mayhem might ensue. Pure ecstasy and joy would reign if Phase I were successful.

The sheep sniffed the straw, stuck its nose up an angel's white sheet, and peed on the slate floor. The choir director yelled something that sounded a lot like "holy sheep." Not sure 'bout that last consonant. Phase I was working as planned.

The sheep nuzzled Joseph aside and snorted a blob of snot on a duly-surprised Mary. The sheep ripped the swaddling clothes off the plastic baby-doll Jesus and chewed its way out the center aisle like an eager bride on her way to her honeymoon.

Phase I you ask: Danny and I had soaked the swaddling dish towels in a salt-brine mixture laced with clover and alfalfa flakes. It was golden. Frankincense, indeed, we demurred.

Ho Ho Ho... MERRY CHRISTMAS!

* * *

THE RARE BOOKSTORE

My Daddy loved me. Still does, in spite of the exorbitant, God-awful tuition checks he wrote for my college education. It isn't the elite Eastern snob college turning me into a left-leaning liberal that eats at him. It's the creative writing major with a minor in 18th century French philosophy that he doesn't get. *Ya better larn how to type or file,* he'd lecture with his faked hillbilly accent. *Or at least marry-up.*

I've yet to marry up. Or down. If ever there were a man in my life, he couldn't measure up to Dad. I've become independent and promise to visit my parents on Sunday afternoons at whatever assisted living hell-hole my brother and I park them.

I have a cozy loft in the up-and-coming Over-the-Rhine area of Cincinnati. I walk to work. And yes, there's a reason it's called work. While I don't type or file, my job is about as rewarding as hopping on and off a Rumpke sanitation truck on a mid-August rainy morning. I write copy for a number of client websites and blogs. I don't actually lie to my dad about my job; he seems to accept that I work for a front-line ad agency. *Good thang ya lernt how ta write.* I love my dad.

Evenings, weekends I walk around my neighborhood. I usher at Music Hall and the new Shakespeare Theatre; I haven't paid for cultural enrichment since my return to Cincinnati. I loiter at a rare book store on Vine Street that interrupts my walks home from my low-rung ladder job. It's spooky dark, cluttered, and dusty, yet holds a charm hard to describe. Not true. As a writer and deserving of being my dad's Little Miss Sensitive College Grad, I can describe it.

Mr. Winston's Books hovers in a no-man's land between used and rare. Because it's Cincinnati, Mr. Winston's leans—leans hard—toward the used end of the spectrum. Unlike its counterpart in New York City or Boston, not a single volume is rare enough to be "under glass" or available on a "white-glove-only" basis. I can touch and peruse anything I want in the claustrophobic tombs at Mr. Winston's.

Shopkeeper Molly knows my backstory and leaves me alone unless I have a question. While I do buy something—every once in a while—Molly lets me browse. Molly reminds me of Mr. Rogers. I doubt she sleeps in her tattered cardigan sweater, but she wears it every day, under a touches-the-knees apron that's a holdover from an earlier day as a coffee shop barista. Premature salt and pepper hair might improve with a trim, but looks the part on a fiftyish lady as she balances half-frame bifocals astride her patrician beak of a nose.

About a month ago, ten minutes before a not-so-fixed-in-stone closing time, I stopped in Mr. Winston's. The bell above the door announced my presence.

"It's me, Molly," I announced.

From the back storeroom I heard a faint reply, "Hi, Rebecca. Make yourself at home."

I did. Nothing in particular on my wish list. I proceeded to wander through the shadowed stacks.

"Excuse me, Miss," he said.

Startled, I whirled around, clutching a dusty volume to my chest.

"Oh, I'm sorry, didn't mean to, scare…"

"Just a little," as I caught my breath.

He sported his own barista touches-the-knees apron. Beyond elderly—I envision him playing chess with my dad—an argyle sweater vest peeking atop the wrinkled apron. A learned look, unlit pipe clenched between teeth framed by a professorial goatee.

"You new here?" he asked.

"Returned after college," I offered. Intrigued, I gave the distinguished gentleman a genuine smile. The apron implied that Molly had hired the oldest intern in Southern Ohio.

Retrieving a book hidden behind a larger volume, he dusted it with his apron, handed it to me, "You look like a girl who would appreciate French philosophy."

"Thank you, sir," I smiled. "I'm Rebecca."

"Peter. Pleased to meet you, Rebecca." He leaned closer and whispered, "Tell Molly it's on sale," as he tapped my Voltaire.

My new friend Peter shuffled from my stack. The bell above the door performed as designed.

Molly walked from the back store room, "Goodbye, Rebecca."

"I'm still here," I announced.

Puzzled, seeing no other customer in the stacks, Molly wiped her hands on her apron.

"I'll take this," laying my new treasure on the counter. "Your new guy, Peter, said to tell you it is on sale."

Flushed, Molly replied, "Excuse me?"

Not quite finished describing Peter, Molly interrupted me.

"Peter Winston, my father? He died three years ago... three years ago... today."

* * *

THE RUSSIAN EMBALMER

"She looks great. Don't you think she looks natural?" the elderly mourner queried.

Positive nods all around confirmed that Serge had once again performed magic. Tears flowed, a lifetime of stories competed with the gentle fragrance of lilacs and fresh-cut carnations. Serge stayed in the shadows and took no small measure of satisfaction in his craft. He indeed had turned the cranky widow Petrov into a prom queen. Tomorrow she would be slowly nestled next to her beloved husband of fifty-seven years who would probably remark, "Damn Natasha, you haven't looked this good since 1957."

In his early forties, Serge had left his family mortuary business in St. Petersburg in the able hands of his twin brother Dmitri. Serge's emigration to Buffalo, New York was part of a larger plan of intrigue and, well, he kept most of his plans to himself. Only fellow mortician Dmitri knew the truth.

The scheme was Dmitri's idea. His close connections to the newly empowered Russian mob, combined with Serge's artistic skills resulted in a dozen small paydays. There had been no glitches. It was all so easy. The aging ethnic population in Buffalo produced a monthly supply of burial shipments back to Mother Russia. Serge would perform his cosmetic magic. A beautiful Buffalo memorial service would end with caviar, vodka, and dancing. The casket would be closed, crated, and shipped to Dmitri in St. Petersburg. The Panolov funeral home would Zoom the internment in the family plot and local Buffalo mourners took final solace that grandma rested in eternal Russia. The old folks needed to be back in the U.S.S.R.

Only Serge and Dmitri knew that grandma's body cavity harbored a treasure of diamonds, rubies, and U.S. greenbacks, all duty free. Russian mob money laundering from Serge through Dmitri. Business was booming. Grandma did indeed look, "oh so natural."

When it was time for Sofia Pushkin's service, Serge and Dmitri agreed to go for the mother lode. Sofia's would deliver $2 million in cash.

Sofia was radiant, not easy for a Russian babushka corpse. Serge had performed another miracle. Her hands folded neatly on the white knit suit that graced her tummy, only Serge knew what she was protecting. The service was lovely. Serge stayed in the shadows, pacing a little nervously. This casket was different. This shipment would be his last. He and Dmitri would retire and distance themselves from the mob. They would skim just enough of the $2 million to make it worth the risk.

As the last mourner left the Buffalo funeral parlor, Serge smiled at Sofia and stroked her cheek. "Safe travels my dear," he said as he deftly closed the casket lid. The catch of the lid clasps sent a brief chill down his spine as the "click" was swallowed by the plush parlor carpet and soft brocade drapes. Serge turned out the lights one last time. Fred and Tom would crate the casket and drive Sofia to the airport in the morning.

Serge slept in. He dreamt of caviar, full-lipped Russian women, and how he and Dmitri would live the high life. Mid-afternoon, he stopped by the funeral home to confirm that Sofia was on her way to St. Petersburg. To his surprise, Fred was pushing a casket through the courtyard to the storage shed.

Puzzled, Serge inquired, "Isn't that the Pushkin casket?"

"It was," Fred responded.

"Was?"

"Yeah, the family changed their mind," Fred said. "When they saw the shipping charges, they changed their mind."

Still not fully comprehending, Serge asked, "Changed their mind? Where's Tom?"

"Oh, Tom's on his way to the airport with the Sofia Pushkin urn. The family had her cremated this morning."

* * *

THE RALLY

Daquan Baker had experienced real fear only twice before. The kind of fear that bleeds beads of sweat on the forehead. The pounding of a heartbeat in the ears. Shortness of breath, clammy skin, goose bumps. Daquan barely lived through his first scrape with danger. When a freshman in high school, Tameka's bra had just come off. Her hand clumsily fumbled with his belt. His pulsing blood was coursing to a destination that firmly begged for Tameka to succeed with her current effort. Just as he imagined his tongue flicking its first bare nipple, the front screen door bounced.

"Tameka, I'm home," Mama Johnson announced.

Never in football practice had he run so fast. Only a finely tuned athlete could sprint down a flight of stairs while simultaneously pulling his jeans over his fire engine red boxers. There would be future, more discreet Tameka adventures, but never again in Mama Johnson's house.

Daquan's second brush with fear came on June 14, 1965, Flag Day. Daquan and best friend Isaiah Thomas were just arriving at South Central High School for summer football conditioning. Now seasoned seniors, Daquan and Isaiah hoped to lead South Central to the Indiana State finals. These two hot-shot jocks were on the same wavelength; they could complete each other's sentences. As the star quarterback, Daquan could read a defense and glance at his favorite wide receiver Isaiah. No verbal commands were needed. It was almost as though these two had been separated at birth and could communicate through the Morse code twitch of a neck muscle.

"Coach Smith is gonna kill us before we ever suit up for our first game," Isaiah complained.

"Yeah, his two-a-day workouts surely be muthas," Daquan agreed. "I've lost ten pounds and it's only June."

Division Two college scholarships were distinct possibilities. As they rounded the corner onto the school grounds, they saw the crowd of reporters, fire trucks, and police. A few broken windows and the Nazi swastika on the front door would make the second page of the next morning's paper. The photographer was now focused on the smoldering ashes on the front lawn, this was the picture that would make the front page.

Daquan flushed as he realized he had just witnessed the remnants of a cross burning at his high school. "Damn!" Daquan was overwhelmed by anger and fear.

It didn't take long for the entire community to come to Coach Smith's defense. He was new. Black football coaches were not that common in 1965; it was his blonde, blue-eyed wife who garnered the most attention.

It was assumed that the kook twenty miles east of town was involved. In your face, he had a Confederate flag painted on the side of his barn, within two-hundred yards of the country road. A highly publicized Klan rally was scheduled on Ken Smith's property for July 4th. Previous rallies attracted the usual nut cases from miles around. The ACLU was torn between freedom of speech and defense of the recently signed 1964 Civil Rights Act. Most locals took the easy ostrich, head-in-the-sand approach; ignore the drunk, obscene uncle at Thanksgiving.

Daquan and Isaiah were cut from a more aggressive cloth. Driving the last half-mile down the deserted road with no headlights proved uneventful, produced irregular breathing, but otherwise, so-far-so-good. Not much happens at 2 a.m. on these country roads. Car parked in the ditch, uneventful.

Exchange of two quick glances, one muscle twitch, uneventful. This was going to be easy.

A July 3rd new moon, tucked behind slow-moving clouds masked Daquan and Isaiah's steady advance. An old farm wagon was parked beside the flag-emblazoned barn. The wagon was loaded with white sheets, cans of kerosene, gasoline, and other paraphernalia in preparation for the next evening's festivities. Leaning against the wagon were huge two-by-fours, wrapped in burlap bags. If Daquan thought the release of eye-hooks on Tameka's bra would cause his heart to nearly burst, that was nothing compared to the thunder claps in his ears now. The uneventful was rushing toward some memorable event.

Isaiah lit the pack of firecrackers and flung it into the center of the wagon. Buying the hundred pack would prove to be a wise investment as the two best friends innocently crawled away from the sputtering fuse behind them. The uneventful turned 180 degrees; the rapid pop-pop-pops behind them quickened their pace until they were in full retreat. Coach Smith's wind sprints were paying off. Like a hot, premature ejaculation, this nocturnal cross burning happened before its appointed hour. Such a shame.

Daquan could feel the heat from the conflagration on his back as he raced toward the safety of their car parked in the country-road ditch. He could see his fire-rimmed shadow winning the race in front of him. *Follow my shadow. Catch my shadow!*

Isaiah cleared the barbed wire fence as if a candidate for a high jumping scholarship. Daquan was half-over and half-not. Then he heard the unmistakable metal-on-metal screech of the pump action of a shotgun. Boom! Buckshot whizzed above his head. As he tumbled over the fence, barbed wire performed its intended function. Daquan's ripping pants were tangled in the fence as he dangled, head first in the ditch.

"Move yer black ass, bitch!" screamed Isaiah.

Daquan cursed in pain as the barbed wire ripped a gash in his scrotum, a badge of honor that Tameka might someday appreciate. Isaiah returned to Daquan's aid. Boom! This shot was closer. Daquan's only choice was to surrender his ensnared pants; not an easy task while hanging upside down.

Multiple shotgun blasts peppered the tall weeds beside them. Isaiah yelped like a whipped dog as some wayward buckshot nipped the back of his hand. Daquan felt the burning sting on the back of his bare legs as another blast hit its target. His red boxers felt damp. He wasn't sure if his bladder had just given up the ghost or if he had been shot in the ass.

Car doors slammed. The engine started on the first try. Buckshot invaded the sheet metal of the getaway car and shattered Isaiah's passenger side window. Spinning tires flung mud, grass, and gravel as the getaway car fishtailed the screaming vandals onto the back-country road.

Safely speeding away, gasping for breath, the two vigilantes marveled at their handiwork and the roaring flames shrinking behind them. An unexpected bonus, the barn was now fully engulfed in flames. The painted Confederate flag seemed to flutter as the waves of heat blistered, distorted reality. One reality was clear as flames exploded through the barn roof. There would be no Klan rally on July 4th.

Daquan suddenly slammed on the brakes and stopped cold as he exclaimed, "We gotta go back! My pants!"

"Shit no!" Isaiah shouted.

"My wallet!"

* * *

Rock Bottom

T he sorrowful glance from the top of his eye sockets might have whispered a feeble "thank you" had the shame not quickened his shuffle to grab the last biscuit within his reach. In his few short months in this new routine, Sam Burkett had learned to avert eye contact – either on the street or in the soup kitchen. He was so wet and chilled he ceased to care if the foul odor was from the poor miscreant ahead of him in line or could it be, emitted from his own soiled pores.

Another verse of *Bringing in the Sheaves* was a small price to pay for one of the last coveted spots in the Salvation Army overnight shelter. Sam didn't mind the naïve Corporal Maryanne's warm hands cupping his as quiet words of comfort were spoken. He avoided the offered counseling on how to make a good first impression in a job interview; he couldn't fathom ever wearing another starched shirt and tie.

The nights on a cot, sequestered in a corner by the steam radiator, were a welcomed respite from his cardboard home under the Elm Street viaduct. The underpass concrete retained a never-ending dampness that penetrated his bones. While safe, the constant traffic, semi-truck jack-brakes, and occasional Harley back-fire flung him headlong back to the Afghanistan desert. The VA waiting list for PTSD therapy grew longer than his salt-and-peppered beard.

Dawn brought another day of sameness. While he was a smidge cleaner and mostly dry, the coffee and eggs would see Sam through another morning of dull, yet throbbing pain. A voucher good for a Happy Meal at any local McDonald's in his pocket, he exited the church basement, shading his eyes from a sun that might offer some hope, to someone. He shuffled past the line already forming for the chance at a lunchtime sandwich. While not really looking, he knew the faces of those who had failed to snag the last cot he had taken: Alice from Washington Park, Josh from Over-the-Rhine, Ken from across the river – he knew them all.

He knew them all, except the last in line. This guy was new. Head down, shoulders slumped, hands in pockets. Too young to be starting on this path. Marine pea jacket. Too young. Sam walked on. Street sweepers polished pavement that no one would notice or appreciate.

Sam soaked in the morning sun and noticed the slump of the shoulders in his own shadow. Reversing course from his rigid routine, he returned to the line of hopeless outside the Calvary First Church.

Making eye contact with the new-guy Marine, Sam pressed his Happy Meal voucher into the ex-Marine's hand, and said, "Listen to Corporal Maryanne, she's good people."

* * *

SANDPAPER

L ots of things are coarse, of course. Sure, there are grada-
tions of coarseness. Not all sandpaper is coarse; fine and
medium, each kind of sandpaper has a specific purpose. "Fine"
doesn't grumble when it has to wait its turn. It realizes the
important role played by its "Coarse" and "Medium" cousins.

Interesting how something this simple, so readily understood by sandpaper, is so misunderstood by the human spe-
cies. Why is our discourse so "Coarse?" What ever happened
to "Medium" and "Fine?" Maybe some of it stems from our
attempts at being "Fair." Something as innocuous as the 1965
Voting Rights Act that assured more equal ballot access, also
resulted in "Safe," inner-city minority districts. The dominoes
fell in weird gerrymandered shapes, resulting in "Safe" con-
servative suburban districts. The two "Safes" don't talk to each
other. They are safe—safe from primary challenges and safely
re-elected—again, and again. Oh, we get a chance every two
years to elect a new House of Representatives. We are so divided
into our "Safe Spaces," only forty or fifty districts out of 435 are
even close to competitive. How is that supposed to be good?

We are separate, but not equal. We have separated ourselves
from each other. "Fine" no longer accepts the need to associate
with, or understand "Medium." They seem to rub each other
the wrong way. Thus, everything turns "Coarse."

We don't talk. We jaywalk with our noses stuck in our
iPhones. Our spines are hunching because we are looking down,
not ahead. A few more decades of this and our knuckles will
start dragging the ground, again. Reverse evolution? We don't

write letters; we are even abandoning email. Conversations are limited to texts of a whopping 140 characters. We are more interested in our selfie than turning the camera around to capture nature's beauty or the glint in someone else's eye.

All this doom and gloom pales in comparison to high level math called "algorithms." Google knows our every move. Facebook sorts us, separates us. Joe blocks Suzie's MSNBC, Suzie blocks Joe's Fox News. "Fine" doesn't even hear or see what "Medium" is doing. That makes us all "Coarse." That's rough.

A self-taught Lincoln never had a laptop to compute calculus or algorithms, but he understood that "A house divided against itself cannot stand."

Try smoothing that with sandpaper.

* * *

THE SNOWMAN

Freddie Foureyes, I can't remember his real last name, was an easy target on the playground. The founder of the seventh-grade chess club and secretary for the recess stamp collectors' guild, he was red meat for the town bully. Freddie's Coke-bottle glasses, held together by a wad of white adhesive tape, made his eyes look like two globs of tapioca pudding. Rumor had it that if he looked directly at the sun, steam would spew from his ears.

No one in the seventh grade knew what an IQ was, but we knew that Freddie was smart. Rocket science smart. Personality more than a bit limited, but ole Foureyes was a wizard. Having befriended the local junk yard owner, Freddie got first dibs on the weird scrap metal that he might someday fashion into his next science fair gizmo. His workshop shed behind his house was crammed with treasures including the chassis of a motor-less golf cart, an hourglass shaped black potbelly stove, a chicken egg incubation chamber, and a one-third scale model of a working guillotine that he had refurbished and sharpened for Halloween. The city Mayor had requested Freddie's father remove Robespierre's contraption from their front yard after pumpkin heads carved resembling town council members rolled down Maple Street and settled in front of City Hall.

The Mayor's son, Jason Punch, was the town bully. Jason and Freddie had their moments, with Freddie coming out on the short end most times. Father Mayor Punch and Freddie's father did not see eye-to-eye on much, so the bullying continued.

Halloween bled into Thanksgiving, signaling the approach of school Christmas break and winter. Snowfall was ample, which boded well for the annual snowman contest. Freddie's entries were the envy of Maple Street. Last year he fashioned a Styrofoam head that rotated 360 degrees before levitating two feet above the snowman's body.

His newest entry was a well-kept secret. Freddie constructed a plywood barrier around his front yard exhibit area and did most of his work under cover of darkness – chicken wire, lumber, buckets of white paint, and wheel barrow loads of tightly packed snow. New Years' Day, the opening of the annual snowman contest, Freddie removed the sight barriers and revealed his masterpiece.

Simple. Elegant. No moving parts. A classic snowman. Perfect shape. Stovepipe hat cocked to one side. Lumps of coal neatly arrayed as buttons, eyes, mouth and an orange carrot nose. A red-wool neck scarf draped down the graceful arc of the tummy, ending at...

Could it be? Yep, Mr. Snowman was anatomically correct in his nether region. Correct might be an understatement as the evidence indicated this snowman was very cold. And misshapen. A yard sign displayed a red arrow pointing to the Mr. Snowman's limited maleness and read... *Jason Punch.*

Scores, hundreds of spectators enjoyed the hot cider punch Freddie sold for fifty cents a cup. Click. Click. The internet would be full of pictures and wise-ass comments.

Mayor Punch and his son, Jason, were not amused. Jason first tore up the yard sign and took a swipe at the carrot nose. The stove pipe hat went flying. The crowd parted as Jason backed up, and with a running start, threw his shoulder into the snowman like an NFL linebacker.

CLANK! A flake of white paint chipped and went airborne as the black potbelly stove held its ground. Jason missed the first two weeks of school with a dislocated shoulder.

Freddie Foureyes' snowman entry was disqualified (the Mayor was a judge).

The bullying stopped.

* * *

SETTLED IN

"Why didn't you turn out the light?" Mary Ann Brooks, Ph.D., quizzed. "And I don't hear the dishwasher."

After six years of wedded bliss, Chuck and Mary Ann Brooks had settled in a routine that would probably carry them to their graves, whether that be ten or sixty years hence. They shared the cooking as neither considered it an actual chore. They both had full-time careers and were equally tired at the end of their day. Dicing an onion and arguing over the difference between a garlic clove and a garlic bulb was invigorating and reminded them why they had tied the knot—best friends and lovers—they were life-partners.

"I did," he insisted, as he tumbled out of bed. "Both, lights and dishwasher."

Mary Ann sighed, pulled the covers over her head, and ignored her husband's plaintive plea. She listened for his progress down the one flight of stairs as they creaked and moaned in protest to his athletic frame. She held her breath to confirm that the dishwasher started; an unnecessary act as the clanging water pipes rattled throughout the century-old house at the newly-requested surge of water. The crystal baubles dangling from the antique light fixture above her bed vibrated every time a new appliance or the water heater needed replenished from the over-taxed lead pipes.

Mary Ann loved her old house; it was her baby. It didn't replace the babies she had thus far failed to keep to term, but it filled part of that emotional void. Perched atop a knoll overlooking the small-town college campus where they both continued their academic careers, the old gray lady begged for a name. As the youngest professor of Hitchcock College's Archaeology Department, she nominated "Neffy," a shout out to Queen Nefertiti, the subject of her doctoral dissertation. Husband Chuck's favorite was "Lizzy," of the infamous Borden family. As the newly appointed head of Hitchcock's Department of Forensic Studies, Dr. Charles Brooks thought a touch of humor appropriate.

Lizzy-Neffy had been well researched. The realty disclosure documents were a boring yet complete summary of no termites, old ceramic insulator electrical wiring, glass fuses—no circuit breakers in this ole lady—original slate roof with no leaks, stone foundation in need of some repair, and a clean title search stretching seventy-five years into a previous century. The new buyers were unconcerned about the undocumented fifty years dating back to the original 1891 construction date. Any deed claims that old would surely be blocked by even the most liberal interpretation of statute of limitation laws.

Lizzy-Neffy's "fix-me-up" list would not fit on refrigerator Post-it notes. The two college professors each added row-up-on-row of repairs to an Excel spreadsheet that seemed endless. It would take years for Lizzy-Neffy to reclaim her 19th century glory.

The harsh winter had put all exterior projects on the delayed priority Excel worksheet number three. It was a cold, dank February Saturday morning when they discovered the old scrapbooks in a dusty corner of the attic. They removed decades, perhaps a century of spider webs and dust from yellow-cracked, faded news clippings and black & white photos. Both professors Googled high-IQ words like "Daguerreotype" and "Calotype." It was Mary Ann who exclaimed, "I want that!"

"What?"

"This," as Mary Ann pointed to an old blurry, faded photo, "I want this garden."

With Lizzy-Neffy's rounded-corner turret visible in the background, it was clear that a once highly-sculptured garden had been on the southeast side of the old brick mansion. Long since abandoned to the current tangle of bushes and undergrowth, the photos depicted grandeur and grace. While the old photo lacked precision and definition, straight rows and evenly spaced trellises provided Mary Ann with her initial landscape layout.

It was detective Chuck who noticed the glaring absence in the photo. Where was the bay window and the first-floor sunroom that should be tucked to the east of the two-story turret? It took until the Ides of March to stumble upon the blueprints for the 1937 solarium addition that brought half of the garden inside. Mary Ann spent the balance of March and early spring revising her garden landscape plan based on the smaller exterior space. Grand oaks with hanging moss and an abandoned concrete koi pond defined the outermost limits of Lizzy-Neffy's restored garden. Mary Ann had an herb garden penciled in for the repurposed koi pond.

With the arrival of May, the two professors looked forward to a well-earned summer break from academia. They each had summer workshops planned, much less rigorous than the usual academic term. Mary Ann hoped to work in her new garden, while Chuck upgraded Lizzy-Neffy's Excel worksheet priorities.

Chuck's second and third trips downstairs to turn out the lights and re-start the dishwasher had become so frequent as to become the irritating nightly routine. While frustrating, he wrote it off to old electrical wiring. Other weird things occurred on almost a daily basis, most persistent as Mary Ann raked and hoed in the garden. Small things, but unexplained. Weird.

Taking a deserved break on an unusually hot June afternoon, Mary Ann settled into a wicker rocker on the wraparound porch, sipping lemonade. Straw hat tilted over a work-moistened brow; she would have taken a quick snooze had the crack of a large tree limb not disturbed her peace. She scrambled to the garden to find the handle of the hoe she had swung nary moments earlier broken in half by the fallen limb. Coincidental timing aside, she shook it off, until later that night, another oak tree crack caused her to sit straight-up in bed. The next morning, she discovered her half-completed koi pond herb garden destroyed.

"It's as though the gods don't like my garden," she lamented as she shared a morning coffee with Chuck.

"Ooo, heebie jeebie," came the unappreciated attempt at humor.

"Go to hell."

"You're the archaeologist, dig around a little."

"That's your job, wise ass," Mary affirmed. "They're delivering the Bobcat this morning at nine."

"Been looking forward to this."

"Easy, farm boy, down," she laughed.

"You'll see," Chuck insisted, "once a farm boy, always a farm boy."

As the bantering continued over coffee, Mary Ann reviewed her garden landscape design layout with her braggadocios farm boy. Covering the rustic wooden breakfast table, the furled corners of her plan secured by salt and pepper shakers, coffee mug, and sugar bowl, Mary Ann highlighted how she wanted the dirt moved around her quarter-acre garden. Depression here, three-foot rise there, gentle slope down to the herb garden. Chuck nodded and asked a few relevant questions to demonstrate interest and confirm that he understood.

Sunbelt Rentals had the Bobcat unloaded by 9:30 a.m. To Sunbelt's surprise and relief, farm-boy Chuck demonstrated an adroit mastery of coordinated hand and foot movements to make the miniature bulldozer do its thing. Rental agreement signed, including insurance, just in case, Chuck was moving dirt. Ear plugs in place, he and Mrs. Archaeologist had agreed on hand signals, except the single-finger salute would not be permitted.

By noon, Chuck had skimmed a foot of top soil off the quarter-acre space. He had created a gradual rise to a three-foot high plateau, exactly as designed by Mary Ann. Eye contact affirmed satisfaction with Mr. Farm Boy. Chuck twirled the Bobcat 180 degrees, lowered the bucket to charge toward the taunting matador that was his next objective, when BAM! Whatever he hit, submerged about a foot deep beside a strangle of honeysuckle, was stubborn enough to kill the Bobcat dead in its tracks. A quick motor restart and Chuck charged again. BAM! Same result. Knowing the definition of insanity, Chuck's technique became more nuanced. A gentle jiggle, up, down. Jiggle again. He lowered the bucket beneath the obstruction. A subtle dance with foot pedals and hands, the Bobcat responded like an eager tango student. Rewarded for his patience and farm-boy persistence, Chuck raised the flat obstruction into the sunlight.

As lunchtime communicated a rumble in his stomach, he killed the engine and climbed down to examine his find. The farm-boy and his garden landscape supervisor arrived at the front-loader bucket together. Nestled amongst dirt, stones, honeysuckle roots, and chips of broken limestone was a flat, board-like stone. Rounded at the top, the dirt-stained slab of stone revealed an inscription as Chuck roughed the surface with his leather work gloves. Archaeologist Mary Ann poured her glass of iced tea over the limestone surface: *R.I.P. 1894 Infant Brooks.* A chill shivered down her spine as a lump settled in her throat.

Lunch lasted two hours. How large was the cemetery? Yeah, the title search should have revealed this? No, it's not my fault. You wanted the damn garden. Who was the Brooks family? Too much of a coincidence.

"It's haunted," Professor Chuck whispered.

"It's just a cemetery, Professor Wimp," she retorted.

"Not the cemetery," he continued, "the house. Remember the photo?"

"What about the photo?" She asked with a furrowed brow.

"The sun room addition," he insisted. "The bay window, 1937. I'll bet it was built over a portion of the abandoned cemetery that was never a sculptured garden. The damn house is haunted."

"Now who's the weirdo archaeologist?"

"It's only a crawl space, no slab, no basement. The original house? It has stone walls, seven-foot-high ceiling in the basement. The 1937 addition was never excavated."

"One way to find out," Mary Ann insisted.

"You archaeologists have a one-track mind. Dig."

"Since it's only a crawl space, can you reach the bucket under to pull out...?"

"... yes, dear." Chuck surrendered. "I think I can pull out a foot or two of dirt."

Hand signals confirmed, ear plugs re-inserted, Chuck eased the Bobcat away from the honeysuckle grave to the foundation of the solarium. Extend. Scrape. Reverse. Repeat. Foot, foot-and-a-half deep. The front bucket hit something solid. Another headstone? Chuck idled the engine, shifting the Bobcat into neutral.

Mary Ann heard the crack as another limb broke loose. Waving and hand signals were useless, Chuck had crawled under the solarium. Bobcat engine and Chuck's earplugs swallowed Mary Ann's warning scream. She ran toward the Bobcat. The oak limb clipped her shoulder, sending her head-long into the honeysuckle grave. The hundred-year-old oak tree signed a moan of death as it fell across the garden, crushing the 1937 bay window and solarium.

The Bobcat shuddered, slipped into gear, depositing a load of dirt into the cemetery's newest grave, under the solarium.

The Brooks family plot welcomed two new eternal residents.

* * *

SOUL BROTHERS

"Sure, one more Guinness, sounds good," the out-of-towner agreed. As the happiness purveyor worked his magic on the perfect pour, Mr. Guinness surveyed the comings and goings in the dark, mahoganized bar. The bubbles do-si-doed up and down in their rhythmic dance. The four-leaf clover floated, kissed the foam at the rim of his glass. "Truly a thing of beauty," he said as he worshipped the glass to his eager lips. He gently swiped his tongue across his promise of a mustache, savoring each toasted barley nuance.

"Joyce Kilmer might have mused that only God can make a tree. But God surely must have toasted barley in His spare time," he praised as his hands caressed the glass to the bar counter top.

"Excuse me?" barked the newly-arrived and obviously skeptical lonesome soul to his left.

"Pardon me?" Mr. Guinness burped back.

"Do you think that god really had anything to do with your perfect beer? Why is a 'god' even needed to brew beer?"

One more sip for courage, Mr. Guinness accepted the challenge. "I see a delicate butterfly, a rainbow, a newborn baby, and I know that there must be something larger than just man involved."

"Nope. It's all physics and chemistry."

"Physics, huh. Who invented physics? Gravity, oxygen, all just accidents?"

"Pretty much," as the doubter paroled an olive from its toothpick prison. "You're probably gonna try to convert me to the afterlife and eternity next. Bunk. Death is final. Then nothing."

"Really? So, you have no soul?"

"Nope. When I'm through with this crap-high pile of protoplasm, just sprinkle me around some petunias."

"Hmm, no soul. So, you wouldn't place much value on your soul?"

"How can something that doesn't exist have any value?"

"Tell you what, if you're not going be using your non-soul, I'll take it."

The God-Doubter slapped his chest twice, then grabbed at his heart, extending a closed fist. "Here, it's all yours."

"Gratis?"

"Yep, no charge."

"Let's make it legal. A contract requires consideration. Here," as he scribbled on a bar napkin and slid a five-dollar bill to his new friend, "you get five bucks, and I get your soul."

The closed fist opened, accepted the $5, and willingly scribbled his name to the bar napkin contract. "Sucker. Never met anyone quite like you before. What's your name, man?"

The signed napkin contract safely nestled in his breast pocket, Mr. Guinness rose, downed the last guzzle of god's nectar, and as his shadow left the bar, he smirked, "Damien, Damien Faust."

* * *

THE WEDDING

The courtship had been uneventful, almost routine. Not one of those dark, noisy bars where shouting left you hoarse within an hour. No highly-structured speed dating with its musical chairs and ninety-seconds of lying and sneak peeks to the next victim to the left before the bell rang. Suzanne and Ed had been introduced by mutual friends. A double-date of sorts. No one jumped into bed on this first date.

Suzanne liked Ed. She would learn to love him. He had a master's degree, great job – actually handsome. Just coming off a bad relationship, she was gun shy and hesitated initially when Brooke had said, "Come on, I know that you and Ed will hit it off."

"Not sure I'm ready, not yet," Suzanne had pleaded.

As we skip ahead a year, this story is, after all, about a wedding. The big day having arrived, the happy couple stood at the altar. It was lovely. Flowers. Only three bridesmaids, not a circus. The minister welcomed everyone and then slid his hand to his side, under his robe, and turned off his microphone. Not even the best man or the maid of honor were privy to what the minister was saying to the bride and groom. Suzanne and Ed leaned in, brows furrowed, listening intently. Two-hundred curious attendees couldn't wait for the reception where, in addition to the usual libation, the private conversation might be revealed.

Pastor Nelson asked the question again, "Are you sure?"

Suzanne and Ed stared at the minister in disbelief. No rehearsal, no warning. They sheepishly made eye contact with each other, both blinked, and then nodded in the affirmative.

Pastor Nelson continued, "Really? Because now is the time. I don't know exactly what I'll say to the congregation, but I'll think of something. We can then all adjourn to the reception, open the bar, and you'll save fifty-thousand dollars in attorney fees. Do you want to tie this knot?"

This whole discussion and almost-public counseling session took three minutes. Excruciatingly long for the congregation. An eternity for the parents of the alleged happy couple. Only the organist knew that this was normal for Pastor Nelson.

Ed broke the silence as he whispered, "Yep, let's do it."

Suzanne nodded agreement. They took a step back, faced each other and held hands. The good pastor started with, "Dearly beloved." That's when the parishioners in the first five or six pews noticed that the bride was turning more and more pale. In another twenty seconds her wedding gown would have more color than she would. The men noticed that the groom was breathing okay, except his lungs were probably full. He had the inhale part down pat. It was the exhale that needed more practice. The men in the congregation were silently mouthing the word, "breathe." They hoped that Pastor Nelson knew CPR.

Then it happened. Everything went black. This wasn't Pastor Nelson's first rodeo. He had experienced a fainting bride. And a groom so drunk from a bachelor's party that he passed out. But as the bride and groom in front of him now both crumpled to the floor at the same time, he bowed his head and closed his Bible. The bridesmaids and groomsmen created a rugby, scrum-like huddle, blocking everyone's view of what needed to be seen.

Pastor Nelson calmly announced, "Folks, we're gonna take a quick break. Let's hear a word from our sponsor."

Whereupon the organist played *Nearer My God to Thee*.

* * *

I'LL TRY

"You want me to what?!" I exclaimed.

"You heard me," my somewhat embarrassed but persistent neighbor implored.

I was two-years new to Cincinnati—the Six and Eleven O'clock TV weatherman—moving my way up from Des Moines. In addition to my undergraduate and master's degree in meteorology, I had all the TV personality attributes: handsome beyond repair, glib, your basic "made for TV" formula. I had it all.

The Wilsons were great neighbors. They understood my weird schedule and instructed their gardener to do his thing afternoons only. I always slept-in late. Sam Wilson was a banking executive who spent a lot of time on airplanes back-and-forth to Chicago. Wife Susan worked from home, some kind of IT consultancy that I never tried to understand. Golden retriever named Rex. Really? Yep, this is a Midwestern story. No kids. Yet. Thus, the rub.

"That's a first," I admitted to Sam. "I like you folks, but this is a bit strange."

"It is Susan's idea," Sam offered.

"And you're okay with this?"

"It's better than the pig-in-a-poke turkey baster crap shoot."

"Let's see if I understand," I stumbled. "You had adult mumps that fried your nuts, left you sterile and you want me to impregnate your wife?"

"Simple, right?" Sam confirmed.

"You gonna... watch?" I challenged.

"Heavens, no! You'll do the deed while I'm out of town."

I was reluctant, but agreed, saying, "I'll try."

My first couple of hay-roll tries with Susan were somewhat awkward. It's not like I didn't know the territory; the arrangement seemed a bit, how shall I say, "*sister-like*"? Ew, that was a tad too descriptive. As the weeks progressed with my weathervane getting to like the activity, Susan still wasn't pregnant.

After six futile months, Sam wanted me to get tested. I demurred, apologized and suggested they resort to a med-student turkey baster. I didn't have the courage to admit that I'd had a vasectomy last year.

I only said, "*I'd try.*"

* * *

DREAMS OF RUSSIAN SPY SCHOOL

The training had been rigorous. Vladimir had finished first in his class. Not your usual valedictorian. He had success; broken more necks, gouged more eyes, and killed more competitors than his classmates. His post-graduation foreign assignments could probably be classified as more cerebral, not eye gouging. Computer hacking and currency destabilization played on his London School of Management MBA more than any rough and tumble skills. In his first ten years with the KGB, Vladimir had not been in a single fist fight. While his James Bond career choice did involve some seduction and womanizing, he'd only seen an Aston-Martin in the Washington D.C. Spy Museum five years ago.

"Give him another 20 cc's, George."

"He'll pass out. He's no good to us dead," Agent Foster grumbled. "Russkies know how to train their creeps."

"Just give him the extra sodium potassium," Agent Spacey implored. "Vladimir's the last piece to our puzzle. He knows more about our Federal Reserve's source code than any MIT professor."

Vladimir only smiled. He could hear his captors discussing how to break him. The room seemed to spin more with each injection. Through his blurred vision he saw stars. He twisted his wrists and ankles against their restraints. He wasn't in pain, but he sensed that his breathing was becoming more labored. He could still win. His training would pull him through.

Then it all changed. The change had a name. They called her Wanda. Wanda pressed the scales at three-hundred pounds; she pressed it hard.

Why were his wrist and ankle restraints removed? The room was full of laughter. His body seemed contorted. He was free, but was he really? While he wasn't tied down any longer, he couldn't escape. It was Wanda. She had him pinned to the floor.

"Move his arm," a panicked voice exclaimed. "She's going to break his arm."

Someone laughed that laugh one laughs when a chair is pulled out from an unsuspecting victim holding a bowl full of Jell-O. And both the victim and bowl contents wiggle their way across a freshly waxed linoleum floor. The laughter stopped when Vladimir's shoulder popped out of socket. An involuntary yelp escaped his pursed lips when his ACL was stretched beyond its limit.

Wanda used her weight to her advantage. Her three-hundred pounds were firmly planted on Vladimir's rib cage. Vladimir gave up the ghost, he finally blacked out. The stars turned to circles. Even though unconscious, he would remember the circles circling. Primary colors of yellow, red, green. He felt cold.

"He's going into shock," someone shouted.

"Roll her off. Off, off!" the chorus rang out.

The cousins helped Wanda crawl to her hands and knees. Air seeped into Donnie's lungs as his rib cage gristled and cracked its way back to its pre-Wanda position. The welcomed inhale interrupted his Vladimir, Russian spy dream.

"He's blue! Uncle Smitty, call an ambulance," came the cries from the basement rec room.

The next thing Donnie saw was the ceiling tiles passing over head as the hospital gurney was wheeled to the emergency room. He clutched the plastic sheet close to his chin. His unconscious dream of Russian spies and vodka was replaced with a throbbing headache.

The ER doctor complimented Uncle Smitty on keeping Donnie warm with the plastic sheet; early treatment of shock victims is critical.

"Tell me again," the good doctor inquired. "Why you didn't use an ordinary blanket?"

Embarrassed as the adult spokesman for the gaggle of adolescent nieces and nephews, Uncle Smitty confirmed, "The plastic Twister game sheet was already stuck to his chest."

* * *

THE VAGRANT

New York City was alive. Ever since 9/11 it had actually become much more civil. Paul Cox confirmed this when he and his wife Francine moved to their $5,000 per month apartment on the Upper East Side. Paul had been coming to "The City That Never Sleeps" for twenty-odd years on business trips. They both regularly came to New York to take in Broadway, museums, and the occasional Opera at Lincoln Center. Francine could jump out of a cab, amble up the steps at the Metropolitan Museum of Art, and get her much-needed Monet fix in four-minutes and thirty-seven seconds. She answered docent questions.

They both knew the city like the backs of their hands. Patsy's had the best pizza because it was baked in a coal-fired oven. David Ippolito, that "Guitar Man from Central Park" could always be found on Sunday afternoons on the grassy knoll just south of Strawberry Fields on the West Side. It only took one E. coli experience to swear Paul off the wiener wagon in Midtown at 52nd Street. He always suspected some wayward pigeon might have been involved.

Baker Enterprises transferred Paul for only a two to three year "fix-it" assignment. The Northeast Region of this multi-billion-dollar financial services giant needed some fresh blood. Paul tested A-positive. The money was great, much needed if one wanted to survive in New York City, plus the extra stock options, and a bonus guarantee that probably added a summer or two in Tuscany to his retirement plan. Life was good. Handsome, well spoken, confident, except he was a bit self-conscious about a slight deformity in his right hand. He practiced his hand shake incessantly, so no one actually noticed.

No town cars or limos for Paul. He enjoyed the one-mile walk to work down Lexington Avenue. He even sloshed in the snow. Rain chased everyone, including Paul, into the tombs of the Lexington #6 Line. Nothing like the smell of a little subway ozone to start the day. Paul always had a quick buck to drop in the guitar case of a particularly talented dude in the 2nd Avenue and 68th street tunnel. On one monstrous wet day, Paul paused as the stranger was strumming away and asked, "How long you been doing this?"

Without missing a beat, the answer, "Seventeen years," came with a grin.

"You ever do gigs or parties?" Paul asked.

Now a beat was missed, just a dotted quarter note, as Paul's new friend Tom deftly produced a business card.

Impressed with this entrepreneurial flare, Paul volunteered, "I may need someone for an office party. Do you do that kind of stuff?"

"Sure do," came the rhythmic reply. "Tuxedo or sport coat? Call the cell phone, I'm kinda booked next month."

Grins exchanged; they would meet again.

New York morning walking commutes were focused. Heads down, same route, coffee purchased at the same wagon every day. Never a conversation other than an occasional elbow in the ribs, nothing serious. The walks home were exactly the opposite, more like a saunter. Paul always zigged and zagged, varied his route. Window shopping wasn't out of the question. People actually talked.

Last week Paul shuffled up to a display window at a chic boutique on Park Avenue, stood beside a young lady half his age and smirked, "Would anyone actually wear that thing?"

Quick on the trigger, she weighed in, "I'd have to lose twenty pounds and never inhale all night." New Yorkers could actually be open and quite witty.

Paul usually ignored the occasional panhandler. The aggressive beggars were somewhat reigned in during the Giuliani years. When pressed, he never, ever gave money; he knew it would get shot up a vein or guzzled down a gullet. If his stroll home was particularly unrushed, he might reward a clever line with a detour to a corner deli and buy the grubby comedian whatever he or she ordered. Ten bucks here and there seemed appropriate.

That was until November 14, 2008. In a hurry for a dinner party, the walk home on that chilly fall night was straight and to-the-point. Paul had always ignored the vagrant in his usual spot on the warm sidewalk grate on 57th and First Avenue. Maybe it was the chill in the air, maybe the threat of a spirit-damping drizzle, but something caused Paul to offer this perfect stranger cash, actual cash. He leaned down and gave the downtrodden soul two or three bucks.

Paul could feel, and smell the warm air rushing around the bum's dirty carcass as he offered the crisp bills and said, "Here buddy, get yourself a cup of coffee." As Buddy extended his left arm to receive the hand-out, his dirty forearm stuck out the sleeve of his tattered coat.

That's when the chill ran up Paul's spine. Buddy had a scar on the top side of his left forearm that ran from the elbow and stopped at the joint of his wrist. As their eyes met, all the dirt and grime couldn't deny that... that. Paul couldn't finish that thought. There was a Twilight Zone quality to the encounter that he couldn't describe.

Buddy reached up, touched Paul's shoulder. Expecting a simple thank you, instead Paul heard Buddy whisper, "I know you."

The chill reversed course and darted back down Paul's spine with a companion flush of his cheek. As Paul dashed home, he reflected on his success. All the money, the millions in his stock option account, the two daughters at Yale. He had it all. Raised by a single-parent Mom, an only child, he always felt something was missing. Mom couldn't afford more than one child. Below middle class, his Mom sacrificed everything for Paul.

From his mother's death bed, he heard her whisper, "Find him."

"Who?"

"I had to let him go."

Then she slipped away, quietly into the night. The gap. I felt incomplete, disconnected.

Francine was fit to be tied as he lumbered into their apartment, "You barely have time to change clothes. What took you so long?"

Ashen and shaken, Paul responded, "I think I met him."

Francine gasped, hands to her mouth muffling her, "Oh, my God."

Paul quickly went into the bedroom, clothes flying left and right. He stepped into the hot shower. As the steam and soap suds did their thing, he gently scrubbed his right arm and gazed at the long scar – elbow to the missing pinky on his hand.

He raised his head to receive the gushing water in his face and exhaled, "Now what?"

* * *

GREAT JOSEPH'S FAT

D uck fat fries. The Pilgrim. Downtown Des Moines on Elm Street. Who'd a'thunk that middle-America consumers would flock to pay $11 for a hot dog and $6 for French fries crisped in duck fat?

The lines out the Pilgrim door spoke volumes to Joseph Frank. Entrepreneur Joseph was ready for a new gig. Having just deposited a $500,000 severance check and exercised a few hundred-thousand stock options, this fifty-year-old was too young to retire; he was chomping at the bit to get back in the game.

Mrs. Frank was a renowned plastic surgeon. A Miss America runner-up, Dr. MaryEllen was all natural. A runway knockout, she never needed to "self-medicate." Nothing needed nipping or tucking on Des Moines' most sought-after beauty enhancer. Coolsculpting, face lifts, tummy tucks, liposuction, breast augmentation; Dr. MaryEllen did it all. Her medical practice income was more than sufficient to support an extravagant lifestyle and she encouraged her newly-retired husband's entrepreneurial spirit. She tolerated a certain level of irrational investing exuberance; just to get her husband out of the house.

Dr. MaryEllen expressed a word of surprise and caution at her husband's project choice, "Restaurant?"

"Yes, a restaurant," he retorted.

"Don't restaurants have the highest rate of bankruptcy of any business venture?"

"Wow, there's a vote of confidence."

* * *

ONE YEAR LATER

The camera crew and production staff resembled a swarm of Serengeti locusts. Wires, lights, microphones, cameras. *Diners, Drive-Ins, and Dives* host Guy Fieri had heard about the best French fries in America and wanted the scoop.

"Interesting name for a restaurant," Fieri dead-panned, as the cameras rolled. "Great Joseph's Fat."

"It's all in the fat," Joseph said.

Shoving his third fist-full in his mouth, Guy continued, "These are the bomb, phenomenal. What kind of fat?"

"Secret. I'd have to kill you," Joseph smirked.

"Remember, you're on live camera," Guy teased.

"Let's just say, it was my wife's idea."

"Does she work here, too?"

"Oh, no. She's a first-rate plastic surgeon."

Devouring more fries, Guy continued, "Must be expensive oil."

"Not really. And it's not oil."

As the camera panned the storage shelves above the deep fat fryers, the sound boom operator directed Guy's attention to the row of plastic jugs. Guy reached above his head and retrieved a gallon jug. "Whew, this is heavy. Is this the magic juju?"

"Magic. Great word," Joseph agreed, as he reached for the jug.

Guy refused to surrender the jug as he turned the label toward his cameraman and read, "Frank Surgery Associates?"

Failing in his attempt to block the camera, Joseph shrilled, "This ingredient is proprietary. Stop the camera."

Fieri eyed the jug, squinting as he read the fine print, "Liposuction Lab?" He tossed the last French fry in his hand aside and swiped his hand across his throat as he instructed his cameraman, "CUT!"

Great Jehoshaphat, indeed.

* * *

WHAT IF?

"King Charles, who?" the drunken colonist slurs.

"Come on, Edward, how many times are we doing this?" the Point Comfort, Virginia Innkeeper Johnson whines.

A burp and a foam wipe on his sleeve, Farmer Edward retorts, "See if I understand. A hundred years ago the King of Spain..."

"Good, King Charles I."

"Let me finish, the King of Spain issues a decree allowing the slave trade direct from Africa to the Americas."

"The Caribbean," the innkeeper adds.

"Carry bean."

"Car-e-be-ann?"

"What do I care what happens down there?" Edward quizzes. "As long as you can import that good rum."

"How long we been here Edward?" the impatient innkeeper muses.

"Jamestown settled... 1507."

The innkeeper pulls the farmer's pint away from him, "You've had enough, Edward. Jamestown Settlement, 1607."

Edward retrieves his rum, "Oh, yes, and we arrived two years later. That makes it," he counts on his fingers, "makes it... we've been here ten..."

"Ten years we've been working this land," the innkeeper laments.

"What's that have to do with King Charles?"

The innkeeper leans in closer, hand across the bar to Edward's shoulder, "They are coming here."

"Who?

"A slave ship," the innkeeper grumbles.

"Here? Virginia? How did you hear that?"

"That rum you're destroying'? Barbados. Ship's mate told me at the dock."

"So?"

"The White Lion... English privateer schooner bringing twenty-or-so captives. Direct from Africa. Flying a Dutch flag."

"Maybe you buy yourself a little barmaid or acquire help cleaning those chamber pots."

The innkeeper once again slides Edward's pint aside, "Listen here nincompoop. It won't be just one ship. Hundreds. They will breed like flies. Take jobs away from your sons. Plus, it is evil. Against God. We have to do something."

"You and what navy?" Edward steals his pint back.

"Don't need a navy? Remember when we Brits defeated the Spanish Armada?"

"Way before my time."

"Nimble. Dart in. Dart Out."

"And what?" Edward shows keen interest.

"Five, six guys. Half-full barrels of rum. Gunpowder. A few rowboats. Before the White Lion can offload its sinful cargo."

Edward mimics a huge explosion with both hands as he jumps off his barstool, "Kaboom!"

The innkeeper settles Edward back to his stool with hands on each shoulder, "Shh."

"But, that could kill innocent souls..." Edward shivered.

"Kill the profits too. Nip this thing in the bud. Maybe save thousands of lives. It would be a holy sacrifice."

"We would be heroes," Edward beamed.

"Shh, unsung heroes. The privateers would string us up."

"Now what? Edward was ready for action.

"I'll work on the rum kegs and gunpowder. And find two more blokes."

"I have dock access. I'll get two skiffs."

The innkeeper draws two more pints of rum and clicks mugs with Edward.

THREE DAYS LATER

The sliver of a new moon pierces a settled sky. A midnight breeze over the mouth of the James River teases the Dutch flag atop the English schooner as it nestles into port. The wind freshens, rippling the river's surface and wafts an indescribable stench into the sleeping Virginia hamlet.

The deafening explosion shatters windows throughout the valley as the White Lion roars. Chains rattle and screams from the ship's hold beg for freedom that would be denied. Profits denied.

Across the Atlantic, under the same new moon, village shamans throughout a mysterious continent exit their huts. They couldn't explain the newfound freedom that enveloped them from the West. They would try to explain a new meaning of sacrifice on a new dawn.

* * *

SUSPENDED

John Roebling created something historic. Romantic. The initial pedestrian toll in 1867 was only a penny. Absent the cost of the ring, a moonlight stroll mid-bridge above the Ohio River was a memorable way to propose and begin a new life together. Over the years, this first suspension bridge in America also accommodated those concluding this was the spot to end it all. The confluence of beginnings and endings. The swirl of joy, sorrow, pain, relief, and peace.

Tom Simpson had served honorably. Two Marine tours in Iraq, one in Afghanistan. He had witnessed the best and the worst of the human spirit. Packaged in the experience of a single day he had saved an Afghan child from the grinding tread of an Army tank and had a nearby IED burst his eardrum. He was lucky; a platoon buddy lost both legs.

Tom would survive, eardrum healed, to hear the officer's graveside words of comfort to another Marine's mother: *On behalf of the President of the United States, the Commandant of the Marine Corps, and a grateful nation, please accept this flag as a symbol of our appreciation for your loved one's service to Country and Corps.*

Tom was ready for his discharge when his Afghanistan deployment concluded. He wasn't sure he was ready for the challenges of civilian life. His repaired eardrum was only one of his invisible battle scars. Family and drinking buddies didn't notice anything out of the ordinary with Tom's transition home. They couldn't see the inner turmoil that was eating at his core. Day-by-day, incrementally, Tom was losing it. The erosion was so slow, like the gradual widening of the river, even Tom didn't notice he was drowning in his own whirlpool of despair. He was suspended between military training that taught hesitation meant death, and Cincinnati sidewalk courtesy where a bump on the shoulder elicited nothing more than an "excuse me." *Pull the trigger. Pull the trigger.*

Some people take walks in the park. Others pedal the bike trail that hugs the Little Miami River to Fort Ancient. Tom would walk to Kentucky and back home to Ohio on the suspension bridge. Daytime, dusk, sunrise, midnight; it didn't matter. Tom strolled the same route. Peering down at the water, he could feel life's burdens leave his shoulders. Almost every burden.

Coal barges passed beneath his vantage point as he leaned over the bright blue railing. He felt less alone when the tug pilots gave him a horn blast. It made no sense that coal went east and west. Tom pondered why the western-most buyers didn't contract with suppliers shipping east and vice versa. If he skimmed a penny royalty per shipped ton for this stroke of genius he'd be rich.

The Ohio had a rhythm. A constancy. The water below wasn't just water. Some of it came from the Allegheny, some the Monongahela, their confluence in Pittsburgh. After flowing into the mighty Mississippi, do the three rivers retain any of their original character? Maybe the Ohio is merely an intermediary to deliver the essence of every feeding stream and creek to the Gulf of Mexico. *Hell, if my bloated corpse is gonna end up in the Gulf of Mexico, I might as well book a cruise and enjoy it. Get drunk on the bargain cocktail of the day, and then jump right into the Gulf.*

Clear, full-moon nights imparted the greatest comfort. A summer breeze kissed ripples atop the muddy waters as a slow-passing barge forced triangle wakes. The moon's reflection became tentative, uncertain. Forearms pressed against the lingering warmth of the 150-year-old ironwork railing, Tom counted the seconds, minutes until the moon sharpened its glow as the river settled and recovered from its passing intruder. He hoisted himself to a seated position. Balanced on the railing, he studied the flowing peace below.

The Great Ohio always won. The rusted coal barges might create wakes persistent enough to erode a millimeter of silt from the clay bank, but the water always streamed its calm on all. The river always won. Tom relished that tranquility, that victory. A quick forward tumble and his pain would end. The one-hundred-foot drop to the water's surface would stun, initiate the peace. The cool water would caress his pain and envelop his soul. There would be no more Afghan children to save. No more IEDs interrupting his sleep. No more military funerals. No more Marine buddies calling in despair. So cool. So peaceful.

He bowed his head, flung one leg over the railing as if riding a horse given free rein to choose its own destination. *Back to the barn and a bucket of oats? Or gallop off over the horizon to a new adventure?* He raised his leg back over the railing and dropped to the safety of the bridge. Would he ever drop to the safety of the river?

The weeks, months passed. Ten full moons and countless river walks brought Tom closer to the serenity he desperately sought. He added casual walks beside the beginnings of the Little Miami as it sliced through Clifton Gorge. Sitting on a moss-covered boulder at the same Blue Hole that had inspired painter Robert Duncanson, he tossed a leaf in the cascading rapids and watched as it disappeared toward his spot beneath the Roebling railing. Would it make it? How long would it take? Would he recognize the same leaf should it pass beneath his bridge?

It hadn't taken Tom long to land a job in Cincinnati. Local employers were eager to interview and find slots for bright, willing veterans like him. He interviewed well and received credit for his military leadership experience. Tom found a simple loft apartment on the fringes of the changing Over-the-Rhine neighborhood. He thought about doubling-up and waiting tables evenings in one of the fledgling restaurants on Vine Street.

Tom decided to delay moonlighting. He was hesitant to forego his downtown Cincinnati walks, his meandering around Fountain Square, and the raspberry chocolate chip ice cream cone at Graeter's. There was something about finding the enormous chunk of chocolate in the bottom of his sugar cone. He was convinced it appeared more frequently when Susan controlled the dipper. As he walked toward the river, tongue caressing the frozen delight, he was certain. The smile. The sparkle of her brown eyes. Her fingers always seemed to touch his at the passing of the cone. The toss of her head to free her brow of her midnight-black bangs was when he usually dribbled a new raspberry stain down the front of his shirt.

Close to the river, Tom could watch Reds fans leave Great American Ballpark. He could predict by the presence or absence of post-game fireworks whether he would be greeted by smiles or grumps. The Reds were on the road in Pittsburgh so there would be no riverside fireworks tonight. At least not in Cincinnati. The full moon concealed the Milky Way. He made a mental note how the city lights drowned Orion's Belt. To really see stars, he needed the seclusion of Montana, but not the Afghan desert.

He climbed the railing and sat, bowed his head and watched the inviting shimmer of the moon's reflection between his dangling feet. It was midnight. He jerked to protect his ear from an IED. It was only the backfire from a passing motorcycle. A tugboat blasted its horn, twice. Or was it the thump-thump of a helicopter rotor?

A high-pitched laugh – more like a spontaneous giggle – interrupted his silent prayer for relief from his torment. Raising his head from the shadows that secreted his position, he knew the young couple would remember this night. The girl cupped her hands over her mouth. *Was that a gasp?* The boy, not yet a man, was on a knee, outstretched hands offering a hinged, velvet-black box. So traditional. The couple held a pose as if Norman Rockwell had requested it.

Tom lowered his chin to his chest and swore at the raspberry stain on his shirt. One last bite from his cone revealed the lump of pure chocolate. He turned his head in time to see the young couple embrace.

The river always won. Always delivered peace. Victory. Tom swung his legs back over the railing and dropped to the bridge walkway. He swirled the dissolving chocolate with his tongue as he quickened his pace back to Ohio. He felt a peace, a constancy, a victory. His victory.

Her name is Susan. He will wear a clean shirt. Tom Simpson resolved to say hello to her tomorrow.

* * *

TURKEY IN THE STRAW

Going home. Finally going home. Two flag-draped coffins in the baggage car. I dreaded seeing Isaiah's mother and father waiting to greet our train. Isaiah and I had been inseparable since we shared a crush in the third grade on our small-town Greenfield, Ohio schoolmarm. She broke our hearts when she ran off with the Goodies Dress Pattern drummer. I knew Isaiah rested, at peace in one of the coffins.

Inseparable. After Fort Sumter, we both lied about our age – fifteen – and joined up with other farm boys in the Ohio 54th Regiment. The night before our deployment, we lost our virginity under the old Sycamore tree in the township cemetery with the ever-willing Whitehouse twins.

As we said goodbye in the summer of 1861, at this same train station I now approached two years later, the village band played my favorite song. Isaiah and I acquired a certain degree of local notoriety with our raucous rendition of *Turkey in the Straw*. With a final hug, Isaiah's mother handed him his harmonica and my mother released her grip on my trusty fiddle. Fathers shedding never-before-seen tears, admonished us to stick together.

We did. Through thick and thin, we stuck together. Little skirmishes at unimportant bridges and Shiloh battles alike, we remained inseparable. The big battles eluded us – the mud and mosquitoes did not. Whoever thought blue wool uniforms made sense in July and August never served on a front line. The highlight of each day, evening campfire cast a spell. A young corporal from New Hampshire sang the wings off an angel. The old sergeant from Maine made us all blush with his first-hand stories about the 300-pound hooker-madam in his home town brothel. To cap the evening, I coaxed a plaintive ballad from my fiddle and Isaiah's harmonica introduced *Turkey in the Straw*. Flames shot from Isaiah's mouth organ and smoke billowed from my horsehair bow.

Clickity clack. The coal smoke caught up with the slowing train as we braked into the Greenfield, Ohio depot. What would I say? I envisioned his mother's swollen eyes, his father's stiffened spine, hand over heart seeing his son's flag. Where would I find the words? I pledged to protect Isaiah. He would protect me. That final day on July 3rd at a farmer's cornfield in Gettysburg, I failed. Isaiah was now in the baggage car – at rest, at peace – my thoughts harkened back to July 3rd.

A trumpet signaled the assault. The rebel yell raised goose-bumps atop goosebumps. While we held the higher ground, Johnny Reb had the numbers to overwhelm our flank. I was hit first. Shoulder blown out. I imagined, dreamed, dreaded being shot. Reality was different. Light headed. Pain so brutal it faded into nothingness. The last thing I remember was a cannon ball roaring over our position and Isaiah spreading his body over mine. Stick together. Protect each other. Always. Isaiah was my best friend.

The train jerked to a stop. The band played a spirited *Yankee Doodle*. The steam engine surrendered its last scalding vapor surge. The cars emptied of their passengers and wounded soldiers able to walk. An honor gauntlet formed from the baggage car to the mortician's funeral bier wagon. As the baggage car door was pulled open, the band blared *Turkey in the Straw*. Ohio's 54th Regiment old-man retirees saluted and shouldered Isaiah's coffin through the honor guard. Our lieutenant saluted Isaiah's parents and handed his mother Isaiah's harmonica.

As the second coffin was pulled to the baggage car's edge, our lieutenant saluted my parents and handed my fiddle to my mother. She buried her face in my father's shoulder and wept as the band finished the final verse of a mournful *Turkey in the Straw.*

* * *

OVER THE MARS HORIZON

I t took a little less than a year, 260 days to be exact, for the Walston Expedition to flip from Earth orbit via what's known as the Hohmann Transfer Orbit to ease into the Martian orbit. A trip of 249 million miles. The voyage could have been as short as 150 days if NASA had dangerously loaded up on fuel. A precautionary rescue and supply vehicle had been launched immediately after the Walston Expedition deployment to orbit Mars during the planned exploration of the red planet. NASA had a "Plan B" for even the most remote contingency.

Six astronauts, including a married couple, due to the planned Martian conception experiment, had successfully become Martians on October 1. There were no border agents to stamp their passports. No Native Americans to teach them how to fish, grow maize, or a sleek Pocahontas to lament the felling of a mighty sycamore. It had taken a month to construct their living pod – quite an ingenious contraption. NASA had conducted a global contest won by an eight-year-old autistic boy from a rural community in Iowa. His thousand square foot living pod was basically a transformer constructed of Lego-like Teflon blocks. The $1 million tax-free prize was invested in gold futures that would accrue to the young inventor on his twenty-first birthday.

Even though the Martian days were twenty minutes longer than those on home Earth, the labor seemed easier as Martian gravity was sixty-two percent less than Earth's. The Martian 687-day year was irrelevant as the surface mission would only last six Earth months.

One of the more interesting adjustments came after sundown. Hopeless romantics might wax poetic about a Martian moonrise. It occurred three times nightly for Phobos and every 1.3 nights for Deimos. Two moons. Weird, oblique. Not round. Both Martian moons were captured asteroids slung in very low orbits. At only 5,827 and 14,562 miles above the Martian rocky surface, they were almost "duck-your-head" events.

The expedition had entered its third month. A hydroponic greenhouse fueled by astronaut excrement and water recycled from urine was producing spinach, hybrid carrots, and a mush-like grain they joked probably tasted as blah as manna. The conception project, nicknamed Genesis, was energetically pursued with natural success by the honeymooning astronaut couple.

The third month also signaled the planned delivery of a surface rover from the orbiting rescue and supply craft. Holdover technology from the last three Apollo missions in the early 1970's, this updated rover buggy would enable the astronauts to finally cross the mountain range over the horizon. Aaron the geologist and spouse Elisabeth, the archaeologist, would lead a three-day dig in the foothills surrounding an ancient sea-bed. Contingency plans were confirmed and off they went. Conjugal duties and experiments aside, this was their first time alone, together, in almost a year.

The solar powered rover performed as expected. At programmed intervals, the intrepid explorers gathered samples, banged on rocks, and used instruments designed by adult autistic scientists who didn't have gold futures trust accounts. All went as rehearsed. When something appeared unnatural, a gauge or nuclear instrument solved the mystery: *this glass-like blob is a ten-million-year-old meteor from another planet,* or *the composition of this rock is representative of molten lava, probably volcanic.* Evidence of ice or water was particularly exciting.

On the last day of their adventure, it was Elisabeth who discovered it. The "it" would define their mission. Ever the archaeologist, dig she must. She had removed two feet of surface dirt, dust, and rock when her titanium pick hit "it." A gentle vibration of a quiver was sent through her wrist and settled into her elbow; there was a spark. No sound, as the predominantly carbon dioxide atmosphere was inefficient in carrying a sound, even if there were one. Another stab. Another spark. Unusual. Elisabeth pried, dug, dusted away a greenish fuzz, almost like dried moss or mold. "It" was hard. The shard belonged to a larger something that was not to be found. Its surface had fossil-like rivulets, designs like a fern. But it was ordered, not random. Elisabeth secured it in the rover buggy trophy pouch for the drive back to home base. She pondered her find as Aaron bounced over the red planet's rugged terrain. *What could it be?*

Elisabeth let Aaron do the heavy lifting to unload the rover buggy. She was pregnant and would play that card often over the ensuing months. She was eager to seek out Adam, the philosopher astronaut. She placed her "it" on the lab table in front of Adam.

"What do you think?" she queried.

"Interesting," he said as he fingered the playing card-sized mystery.

"Look at this corner, like it's broken off," Elisabeth puzzled. "Where's the mate?"

"Wasn't any. I searched a three-foot radius."

Adam gently nestled "it" in the carbon dating chamber and keyed instructions. After a whirl and a blip, the rounded number 100,000 appeared on the screen. "Huh?" he pondered.

"Huh, what?"

"I would have expected some of your dig crap to be a hundred thousand years old. On earth, but not Mars."

Adam extracted "it" from the carbon dating chamber and laid it on the scientific table. He rubbed a common cotton swab over a corner of "it." "That's not a fern fossil," he observed.

Elisabeth's pulse quickened as she gasped, "Oh, my God."

"Ditto," Adam agreed. "You better sit down."

Adam's cotton swab revealed something specific. Something intentional. No random fern design here. "It looks like…"

Elisabeth stammered, "That squiggle looks like an…"

"Yeah. An 's'."

"Then," Adam scrubbed, "a 'u'."

Elisabeth was ready to throw up. Letters were forming a definite pattern. "Not words," she said. "More like code."

"Maybe the Mayans or Aztecs beat us here," Adam laughed.

Shivers ice-skated up and down Elisabeth's spine. "Very funny," she quipped.

Adam was done with his scrubbing. The shard gave up the entire code: *sueD tivaerc oipicnirp ni.* They each fumbled and failed to make any sense of "it."

"My first shock is the English alphabet," Elisabeth observed.

"Latin, actually," the philosopher turned astronaut corrected. "But this is gibberish."

Archaeologists being code breakers at heart, Elisabeth turned pale. She removed a small mirror from the lab table drawer and positioned it for Adam. "Okay, Leonardo da Vinci, read it now."

The reversed image revealed: *in principio creavit Deus.*

* * *

ROOM 207

An easterly breeze flirted with the Spanish moss that graced the stately sycamores flanking the gravel lane. We had planned to arrive earlier that afternoon, but Saturday antiquing between Charleston and Savannah proved a worthwhile diversion. The setting sun cast long shadows as the roadside enameled sign pointing to the Pirate's Cove Bed and Breakfast screeched a rusted plea announcing our arrival.

As I rounded one last bend through the wooded estate, I quizzed my wife, "You did insist on room 207?"

"Yes, dear," came the insulted reply. After twenty years of marriage and countless weekends on our quest, she wasn't about to dignify my inquiry with anything more than yes, dear.

Most of our friends agreed that our search for the occult and the paranormal wasn't exactly normal. We didn't have electronic gear. Nor did we wear ghostbuster backpacks or worry about crossing any streamer beams. We didn't traipse through haunted houses intent on bringing Casper home in a Mason jar. A rudimentary Boy Scout compass and a not-so-simple Canon SLS 35mm camera were enough. On previous adventures, we had seen the compass go drunk with confusion over true north. Our scrapbook documented a few orbs caught on film, but a clear image of an apparition had not yet developed.

After a traditional Southern dinner of shrimp and grits, cornbread, and collard greens, we settled into room 207's four-poster bed. The compass at our bedside foretold a not-so-unexpected disappointing night. We had experienced many a bust on these weekend sojourns, so we adventured to a roll in the hay that might salvage some of the trip. The old feather bed was protesting one of my better moves when lightning struck the oak tree outside our window. Crack. Sparks. Fire.

"Oh, honey," my wife faked a moan. "I always knew it could be like this."

That's when it happened. With each lightning flash, it moved closer. Closer. Crack. Closer. I could hear the compass spinning, vibrating on the nightstand. The needle scratched the glass lens. Lightning etched its fingers across room 207's ceiling. A flowing shimmer erased the darkness. There she was. Standing at the foot of our bed. Bathed in the eerie, reflective glow of the lightning. The bride of room 207. Veiled, dark, deep-set eyes. White lace and satin wedding dress caressed the hardwood floorboards, creaking a plaintive sigh, as she swayed to-and-fro. Bare feet. A ghostly drool of blood escaping from the corner of her coal-black lips.

I slipped out of bed and tip-toed to the young virgin's side. I slid my arm around her waist as she rested her pale, chalk-like cheek on my shoulder. Flash. Click. Flash. She vanished as innocently as she had appeared.

CVS didn't open until ten a.m. on Sunday morning. "Do you think you got it, honey?" I asked my photo journalist wife.

She had not yet won a Pulitzer, but if a picture were to be captured, my wife would get it. "Just relax," she retorted. "I probably got five or six good shots."

The CVS clerk slid the packet of developed film across the counter. My fingers fumbled with the gummed flap as I arrayed the deck of photos on the cold glass countertop. There I was, my arm around the waist of NOTHING. I was clear as a bell. But no white wedding dress. No ghostly virgin bride.

"Huh," my wife, ever the photographic technician dead-panned, feeling underexposed. "Looks like the spirit was willing, but the flash was weak."

* * *

GRANPA'S TRUNK

Dignified. Poignant. The military funeral strikes all the right chords. The rifle salute. Crisp folding of the flag. The Army officer bends at the waist, whispers words of honor and thanks from the President of the United States as he touches Grandma Yvette's hand. Taps echoes in the hearts of all in attendance.

Fifteen-year-old Craig opens the car door for his great-grandmother as his fellow cousin, and erstwhile partner in mischief Luke, also fifteen, offers his hand to the new widow. Clutching the folded flag to her breast, Yvette Graham is flanked by these strapping teenagers up the front walk to her stately, yet soon-to-be-lonely Victorian home.

Midwestern family funeral gatherings are joyous occasions when a life well-lived is celebrated. Ben Graham's family has every reason to celebrate. Slipping away silently in one's sleep at age ninety is a good start to any celebration. Grandpa, or Great-Grandpa, or just plain ole Dad was as common as dirt. Successful local businessman, soft-spoken town council head, church elder. It took some coaxing and begging; old World War II stories of glory and heroism were hard to drag out of Ben Graham. But when he got started, wow, could he spin a yarn. A daredevil pilot flying spies and contraband into 1944 German-occupied France. Supporting the French Résistance. Crash landing in a foggy sheep pasture on one midnight mission. Broken leg, he was pulled from his flaming British Lysander by the head of the local Résistance. Fell in love and married her. Yep, Grandma Yvette was a war hero too. Married sixty-five years.

Every horizontal surface in the rambling, fifteen-room house is covered with food. Casseroles, pies, cakes, meatloaf. Kids, cousins, aunts, uncles, neighbors everywhere – and one dog. Laughter and joy in every room. Great-grandchildren feed cookies to the dog. Old Uncle Joe once again forgets punchlines to jokes he has been telling for fifty years.

"Craig," his mother instructs, "zip up to the attic and bring down that old French serving platter."

"Where is it?" Craig quizzes.

"Look behind the iron parrot cage."

"I think I know where it is," cousin Luke brags as he races Craig up the stairs.

The attic covers the entire third floor of the regal old Victorian house. Luke is in the lead as he opens the door to the steep attic stairs. As he flips on the never-enough solitary light, Craig elbows him aside and scampers past him. They tackle and push each other into the tomb of clutter and treasures.

To say that these two are competitive is an understatement. Best friends, but not beyond blackening an eye here or there, they could finish each other's sentences. Craig is the quarterback on the JV football team. Luke is a wide receiver. They don't need to wink or twitch an ear lobe. A quick glance at the defense and Luke would run a precise pattern and catch Craig's perfect pass. The high school coach is already salivating.

The two cousins maneuver over boxes and weave a path toward the iron bird cage in the far corner. Craig picks up a pair of binoculars, blows off a layer of dust. "Craig, focus," Luke orders as he surveys the attic's dark reaches. Backing into a brass floor lamp, he catches it as cleanly as a quick-hitting slant pass. He turns on the three-way bulb, casting haunting shadows around the cluttered attic.

"Shut up," Craig retorts, "forgot these were here."

"We've only been playin' up here our whole lives," Luke laughs.

Craig puts down the binoculars, catches up with Luke, pushes him from behind. Luke falls against the iron parrot cage. The bird cage teeters. In his attempt to steady the bird cage, Luke loses his balance, falls against a book case. The domino effect continues as the book case and books tumble to the floor. Luke is trapped beneath a hoard of books and the bird cage. Craig lifts the book case back to its fifty-year perch against a side wall, enabling Luke to extricate and dust himself off.

The ensuing shoving match ceases as Craig's mother shouts from the foot of the attic stairs, "What's all the racket? Come on, we need the serving platter."

"Coming," Craig yells, as he finds the platter at the base of the bird cage. Craig retreats to deliver the requested china and assure his mother that all is well.

Luke wiggles the book case to a more secure position. He bangs his head on the steeply-sloped attic roof. "Crap," he grimaces as he falls on his butt. Grabbing his head, he kicks the book case with both feet. The book case falls to the floor. Luke flings books and flails at anything else within range in a flurry of frustration.

The fallen book case no longer hides the small, three-foot high door it had guarded for half a century. The door stands askew, held only by a single rusted hinge. He rubs his head and clears the books away from the mystery door. As he pulls on the door, the solitary hinge breaks free and the door lands on top of him.

"Luke, Luke?" Craig yells as he returns to the attic.

"Over here," Luke responds.

Not seeing Luke under the door, Craig scans the poorly-lit attic and quizzes, "Over where?"

"Here," as Luke pushes the door off his chest.

Craig sticks his head into the newly-revealed side storage chamber. "What in the heck is this?" On all fours, he disappears into the small dark space.

"What'cha see?" Luke asks.

Slowly, the corner of a large, rectangular box appears in the door opening. Inch by inch, Craig wobble-slides the box out of its tomb. Luke scooches forward, grabs the leather handle at the small end of the box and pulls. The dry, aged handle breaks in half under the weight of the box. He grasps the edges of the box and helps Craig wiggle it into the attic. Crawling out of the cramped side chamber, Craig settles into an old oak rocking chair with his hands on the lid of the box. The box between them, Luke wipes his hands across the lid and blows decades of dust into his cousin's face.

"Thanks a lot, jerk," Craig coughs as he clears his eyes.

"Sorry."

In all their years of playing hide-and-seek and sneaking a smoke in Grandpa's attic, Craig and Luke had never stumbled upon this treasure. Dull green, brass-edged corners, rivets; it measures three-feet long, two-feet wide, by a foot-and-a-half tall. Craig picks up a wayward cloth and wipes layers of dust from the lid. White lettering solves the mystery: 1st Lieutenant B. Graham, P28749382, U.S. Army Air Corps. Grandpa's trunk is about to reveal its secrets.

"Wow!" Craig exclaims.

"Shhh," Luke cautions as he looks toward the stairs to the second floor below.

"How cool is this?" Craig says as he kneels beside the end of the old Army trunk.

Luke releases the brass clasp on the front of the trunk. Together they open the lid and peer inside. A musty wisp of 1945 air insults the cousins' nostrils. Coordinated sneezes echo throughout the attic canyon of junk. Luke shines his iPhone light in the three-inch deep tray that rests in the trunk. Craig gently fingers through a stack of letters bound with a ribbon. Luke unfolds a silk map of France.

"Carte de champagne francaise du Nord," Luke says.

"Qué?" Craig protests, in Spanish. "OK, showoff. You're fluent in French. Grandma Yvette loves you best."

Fingering the silk map, Luke translates, "It's a map of Northern France."

"Wow!" Craig exclaims. "Back when Grandma was in the Résistance."

"Look at all this stuff!" Luke paws through the tray.

Together, they lift the tray out of the trunk and set it gently on the floor. Slowly, one-by-one, they pull World War II artifacts out of the trunk and examine them. Grandpa's leather Army Air Corps pilot helmet, his flight jacket, brown/green waistcoat uniform. A wool, French beret. A captured German bayonet. Luke picks up a pocket watch, flicks open the scrolled cover. A cautious twist of the stem, he holds it to his ear and nods that it works. Craig grabs it and sets the correct time. He listens to the rhythmic tick-tock and carefully places it on the rocking chair beside him.

Craig's hand trembles as he pulls a scarlet red armband up to the light. As his fingers follow the outline of the black Nazi swastika centered in the armband's white circle, goosebumps rise on his arm. He drops the armband back into the trunk and dusts his hands together as he shudders at this brush with pure evil.

To free a hand, Luke stuffs the silk map into his shirt pocket. He points the light into the army trunk and eyes a small, shiny object. Kneeling beside the trunk, he removes a Zippo lighter. Rising to his feet, he lays his iPhone on the rocking chair and hands the lighter to Craig. Craig examines the brass and chrome-plated artifact. Craig rubs his fingers across the surface and flicks the lighter top open and closed.

Now standing shoulder-to-shoulder, the two cousins breathing in the same decades-stale air, arms touching, Luke grabs the lighter and flicks the top open again. His thumb on the small geared wheel, he gives it a spin. Steel scrapes flint and sparks erupt from the lighter. Had someone been outside the stately Victorian house, looking up at the attic roof window, they would have seen a flash of fire and rushed to call 911.

Luke and Craig fall to their knees, shaking their heads in temporary blindness. Lightning arches through the night sky, illuminating the tin roof of a small farm barn across a meadow. Crawling on all-fours, the wet grass and rain soaks through their khaki pants and oxford blue shirts. They roll to their feet and run to the safety of the barn.

Panting, out of breath, the cousins hide in a horse stall. They bury their legs under dry straw and sit, backs against the interior wall of the barn.

"What in the heck was that?" Craig demands.

"Damn if I know," becomes Luke's honest reply. He looks at the Zippo lighter in his hand. He switches it to his other hand, then back and forth to lessen the impact of the residual heat coming from the lighter.

As Luke places his thumb on the geared wheel, Craig screams, "No! Once is enough."

The darkness in the horse stall is swallowed by flashlights in the boys' faces. "Haut les mains!" came the command.

Luke raises his hands over his head.

Craig, follows suit, quipping, "Obviously, that means hands up."

Secreting the Zippo lighter into his pant pocket, Luke responds in French, "Je ne tire pas, je ne tire pas."

"What'd ya say, what'd ya say?" Craig pleads.

"Don't shoot."

"Yeah, Je an tore pu," as Craig butchers the French language.

Luke gives Craig a sneer and says, "Let me do the talking."

Flashlights still in their eyes, there is enough light to discern that the cousins are held at gunpoint by 9 mm sub machine Sten guns. One of their captors walks up to Luke and pulls the silk map out of his shirt pocket. He examines the map and hands it to his partner. The Sten guns are lowered to their sides as they relax. Laughter is shared as the taller of the two men yells over his shoulder, "Agneau."

"Lamb," Luke whispers to Craig.

A young woman, probably about twenty-two or three, enters the horse stall. As she studies the silk map, Craig and Luke study her. Despite her dark, drab clothes, and the charcoal camouflaged cheeks, she is beautiful. The beret cocked over her forehead cause the boys to glance at each other, puzzled. The beret looks just like the one from Grandpa's trunk. From the wedding pictures, is it possible? "Yvette?" Craig whispers to Luke.

The Sten guns level in a reflex. Flashlights in their eyes. Hands again rise over their heads. The young woman stops in front of Craig and whispers, "Jamais les noms réels, toujours nom de code. Agneau."

"Luke?" Craig pleads for help.

"Agneau," Luke acknowledges.

The young woman leader of this small patrol of the French Résistance does not act like a lamb. She takes charge. The French men lower their weapons and sit on the scattered straw in the horse stall. Agneau motions for the two boys to sit down. She hands the silk map back to Luke. The boys look at each other as if they couldn't read this complex football defense. They conclude they have just been accepted into the French Résistance and are being sent on a mission. The leaders finish their sidebar whispers and circle the two boys.

Agneau snaps her fingers at Luke and requests Luke's map. In rapid fire French that Craig assumes Luke will summarize for him later, she taps her fingers on a corner of the map and issues instructions. She hands him a canvas pouch. Luke nods understanding and rises. Agneau grabs him by his upper arms, pulls him to her, and kisses him on both cheeks. The quick brush of her cheek to his raises the hair on his arms and causes a nervous swallow. Craig rises to accept a similar farewell. Luke and Craig had yet to comprehend what just took place when the two male patrol members kiss them farewell. This causes an embarrassed pinking of their cheeks.

Luke leads the way as they exit the barn into the rainy night. Craig stumbles across the ankle-high wet pasture. "Luke, stop," he pleads.

"Not yet."

Craig tackles Luke around the ankles. Rolling on the ground, Craig ends up on top. "Damn it! What's going on?"

"She gave us an assignment," Luke said, under his breath.

"This isn't real," Craig implores.

Luke raises a knee and catches Craig firmly in the crotch as Luke assumes the topside position. "Does that feel real?" Luke runs and tumbles behind a hay stack that could have been painted by Van Gogh.

Still reeling from the knee in the groin, Craig sits down beside Luke, backs resting against the hay stack. "Okay, what gives?"

"You tell me?" Luke queries.

"You're the Frenchie," Craig pleads. "What did they say?"

Luke retrieves the Zippo lighter from his pocket and flicks open the top.

"Don't you dare!" Craig barks. "We might end up as cave men."

Re-pocketing the Zippo, Luke brings Craig up to speed. "Agneau, Lamb, is her code name. She scolded me for using her real name. Résistance groups, patrols, are small. She leads those other two guys."

"And us?"

"Appears so," Luke confirms. "They hide in the woods. Maquis. We are to sneak into a nearby village. Reverse road signs and drop this pouch beside the well in front of the baker's shop. If we have time, cut some telephone lines."

"That's it?"

"Yep."

"What's in the pouch?"

"She said 'mimeographed underground newspaper'."

"What's a mimeograph?" Craig asks.

"Maybe my French is bad. We'll Google it, later."

"Let's go home now," Craig suggests.

"That woman is counting on us."

"That woman? What do you mean, that woman?"

"Agneau."

"Luke, you damn well know what I mean."

"It can't be," Luke insists.

"I don't speak French, but I'll tell you what. It's 1944. Before D-Day. That woman is Grandma Yvette!"

"I know," admits Luke. He pulls the Zippo out of his pocket.

"Put it back. We gotta figure this out, before we try flickin' that lighter again."

Luke put the Zippo back in his pant pocket. Let's get to the village and then head to the woods. "Agreed?"

"Agreed."

They shinny up telephone poles at the edge of the village. The night is greeted by low cloud cover; it's as dark as a dead-end cave, perfect to mask their ornery deeds. Road signs pointing south are reversed to north. East becomes west. It's like Halloween, but all tricks with no treats. The village is small, quiet. Even in the darkness Craig could tell the difference between a cobbler and a butcher. Just as he was laying the canvas pouch at the base of the baker's well, car headlights blinded the Graham cousins.

"Geler! Haut les mains," came the harsh, guttural command.

It didn't take English, Luke's French, or Craig's Spanish to recognize German orders yelled by the black-uniformed Gestapo officer. The German SS Officer approaches the well and opens the canvas pouch, thumbs through a dozen copies of the latest Résistance propaganda newspaper, and smirks.

"Weiter!" He orders, with a gun in Luke's back.

The small band of Gestapo SS troops march the Graham cousins to the village center, and push their backs against the courtyard gazebo. The German SS Officer snatches the silk map from Luke's shirt pocket, ripping his shirt. He removes a pack of cigarettes from his coat pocket, laughs, and offers the boys one last smoke. Craig initially declines, but follows Luke's lead in taking a cigarette after he notices four German soldiers forming a firing squad. The German SS Officer lights his own cigarette and blows smoke in Luke's face. As he proceeds to light Craig's shaking cigarette, a quick breeze extinguishes his lighter. He flicks his German lighter again with no success.

Luke, slowly, reaches into his pant pocket and offers the Zippo to the German SS Officer. The Officer flicks the top open and inspects the gleaming chrome and U.S. Army Air Corp insignia. "Yankee!"

Luke and Craig make eye contact, touch shoulders, and lean in close to the accommodating German SS Officer. Smug in his arrogance, the Nazi spins the geared wheel as he reaches to light Luke's cigarette. Sparks fly as lightning strikes the village gazebo.

Partially blinded and more expectant of returning to an attic in America, Craig knees the German Officer in the groin. Luke reaches into Grandpa's trunk, retrieving the German bayonet relic. He plunges the bayonet into the neck of the Gestapo officer. Another burst of sparks and a puff of smoke reduces Herr Hendrik to ashes. Only his brass belt buckle and Grandpa's Zippo remain. The belt buckle, a too-hot-to-handle souvenir, chars the attic floor beside Grandpa's trunk as it spins to a stop. The Zippo lighter is once again nestled in Luke's pant pocket.

Panting, short of breath, the two cousins fall to their knees. Craig touches the still smoldering belt buckle and jerks his hand back, reacting to the heat. Luke rises and sits in the rocking chair, shifting to retrieve the old pocket watch. He cups the watch in his hand, puzzled.

"How long ya think we were gone, Craig?"

Finally successful in picking up the warm belt buckle, "Oh, three, four hours," Craig responds.

"Look at this," Luke says as he hands the pocket watch to his cousin.

"Only two minutes?" Craig questions as he furrows his brow.

"And look at our clothes."

"Dry, no dirt, no mud. Your shirt pocket isn't torn," Craig observes.

Patting his shirt pocket, Luke retrieves the silk map of France, placing it beside the ribbon-tied letters on the rocking chair. Retrieving Grandpa's Zippo lighter from his pant pocket, he flips open the top.

"No!" Craig yells, as he cups his hands around Luke's. "We've had enough adventure for one day."

"What's the racket up there?" Craig's mother yells, her foot on the first attic step. "Don't make me come up there."

Typical of their quarterback - wide receiver second sense communication, the cousins make eye contact, confirming that they'd clean the attic mess up later. Luke places the lighter on the rocking chair; as the boys evade discovery and tumble down the steep stairway.

The afternoon returns to good food and a rehash of old Grandpa Graham stories. Luke and Craig avoid each other in fear of tipping their hand. They had no experience in how a killer of a Nazi Gestapo officer should behave or react to Résistance stories or Grandma Yvette's retelling of how she first met Grandpa. Only Yvette, and now two of her great-grand-sons had any first-hand knowledge of 1944 occupied France.

It is now that awkward time following a funeral – when to leave? No one wants to be the first to leave. Leaving last is no good either. Especially with a close-knit family, it would be hard to give Grandma Yvette that last hug before abandoning her to the loneliness of her Victorian house.

"I'm fine," she smiles as the last of her children ease down the steps from her front porch.

"Love you, Granny," seems particularly heartfelt as Craig and Luke accept the new widow's French smooch on each cheek. A chill touches spines as they recall a younger Agneau sending them on their first WWII mission.

The tired, weary widow contemplates her first night in sixty-five years without her beloved Ben. The usual bedtime routine is history. Ben doesn't put the last coffee cup in the dishwasher. Yvette returns twice to confirm that the front door is locked. Halfway up the stairs, she returns to turn off the living room lights. On her last pass through the darkened lower floor, she stops at the table displaying Ben's Army medals and memorabilia. Her fingers grace the fabric of the folded American flag. Clutching it to her breast, she glances at the picture of her young Army Air Corps fly-boy. Tucking the flag under her arm, she limps up the second-floor stairs.

Ready for bed, she notices that the attic door is ajar. Easing the door shut, a remnant of light seeps through the ill-fitting door jam. An involuntary whisper of "fichu" communicates her displeasure at one more task delaying her first night without spooning with Ben. She opens the door and turns off the attic light switch. Light still cascades down the steep stairway, eliciting a second "maudire." This time, less involuntary and much less of a whisper.

The attic stairs had obviously been designed by an architect younger than ninety. Succumbing to the steep stairs, Yvette ascends to the third floor in more of a vertical crawl than upright. Folded flag still tucked under her arm, she meanders her way around junk she now voluntarily "damns" she should have pitched decades ago. Hand on the brass floor lamp's knob, she gives a twist. The three-way bulb brightens. For the first time in ages, she sees Ben's WWII Army trunk. Her breath momentarily stolen, she lowers, kneels beside the open trunk. As she sorts through the dust and memories, she places the folded flag in the trunk. Her legs fail her in her first attempt to rise. She steadies herself with a hand on the edge of the trunk. Not as steady as she would like, her hand slips into the trunk and comes to rest on the trunk bottom. As she extricates herself from falling into the trunk, she grabs at something soft. It is her beret.

Justifiably short of breath, Yvette kneels beside the old oak rocking chair. Gathering the objects blocking her derriere aside, she settles into the chair. A brief exhale and rock back and forth provides a respite. Her only objective had been to turn out the lights. She is now immersed in the 1944 French Résistance. Continuing a slow rock, she fingers the beret, brings it to her face and inhales the French countryside. The beret now cocked astride her silver-gray hair; she unfolds the silk map of a French village she had once called home. She lays her hands on the bundle of letters in her lap. Sliding the top letter free of its bowed ribbon, she reads sweet words written in a bygone century. A tear moistens her cheek as the letter drifts from a quaking hand to the attic floor. As she bends forward to pick up the letter, another object falls from her lap to the floor with a metallic "clink."

The emotions of the day, the years, the decades pierce her heart. She returns the letter to its bundled home. She tucks the silk map under the sleeve of her blouse. She rocks forward and picks up Ben's Zippo from the attic floor. A strange, yet comforting warmth soothes the aged stiffness in her fingers. Her heart races as she flips open the Zippo. The three-way bulb in the brass floor lamp dies, exhausted. Nimble fingers spin the Zippo wheel against the eager flint. Wrinkles fade. Lightning etches jagged shadows across the attic floor.

A bundle of ribboned letters is illuminated in an otherwise empty oak rocking chair that slowly comes to rest.

* * *

SHOVEL-DUG GRAVES

B link twice, it's missed. Three times, best viewed through the rearview mirror. Still Creek, Indiana wasn't highly regarded for anything important, other than solid family values. The locals were equally split over the village name "Still." The creek bed at village edge was drier than ole-man Foster's sense of humor. Never enough water flowing to ever settle still in any one spot long enough to wet a frog's lower lip. Other theory hinged on copper kettles and illegal moonshine runnin' that required considerably more water than the first frog-lip theory.

An eighth-grade social studies project had Jessie Plunkett wandering all the Still Creek back alleys in 1960, conducting an unofficial census. One hundred ten, not counting dogs and cats. It took longer to conduct the census than one might think as Jessie suffered through a feigned courtesy of decades-old stories 'bout half a dozen blacksmith shops—three still existed in 1960—two long-gone eateries, and the haunted hangman's tree that moaned at the slightest breeze through its hollowed trunk.

Jessie was a patient and courteous interviewer as he knew where he could get all his blanks filled in, discrepancies resolved, the truth confirmed. He saved his next-door neighbor Charlie Knox for last. Charlie Knox didn't mind the kids calling him Digger. Charlie didn't mind much at all, he pretty much kept to himself. Digger Charlie had two jobs: best strawberry patch in the county and township cemetery grave digger. Digger Charlie's life was ordered, organized into narrow, straight rows of strawberries and perfectly dug, vertical rectangles precisely six feet deep. Since Digger Charlie dug the graves, he knew every square inch of the cemetery. Jessie got an A+ on his 1960 census project.

The Still Creek old-timers respected Digger, understood him, could carry on a conversation with him. But they were a dying breed. The up-and-coming generation was scared of him, couldn't relate. Probably the lack of eye contact. Ya see, Digger Charlie was only four-feet high. Digger had spent so much time hunched over 'tween his rows of strawberries with a hoe, he couldn't straighten up. He might have been six-feet tall, but he was bent over into two, irregular sections. Each section at a perfect right angle to the other. A T-square's ninety-degree angle could be plumbed using Digger Charlie as the template.

Digger spent his entire existence looking straight down at the ground. Okay if hoeing weeds out of a row of strawberries or possibly crunched six feet deep in the cool of a perfectly-spaded grave. Talking with Digger was difficult. At eighty-plus years old, he did his share of grunting, with little to no gesticulating. Unless you laid on your back and looked up into his face, lip reading was impossible and eye contact never happened. If a stranger offered a Still Creek resident a thousand dollars to create a police artist sketch of Digger Charlie, the stranger would leave with his money in his pocket. No one knew what Digger looked like, except Jessie Plunkett. No one except Jessie could translate Digger's gruff mumbles and grunts into intelligent thoughts and intriguing life lessons.

When Digger Charlie loaded his 1949 Ford pickup with pickaxe, assortment of shovels, burlap sacks, and perched a six-foot ladder 'cross the back tailgate, everyone knew someone had died. No need to wait for an obituary. Just follow Digger Charlie—at fifteen miles per hour—the half mile to the cemetery. Yell down the hole, "Who's gonna be sleepin' here, Digger?"

and he'd mumble something like, "Wid'r Johnson, in 'er sleep last night."

Jessie's classmate hooligans would terrorize Still Creek on their bikes. You could hear 'em coming—baseball cards clothes-pinned—flipping and flapping in the spokes. You could also smell 'em. Mostly because bathing wasn't perfected or even practiced on a daily basis, but, also due to the squirrel tails dangling from each bike's handle grips. This juvenile delinquent biker gang-of-five-in-training would loiter and watch Digger Charlie tend his strawberry patch for hours. Amongst themselves they would ponder stuff like, "How the mortician gonna lay out Digger?" "Haf ta bury him sittin' up." Mostly ignored, stealing strawberries from Digger's unfenced patch crossed the line. The young miscreants would scatter like fleas off a kerosene-soaked mongrel when they heard the closing breech of Digger's double-barrel 12-gauge shotgun from his back porch. Digger never fired a shot at anyone, only raccoons.

It was a foggy Thursday morning in July when Jessie saw the 1949 Ford pickup loaded for the cemetery. He yelled over the hedge but, out of character, he couldn't understand the grunt that came back at him. It was late afternoon when Jessie got around to pedaling his Schwinn to the cemetery. 'Bout halfway, he met the returning biker gang of five that informed him that Digger wasn't talkin'.

Jessie turned his bike into the gravel lane that meandered through the hundred- and fifty-year-old cemetery. Flopping his bike on the lush-green grass near the monuments remembering rich farmers, he respectfully avoided walking on the graves of the fallen from the Civil and Spanish American Wars. Nearing the last section before entering the Potter's Field area, he dangled his feet over the edge of the newly-forming gateway to eternity. Only half done, Digger was slow but methodical. His sharpened spade left crescent-shaped indents in the strangely polished clay sides of his project. It was like every grave before it, but different: perfect. Hunched to disappear into the chill of his office, he straightened—just a tad—revealing a weathered, tanned face. A toothless grin and subtle wink to his friend Jessie communicated all that was necessary.

Jessie offered a cautious, yet knowing smile in return and retrieved his bicycle. The pedal home was measured. He stomped a clod of dirt into dust between the strawberry rows and knelt down, picking a fat ripe berry. He raised his face to a warming sun as a solitary tear softened his cheek.

The Still Creek township trustees approved the purchase of a backhoe at its next meeting. Never again would a life well-lived rest in a perfect shovel-dug grave.

* * *

HITLER'S FIRST DAY IN HELL

"The Ride of the Valkyries" blared from the tin-clad speakers surrounding the scorched Quonset hut. April 30, 1945. The 1933 Mercedes-Benz 380K Touring Convertible was pushed into the central courtyard by a menagerie of children, cripples, homosexuals, gypsies, and elderly women – all dressed in tattered, striped prison garb. Uniformed passengers sat erect, encouraged by the freshness of spring: Bormann, Himmler, Goebbels, Goering.

A word of context might be in order. As the embedded correspondent for the Christian Science Monitor, God permitted me unfettered access beyond the gates of hell. Any day of my choosing. What follows is my account of Hitler's first day in hell.

I understood the presence of the Mercedes passengers, but the innocent car-pushers who inhaled their last in the gas chambers of Bergen-Belsen? Lucifer's lieutenant, assigned as my docent, explained, "Oh, they are in heaven."

"Excuse me?" I challenged.

"God's a clever guy. Heaven and hell are personal. Custom-designed for each person."

"Okay?"

"It's really quite simple. If a daisy is your favorite flower and you like fresh-baked bread, your personal heaven is running the flower shop next door to a bakery."

"And these innocent concentration camp victims?"

"Just watch."

The Mercedes settled to a stop. Slowly, methodically, the bedraggled troupe opened the trunk and removed gardening tools. Hoes, shovels, pitch forks. A sack of steer manure. As the sun broke through the low-hanging clouds, offering a glimmer of hope to the four passengers, the gypsy grabbed a pitch fork and gouged out Goebbels's eyes. Goering's head went airborne, bounced off the Mercedes' hood, and rolled into a pigsty. Blood and guts everywhere. After stuffing steer manure down Himmler's throat, the troupe returned their garden tools to the car trunk.

"See, they are in heaven. Custom-designed just for them."

"But, once and done?" I asked. "What will they do all the rest of eternity?"

"Oh," Lieutenant Lucifer responded, "this is it. Every day at sunrise."

"The Nazis?"

"Every day at sunrise. They think they're going for a ride through the Bavarian countryside."

"So, they re-live this hell? For all of eternity?"

"Pretty cool; don't you think? I just love it."

"I came to find Herr Hitler."

"Oh, yes. It's his first day. We were expecting him."

I shaded my eyes from the rising sun, and there he was. The four uniformed passengers had returned to their former Nazi glory. As Hitler approached the Mercedes, his comrades rose as one, raised-arm salutes. Herr Adolph raised his riding crop to acknowledge his henchmen. Standing at the Mercedes front bumper, Hitler inspected the shiny chrome and mirror black finish of the hood. He approved. The ride to Bavaria would be triumphant.

A bustling gaggle of brown-shirted school children ran from the Quonset hut and overwhelmed dear Adolph. Loved and adored, he touched each head with a tender pat. He was then grabbed around the ankles and knees, hoisted on adolescent shoulders. Adolph's smile turned into a look of surprise and confusion as his tunic was stripped from his chest. Spit-polished boots departed his feet as his riding pants were ripped asunder. Before he knew what hit him, he was on his back, spread-eagled on the car hood, buck naked.

"Excuse me," Lieutenant Lucifer demurred. "I'm needed now."

As a young boy retrieved a rusty set of garden sheers from the car trunk, Lieutenant Lucifer led an old blind man to the front bumper, directly at Hitler's feet. The old man adjusted his yarmulke, open and closed his garden tool with a screech that caused Hitler to raise his head. The old man leaned across Hitler's thighs.

Hitler didn't know it, but, this first day routine would be repeated into eternity. Finally realizing what was about to happen, Hitler screamed, "Damn Mohel!"

* * *

DEATH BECOMES ME

I died today. It didn't hurt this time, not like the last time. The next time might actually feel good—being new at this, this death business—I'm not sure about any death feeling good. I've lost track, ten, maybe a dozen. It's happened enough that I expect it again, at least one more time (eternal sarcasm?). Will there be a last time? Everyone reading this will answer, "Well, yeah, death is inevitable." But perpetual death? That's the question, at least for me.

Before we get all hung up about shadows on cave walls and other undergraduate philosophy 101 contemplations, which is more important to my circumstance? Multiple deaths or multiple escapes? Escapes, you ponder? Why didn't I cut to the chase with "resurrection," "re-birth," or a perpetual hook-up with a "reincarnated" Shirley MacLaine?

Don't even ask. Yes, I die, each time. It's not a suspended animation of some sort where the life squad shouts, "*Clear!*" before the magic paddles scare the grim reaper away. I go stone-cold dead. I remember nothing about my dead time. There's no out-of-body experience where I see a perplexed mortician search for my misplaced remains. I die, and then, I'm not dead. There's no building on what I've learned during my "dead time". I can't recall anything I've learned when I'm not alive. When I'm no longer dead, I merely pick up where I left off. A life continuum. No loops of super consciousness or ability to pick lottery numbers. I don't know if it's ten minutes, ten hours, ten days, or a flash of a nanosecond. There are no angels, no black swamps with misty methane fog, and neither St. Peter nor God say, *Oops, wrong guy, go back. See ya later.*

Is that a Mack truck I see in my peripheral vision?

* * *

BELIEVE IT OR NOT

H ands folded in lap, caressing, twirling my pinky ring, I averted the inquiring glares of my traveling coach mates. For most of my 19 years, I was aware of the stares. The birth of the "Roaring Twenties" a short horizon away, a hopeful time; a time of gaiety, acceptance. I prayed for acceptance. The hot, clickety clack train coach was my hope for deliverance.

I am leaving the small town of Morganville seeking a better future. Eyes closed, I reflect on a life of avoidance, shame. With my Chicago destination in mind, I am headed for somewhere, anywhere away – away from my past. Filled with uncertainty, I am following my heart. My betrothed awaits my arrival. Head on a shoulder, my brother's shoulder, we don't need words. We are both ready for a fresh start. I know it will be difficult for him, but he knows I am happy. Checking his pocket watch, I note I will be in my beloved's arms within the hour. While our heart warms, I sense the apprehension in my brother.

Close our entire life, we know each other's thoughts, inner feelings. We are inseparable, but different. He got A's in ciphering; I excelled in literature. He does the heavy lifting; I quilt the finer stitch. On average, we were the perfect student. Some say we had a double advantage. I usually nodded under-standing with my brother turning a deaf ear, as though all in life isn't fair.

We had discussed this new venture. While hesitant at first, my brother agreed the prospects in Morganville were bleak. The entertainment business and world travel might help us achieve our twin objectives. While awkward at first, I am confident my brother will accept my fiancé. Sharing rent and other expenses will help.

My brother has agreed to keep an open mind. The plan is the brainchild of my fiancé. She has arranged an introduction with an entrepreneur who promises a future better than our tormented past in Morganville. Meeting all our needs would be an oddity.

The last to exit the train, we stand on the top step and survey our future. It's as though the world stood still, at least the new world of the Chicago train depot. The pointing, the stares; it was Morganville all over again.

"Jules, Jules," my fiancé shouts. "Over here."

I take control and race to my beloved, we embrace. My brother tilts his head, looks away, affording a moment of privacy as I am greeted with a passionate kiss. A quick, fiancé peck on my brother's cheek was less than appreciated. Interesting how only Jules blushes.

"Good to see you, Jules," my fiancé again tries to win over my brother. "Good trip?"

"It was fine," I interrupt.

"I see you traveled first class," my fiancé notes.

"Might as well," Jules deadpans. "We only need one seat."

"I better figure out your sense of humor if this marriage is to work," my fiancé admits. "Oh, he's here. The man I've been telling you about. Let me introduce Mr. Robert Ripley."

Mr. Ripley bowed, smiled and blinked twice, "I can't believe my eyes."

* * *

An Ode To Brie

Greenleaf, Michigan was so sleepy I could almost hear it snore as I drove through. Not even a stoplight, just a mid-village, four-way stop sign. When my twin sister Chloe called me on her sojourns to the Upper Peninsula, she'd always lose cell service in Greenleaf. No warning. Dead.

Chloe had frequented the Upper Peninsula for the past two years. A writer, poet, and artist, she rented a one-room cabin in the woods four miles outside Greenleaf. She spent weeks alone, isolated with her art and writings. Chloe restocked provisions at Jeremiah's Diner and General Store every other week and treated herself to a toasted cheese sandwich. It was somewhat unusual for both businesses to cohabitate; even more unusual that toasted brie on salted rye bread sandwiches be the delight du jour. Chloe wrote a poem: "An Ode to Brie," in honor of her favorite sandwich.

Some twins have a sixth sense, communication and under-standing that defy logic. To us it was natural. We didn't try to explain it. We still laugh over our lavender sweater incident. I say "incident" because Chloe and I bought the same V-neck sweater from an Amazon Prime mail order vendor. We each ordered two lavender sweaters, a spare to gift to a twin sister. We wore our sweaters and met for a birthday dinner at a restaurant near my home. We laughed 'til we almost wet ourselves as we exchanged boxes adorned with pink puppy dog paper and yellow ribbons with our best friend.

I remember the cool October morning when my sixth sense twitched, missed a beat and stopped. I spilled my morning coffee down the front of my lavender sweater. I cried, swore, and was puzzled when my sixth sense didn't feel right. Something was missing. I tried calling Chloe and wasn't surprised at failure due to the limited cell phone coverage in Greenleaf. I hadn't heard from Chloe in over two weeks. Wearing my extra lavender sweater, I packed an overnight bag and headed for the Upper Peninsula.

Not stopping in Greenleaf, I drove directly to Chloe's remote cabin. Dusk settled over the deep woods. Shadows lengthened and haunted the early evening. Having visited a few times over the past two years, I knew what to expect. No electricity. An outhouse with a bucket of lime. Hand pump to deliver fresh spring water. Where was Chloe's Jeep Wrangler? The front door ajar surprised me.

The front porch boards moaned under my feet. An owl swooped low and announced it owned the night as Splotch, the cat, pawed his empty food bowl toward me. Though an identical twin to its owner, I wasn't Chloe and Splotch knew it. Lighting the coal-oil lantern on the table, I found Splotch's stash of tuna fish. Cat fed, it didn't take long to survey the one-room hideaway. It reeked of men's cologne—English Leather—Chloe hated perfume and cologne. Painting easel, journals. It looked like an artist's studio. It looked like Chloe, but it felt empty. Physical possessions all accounted for, alas, what made Chloe, Chloe, was missing.

Unpacked, I decided that a toasted brie sandwich would settle my nerves. It had been an exhausting drive and I was concerned at not finding Chloe. Our shared sixth sense was off kilter, all questions and no answers. Maybe a Greenleaf local knew something about Chloe.

Now eight o'clock, and noting that Jeremiah's Diner closed at nine, I stopped there first. I didn't have a picture of Chloe. I didn't need one. I wouldn't be a movie-inspired gumshoe detective pulling a picture of Chloe out of my purse and asking, *"Have you seen this woman?"* I would introduce myself and begin, *"I'm looking for my twin sister Chloe. Have you seen her? She looks just like me."*

The bell above the front screen door dinged as I entered Jeremiah's general store. I approached a pony-tailed, thin man wearing a plaid lumberjack shirt. He squatted at a bottom shelf, either chasing a mouse or arranging his merchandise. He smelled of English Leather. He acknowledged he was proprietor Jeremiah without even looking at me. When he rose and looked into my hazel eyes, it was as if he had seen a ghost.

"Oh, my," he stammered. "May I hep, ya?"

Never very good at concealing my emotions, I turned away to mask a face that must be pale as a snowflake. I decided to postpone my probing about Chloe because I was overwhelmed by a vibe of mystery and bewilderment. Throw in a dash of terror to describe my mood. "Just traveling through," I lied. "A salted rye brie toasted cheese sandwich is on my bucket list."

Still as jittery as a cat's tail in an old folk's home full of rocking chairs, pony-tail Jeremiah directed me to the rear of his store. "Have a seat, missy. I'll fire up some magic, right quick." He parted the tattered calico sheet that covered the doorway as he disappeared into his small kitchen.

I heard the clatter of dishes and smelled the frying butter that wafted through the musty store. The front screen door triggered the bell just as Jeremiah got my sandwich started. A pretty young girl, about my age yelled, "Jeremiah, how much for sardines and box of crackers?"

"Just leave five bucks on the counter, sweetheart," came the inpatient reply.

"Need change. I only got a twenty," the young girl pleaded as she walked closer to the kitchen.

That's when my blood ran cold. She was wearing Chloe's lavender sweater. I wanted to look away, but my gaze was frozen. How did she get Chloe's sweater? Jeremiah wiped his hands on a dish towel as he multi-tasked his way past me, grumbling louder with each step. The Michigander banter between two locals born-and-raised in Greenleaf intrigued me. There was a certain beat and rhythm this close to Canada that eased my tension. I understood what Chloe found charming about Greenleaf.

My attention shifted back to the kitchen by the smell of burning rye. "Hey, my brie is burning," I shouted.

"Give it a flip," Jeremiah yelled back from the front cash box.

I pushed my way through the threadbare calico barrier into what barely passed as a kitchen. Folded dish towel in hand, I grabbed the cast iron skillet handle and rescued my rye and brie from the flame. The dangling dish towel was not as lucky. It caught fire, burning the back of my hand. I dropped the heavy skillet on the butcher block table and flung the flaming towel toward the sink. Never an athlete and blessed with zero hand-eye coordination, the flaming towel fell short of the sink and draped over the trash can under the sink.

I rushed to retrieve the burning towel and dropped it in the sink. Running cold water extinguished the flames, but smoke was pouring from the trash can. I pulled the trash can from under the sink and smothered the contents with the wet towel. As I bent down to confirm I wasn't burning the store down, I saw it, under the sink. Wadded in a heap behind the trash can. I freed a V-neck lavender sweater from its rats-nest prison as I rose to my feet. It was unmistakable. The dark stain on the front was definitely a blood stain, in the same location I had spilled coffee down my front two weeks earlier.

I clutched my sister's sweater to my chest and buried my face into the last of Chloe's existence. Damn! English Leather. Shaken to my core, I backed against the butcher block table and turned to face pony-tail Jeremiah. I dropped the birthday sweater at his feet as my free hand rested on the handle of the cast iron skillet behind me.

Could I summon the courage to serve up a salted rye toasted brie sandwich?

* * *

A Grave Situation

"Doc, I tell you, I'm going to die."

"Harold, as usual, you speak the truth," the learned psychiatrist quipped. "As will I. We all will die, eventually."

"Why I pay you $200 an hour to preview your comedy material is beyond me," Harold retorted.

"Point taken. Now, let's review: the first sign of your impending demise, came, let's see...," as the bearded Harvard MD scanned his notes. "Oh, yes, two months ago. Your life insurance company sent you..."

"I didn't request a new beneficiary designation form."

"Maybe we can write this off as bureaucracy. Administrative error, perchance? Don't forget Occam's Razor..."

"Doc, stop showing off. Yeah, yeah, when faced with a complex problem, the simplest explanation is generally the best."

"Shazam, you do pay attention when I pontificate. Did you need to designate a new beneficiary?"

"Well, yes. I was in the middle of my divorce and didn't want the ole hag to get more than she deserved," Harold recoiled in defiance as he recalled this unpleasantness.

"Can we eliminate this episode as foretelling your demise?"

Harold squirmed as he nodded acknowledgment that Occam's Razor probably did explain this conundrum. Noting he still had 15 minutes left in his session, he continued, "And the 'living will' documents my attorney sent me last week?"

"Didn't you just celebrate an important birthday, Harold?

"Yes."

"How old are you?"

"Sixty-five."

"Bingo. Social Security. Medicare. Pension plans. Sounds to me like you have an on-the-ball attorney. Are we done with all of this death…?"

"One more. Look what I got in the mail yesterday," as Harold handed his psychiatrist an envelope.

Dr. Friedbach scanned the enclosed document and folded his glasses, dancing them in Harold's face to accentuate his point, "An invoice for monument engraving services at Woodlawn Cemetery? Four hundred dollars. So what?"

"I didn't request any monument engraving," Harold entreated.

"Do you have a burial plot at Woodlawn?"

"I do," Harold confirmed.

"Time's up," the exasperated counselor sighed.

"That's it? No theory?"

"All right. You have homework before our session next week. I want you to stop by Woodlawn and check out your headstone. Can you do that, please?"

"Certainly. Until Tuesday. Thank you, Dr. Friedbach."

The drive to Woodlawn was short. It was an uplifting stroll on a warm April day as Harold approached his family plot. Generations of ancestors told a story of perseverance, love, and grace as Harold's fingers stroked the smoothness of his granite monument. He felt a peace and comfort – hard to explain – yet real.

Not questioning the heaped flowers on a recently closed grave, he borrowed a wilted lily, his favorite, and placed it at the base of his headstone. It was then that he noticed the newly engraved date of death. It was today. Aghast, he rose and focused his iPhone camera to take a selfie with the engraved date. A quick text to Dr. Friedbach accomplished, he turned his ankle on the uneven ground. He fell, his skull crushed on the corner of his own headstone.

Explain this to what's-his-name Occam.

* * *

Lu Sing Died

Lu Sing's death was foretold on October 1, 1979. Her parents would not cry at her actual death in 2015. The neighbors would go about their daily lives. There would be no calling hours, no funeral, no grave, no headstone. Just gone. Dead. In 2040, Tzu Chen, who normally might have married Lu Sing, as their parents lived next door to each other in the remote China village of Jintang, would get his MBA from Stanford University. He would probably become a millionaire from the stock options a new IPO startup would give him. Chen never thought of Lu Sing. He never met her. She was dead.

When does the medical community officially declare someone dead? Heart beat? Breathing? Rigor mortis? Morticians used to run a string from a casket to a bell above the new grave to give the alleged deceased one last chance to ring home. Embalming replaced this practice.

Who declares a civilization dead? When does a culture cease to matter? Or even exist? Unlike the death of a person, an individual, the death of a culture isn't apparent to most people at the time the last gasp of breath is taken. Historians might assign a date of death – a range of time – centuries or even millennia later. An exception, the fall of Babylon in 539 BC was probably apparent to the Babylonians when they got conquered by Cyrus the Great of Persia. The Roman Empire didn't all of sudden roll over and croak in 476 AD when Romulus, the last of the Roman emperors, was overthrown by the Germanic leader Odoacer. There had been indicators. Adolf Hitler died on April 30, 1945. But when did his Germany die? It started to cough—caught a terminal cold—when the Treaty of Versailles was signed on June 28, 1919. Or, had the German culture started its slow demise decades earlier? Where was the church? Where was the German conscience? Its soul?

Did China cease to exist as an honored civilization in 1979 when it adopted its "one child" policy? Or, did its culture cease to have meaning when Lu Sing's parents reacted with, *If we can only have one child, we want a boy.* Lu Sing was aborted in 2015, because she was a girl.

Also, in 2015, a pregnant Tzu Huan arrived in Arcadia, California, three weeks before her due date. This birthing trip cost the Tzus sixty-thousand dollars. The 14th Amendment to the U.S. Constitution was designed to assure full citizenship to recently freed Negro slaves in 1868. This document of unequaled freedom, has granted citizenship to any child born on U.S. soil ever since. Mrs. Tzu's son, Chen, was an anchor baby, a legal U.S. citizen.

Another piece of China just died.

* * *

LOG CABIN QUILT

She'd sleep by day and travel under cover of darkness. Dusk signaled it was time to head North. Today had been good; about dawn, she happened upon a mama deer and her fawn youngin' mashed down in a thicket. Elsa scared them off and curled up with her sweet baby Louisa-May in the warmed grass that smelled of the love of one of God's creatures. Daytime sleeping was hard at first, but days like today—tucked beneath brambles and thicket—Elsa felt safe. Baby Louisa-May nursing at her breast, they both cuddled and hummed themselves asleep. Dusk. Time to go.

Elsa's journey was not of her own making. She knew no other life. Born into this peculiar institution, as it were, she was third generation. News of impending hostilities was scant and unreliable, but a new tension was brewing. Campfire songs were more plaintive, the River Jordan widened, deepened, became more foreboding. Each chorus mourned an urgency.

Elsa's journey started on a Tuesday. Middle of the night. Her man, John, arms stretched, tied around a blood-soaked ash, moaned a pain that pierced her heart. Back lashed and welted, he hung like a shredded rag doll. Restrained by Ole Hebrew, the plantation's oldest resident, Elsa realized her fate was sealed. John and their son were being sold-off, down river. Elsa wept as she read her man's eyes as they communicated, "Go. Run."

That Tuesday—dark of night—was two months ago. Late fall now surrendered to a morning frost and scattered dustings of snow. While not dressed for the cold, snow meant North. Hope. Elsa was leaving pink snow tracings behind as her rag-wrapped feet trudged through woods, across frigid streams. She foraged on whatever a farmer left behind in harvested fields.

Elsa and baby Louisa-May, secured across her mama's chest with a ratty shawl, usually traveled alone. There were a few days in early December when Elsa stumbled upon a conductor who shuffled Elsa with another family from barn to barn in Southwest Pennsylvania. For a short while, the food was plentiful. Nursing a baby and the nightly struggles with the elements were taking a toll; Elsa got weaker by the day.

More important than the food was the information—codes—clues on traversing from station to station. Bounty hunters abounded and the searching howl of their bloodhounds chilled an already hopeless psyche.

"Look for the quilts," the conductor admonished before pointing Elsa northward. "Look for clotheslines, picket fences, hanging from second floor windows."

"What they say?" Elsa pleaded.

"Star shape, don't stop here; it's not safe. Keep north," the conductor continued.

Elsa's head spun, desperate to remember all the signals. Exhausted, concentration waned. "When will I be…?" she faded.

"Home?" the conductor knew Elsa's heart.

"My baby's terrible sick."

"Glory be yours when you see a log cabin design."

"A log cabin?"

"Yes'm. Quaker family will take you in. Home."

A never-ending two weeks of winter cold and thick woods presented little promise. Despair accompanied each labored step as Elsa longed for her man's broad shoulders and firm resolve. Thoughts of her son being down river would have produced tears but she was too defeated to cry. Forest glens offered no quilts. Isolated crossroads either had no quilts or only star patterns. Keep north.

Elsa knew a mid-December new moon introduced the shortest day of the year. She limped along the country lane and spied a solitary farm house and barn around a bend. A gentle breeze teased wisps of clouds across a starlit sky. Louisa-May whimpered and nuzzled a breast that provided no nourishment.

There it was. On the clothes line. Oh, please, not another star. The clouds permitted enough of the new moon to illuminate a log cabin pattern.

Elsa crawled to the clothesline and clutched the corner of the welcoming quilt to her cheek. Home. Home at last. She tugged and freed the quilt, wrapping baby Louisa-May in a new future. Elsa snuggled beside her swaddled baby girl. The quilt freed Louisa-May. Humming how Jordan was finally crossed, caressing a warmed, cooing Louisa-May, Elsa closed her eyes in a final, peaceful sleep.

While an eternity apart, both Elsa and baby Louisa-May were home at last.

* * *

THE STOLEN BYCYCLE

Not much exciting happens in Possum Corners, Tennessee, population 213. McKever's General Store, its enameled Pure Oil sign creaking in the mid-day breeze, with its liars' bench and pot belly stove, keeps the gossip mill churning. It was Pastor Turner's turn to hold court.

"I tell ya, it's just not Christian," the good parson sulked. "Who would steal my bike? Everyone knows ole Bessie is mine. Just doesn't make sense."

"How long you had that ole Schwinn?" the store owner Pete asked.

"Gosh, forty, fifty years," the pastor said. "I've ridden Bessie all over the county. Original chain. Replaced a link or two over the years. But she's pretty much the same as the day I bought her. Plastic handle grips are a bit cracked. Chrome fenders still shine like a newly-minted dime."

"Seat's broken down," Pete laughed. "Guess that's expected, been rubbin' 'gainst your fat fanny all these years."

"Who would steal ole Bessie?" the pastor queried.

After a good thinkin' and cogitatin', the group settled on a recovery strategy. It was decided that a well-crafted sermon, delivered with appropriate levels of fire and brimstone would out the evil perpetrator. Possum Corners being a one-church town increased the odds the thief would probably be in attendance.

Pastor Turner showed up at McKever's early on Monday morning, astride ole Bessie. No new scratches. She looked no worse for the wear having been missing for almost a full week.

Back slaps and congratulations welcomed the minister as he assumed his assigned seat on the liars' bench.

"Great sermon, parson," Pete offered. "But pretty short. It weren't your usual half-hour stem winder. Thought there were ten commandments. Why'd ya stop?"

Every eye noticed the quick blush in the parson's cheeks, his averted gaze.

"Well," the good parson started to explain. "I thought the thief would get all shy and embarrassed as I worked my way through thou shalt this and thou shalt not that." He paused to catch his breath. "Figured I'd nail 'em when I hit 'em with thou shalt not steal."

"Why'd ya stop in mid-sentence?" Pete implored. "Ya never got to thou shall not steal."

The blush returned to the minister's cheek as he said, "Well, when I got to thou shalt not commit adultery, I remembered where I left my bike."

* * *

UP THE RIVER

Writer's note: This one is technically not a flash or short story. At a robust 12,839 words, this offering is between a novelette and a novella. This story was a contest quarter-finalist in the ScreenCraft 2017 Cinematic Short Story Contest (1,400 entries). That means it is screenplay worthy material. Well, hello Hollywood.

Including "Up the River," I've penned five screenplays. My "Up the River" script earned quarter-finalist status in the 2018 Los Angeles International Screenplay Award (2,500 entries). That, plus "Consider" coverage reports, ranks "Up the River" in the top three-percent of all scripts written.

As you read this one, imagine you're in a movie theater and the popcorn has real butter.

* * *

It had not started out like a day that would change the rest of his life, however long, or short that might be. Josh Whitlock had suffered through another Friday morning of product launch meetings that had yet to solve the outsourced production quality problems half-way around the world from his Pittsburgh corporate headquarters. It was early afternoon as he struggled with his resolve to cut back on caffeine—fifth cup of coffee—and it was only 2:00 p.m.

From the tenth-floor conference room vantage point, he gazed at his Subaru Outback in the parking lot below. Deep in thought about Shanghai and international bureaucracies, the sight of his expedition kayak strapped atop the 4 x 4 zigged him in and out of daydreams of the weekend ahead.

"Where to this time?" an attractive co-worker inquired.

"Excuse me?" Josh fumbled, as he focused on Diane's deep, blue eyes.

"You off with that deputy sheriff buddy of yours again? How far into the backwoods you going this weekend? That kayak looks super sleek."

Body and brain forced back into the present, Josh grinned at his two-year project teammate, "An upper tributary of the Allegheny River. Allegheny National Forest, camping near the New York State line."

"White water?"

"Only stage two. Use my other kayak for the exciting stuff. This is a camping trip. I love mid-summer in the forest."

"How many kayaks do you have?"

"Three."

"That thing looks more expensive than your dinged-up car."

"Not really, only three thousand."

"Three thousand? You're picking up the tab for lunch next time." Diane Clawson knew all about Josh's macho weekends and his competitive nature. She was only two rungs beneath him on the office racket ball ladder. She understood the need to get away from the product launch pressures eating at their entire team. Changes were expected. Burning off some testosterone with an old high school buddy would do Josh some good.

"Been there before?" she asked.

"Brad has. New to me."

"Interesting how you two have stuck together, what, ten years?"

"Interesting? How?" Josh asked with a puzzled look.

"Oh, I don't mean anything by it."

"You must've meant something."

"Brad's a great guy. Just, that, you're a college grad and he's a deputy sheriff, high school grad."

"Been close since grade school. Still on the same under-thirty masters lacrosse team."

"Just sayin'," as Diane tried to extricate herself from the dead end of her class commentary.

"I'd never gotten that athletic scholarship to Penn State without Brad on my wing. He's a better athlete, I just lucked out on gene-pool brains."

"Getting an early start today?" Diane finally succeeded in changing the subject.

"One more meeting with the boss. Five minutes," as he checked his iPhone.

"Careful in those rapids," Diane commented, leaving no doubt she was opining about their new boss and not Josh's weekend adventure up river.

Draining the last drop of Joe from his Nittany Lion mug, Josh stared at his awaiting chariot below. His daydream through the weekend rapids was interrupted by his cell phone timer alerting him to his 3:00 p.m. meeting with Peter Eubanks.

Josh stopped by his cubicle, gathered the binder of reports and Excel spreadsheets that might provide the backup for his latest solution to their China quality control problem and headed for the Peter Eubanks rapids upstream. Eubanks was a straight-enough arrow, but as a boss, the team had yet to figure him out. He had been brought in from the West Coast region six months earlier with a reputation of "this guy can fix anything." Josh had his doubts, but Peter was the boss.

Josh detoured past the break room for one last cup of coffee. As was customary, most, if not all manager doors were open. Josh paused at Peter's door, waiting for the courtesy of an inviting wave—which he received—as Peter shouldered his phone to his ear. The boss showed his frustration with an extended goodbye that seemed to last forever. Josh waited respectfully before taking a seat.

"Thank you for your input, goodbye," Eubanks said for the second time. He cradled the phone and motioned for Josh to close the door.

Josh did a quick two-step as he had expected his next move to be taking his seat. A slosh of coffee was less-graceful than his muscle-memory crossover move as it splashed on the carpet beside the chair he was about to occupy. Door closed; Josh hoped Eubanks hadn't noticed his crossover move.

Josh leaned forward in his chair, placing his report binder and spreadsheet on his boss's desk. As he pointed to a column that summarized his new approach to improve product quality, Eubanks put his elbows on his desk and interrupted Josh before he could make his case.

"Josh, we've decided to go in a different direction."

"I'm all ears," Josh said as he slid back in his chair. "Anything that gets Shanghai on board."

"Josh," Eubanks paused, as he pulled a large envelope in front of him, "I'm afraid that different direction does," another hesitation, "does not include you."

Josh clenched his butt cheeks tighter than a crushed cap on a half-used tube of Super Glue and tried to gather himself. He had never been benched, never cut from a team. He was always the guy taking the penalty shot. Every coach had him in the game to the bitter end. "Excuse me, Peter," as he felt his face go from flush, to blush, and settle back to the chalk-pale of death, "am I being fired?"

Peter slid the large envelope in front of Josh. "As you know, we've had a number of cutbacks nationwide. It's not personal, Josh, it's business reality."

"You're hitting me with 'The Godfather' quotes?"

"It's never easy, Josh. You will land on your feet. Someday you will sit on this side of the desk and have to do what I'm doing now. I'm sorry."

Josh fingered the envelope with his name on it. "What's this?" he asked.

"Forms. Cobra. A release that you should have an attorney review. Confidentiality agreement. Oh, and a check for three-months' severance pay."

Still in shock, Josh was able to editorialize about the severance amount as he sorted through the envelope contents, "I may feel differently four months from now, but three months seems," a hard swallow, as he continued, "seems, fair."

"You'll get a good reference, Josh," Peter said as he gave Josh a look that confirmed it would happen. "It really is just a change of direction."

"How long do I have?" as Josh forced eye contact.

"Now," Peter said bluntly. "Boxes are in your cube and HR is in the ninth-floor conference room to answer any questions you may have."

"Are there others?" Josh softened.

"Yes, but that's a question for HR."

"Well, I guess that's it," Josh acknowledged as he folded his spreadsheets that no one would see or care about, rose, and nestled the stone-cold envelope under his left arm. He turned to leave, paused, faced Peter, and extended his hand, "It's a good team out there," he said, glancing to the cube farm, "keep an open mind." He thought of his high school lacrosse coach's admonition as he firmed his handshake, like it communicated something about one's character.

The ensuing fifteen minutes of packing personal items in nondescript boxes and uncomfortable goodbyes were a blur. Josh was embarrassed and wanted to slither out as quickly as he could. He was full of questions, but the thought of talking with someone in HR at this moment was the furthest thing from his mind. He thought he could schedule an appointment if he had any questions once he'd reviewed the contents of his termination packet. He looked for Diane, but she was now with Peter. A gray-shirted maintenance guy checked his clipboard and left some packing boxes in her cube.

Josh cornered himself in the lobby coffee shop with a double espresso and sorted through the legal mumbo jumbo until he thought a more detailed review might require alcohol. He studied the deductions from his severance check and realized that three months wasn't really three months. For joy, Uncle Sam got fired too, or at least got some of Josh's severance pay. Josh freed the check from its stub at the perforation and whisked it into his bank account at the lobby ATM.

Good news? Josh would beat the Pittsburgh rush hour traffic as he and Deputy Sheriff Brad would speed to the headwaters of the Allegheny. Josh could unwind in his beloved Allegheny National Forest for longer than a two-day weekend, he had all the time in the world. He was unemployed.

* * *

Josh and Brad met at a rest stop ten miles north of Pittsburgh. Josh was ready to explode, unload a shit-load of frustration and he knew that his deputy buddy Brad would be sympathetic. As kayaking required two cars to deadhead upstream for multiple rapids runs, driving separately, he had to wait until they arrived at base camp to vent.

"Got the cigars?" Brad inquired as he leaned into Josh's Subaru.

"Yep," came the less than enthusiastic response as Josh handed Brad a Punch Gran Puro Santa Rita for the road.

"You, okay?" an observant query was posed. "Ya look like hell."

"Bad day at the office," Josh admitted.

"Well, me and Jim Beam will fix that. Nothin' like a weekend dodging sobriety and boulders to cure what ails ya." With a firm, dual-fisted drum roll on Josh's car hood, Brad was off to lead the way, "Follow me, pardner."

The reminder that his hillbilly best friend was indeed his "pardner" provided a bit of good cheer as the two-hour drive to the Allegheny National Forest near the New York state line passed quickly. He thought about his next move. *His resume was dusty, stale. Could he stretch his severance pay to last longer than three months? He thought of Diane. She probably got less severance than he did.*

Brad's tail lights flashed red ahead of Josh as the skilled deputy swerved into the ditch and fishtailed broadside back onto the narrowing National Forest road. Both feet imploring the Subaru brakes to avoid the young doe deer, Josh missed making Bambi an orphan by only inches. He was less fortunate in steering clear of Brad's rear bumper.

"Son-of-a-bitch!" Josh screamed as he leapt from his car. Hands on hips, standing in the middle of the road, he surveyed his broken headlight. He buried his boot heel in the wounded light port twice before Brad bear-hugged both of Josh's arms to his sides and lifted him off the ground.

"Whoa, dude!" Brad shouted. "It's a forty-dollar headlight at Advance Auto Parts. Nobody died here."

"Damn!" Josh blurted as his chest heaved.

Brad gave Josh a firm squeeze and released his grip. "Are you okay?"

Breathing a bit more measured, Josh kicked the ground and examined his buddy's rear bumper. "Sorry about the ding in your bumper."

Holding back a laugh, Brad dug his heel into one of many wounds in his bumper. "This ole Jeep? Hell, ya probably improved my alignment."

Composure regained; Josh knew the weekend with Brad was just what he needed. He would share his newly-gained unemployed status with Brad and Jim Beam with a Santa Rita smoke lit from tonight's campfire. *What are best friends for, anyway?*

* * *

"Wow! For that much severance pay, I'd screw the sheriff's daughter."

"No more booze for you tonight," Josh laughed.

"You're right. It might take six months' pay. Ever seen ole flubberbutt's daughter?"

They each saw the bottom of their plastic Solo cups and agreed that the night was still young. Brad splashed the Jim Beam as Josh subtracted two Santa Ritas from his inventory.

"You know yer gonna be fine, right?" Brad encouraged.

"I suppose. The way things were going, everyone talked past each other. We weren't on the same wave length."

"Tell me 'bout it. Sometimes I think our county commissioners are idiots."

"Enough of this crap," Brad pronounced as he swallowed a serious gulp of whiskey and swished another mouthful like cheap gargle.

"Don't you dare!" Josh pleaded as he drew his feet under his ass, away from the campfire. Friends since grade school, he knew the routine. He had come to expect it – could even predict when.

The night sky blazed as the campfire accepted Brad's spray of 80 proof alcohol. Eye brows singed, Josh curled into a ball and rolled onto his back as he screeched, "That stuff's expensive."

Brad wiped the whiskey residue and snot from his chin onto his shirt sleeve. Doubled over in laughter, he was ready for Josh's rib-busting onslaught that was part of the routine. He had come to expect it – and knew when.

Best friends. Cigars. No cell phone service. Their routine knew to shelve the Jim Beam when they couldn't tell the difference between the Big Dipper and Taurus. They didn't hit the tents and sleeping bags until 2 a.m., an unimportant detail. They'd be up at the crack of Saturday's dawn.

* * *

Both kayaks secured atop Brad's newly aligned Jeep, four-wheel drive engaged, two somewhat hungover friends ducked as low-hanging branches blocked their view of the narrow fire road. Leaves scattered; birds flew to higher reaches to evade the punishing glee of the two weekend adventurers. A limb exhibiting more spunk than anticipated arced a new web of splintered glass across the Jeep's defeated windshield. Dappling morning sun was erratic as it chased its first shadows of the day.

"Shit, Brad! I'll be one of your pallbearers, but don't take me with you."

Brad laughed, laid on the horn, and spun the steering wheel hard left to mostly avoid a rotting tree stump at the edge of the narrowing fire road. The stump exploded in a mash of fungi, lichens, and decomposing bark.

Josh dug his fingernails into the Jeep's disintegrating dashboard as his ratty bucket hat brushed the sagging headliner. His termination packet and Cobra forms couldn't be further from his mind; he was focused on surviving Brad's brush through the gates of hell. Guiding his kayak through plunging rapids and kissing moss-covered rocks would be a piece of cake – compared to this current roller coaster. If he could spray an alcohol fire ball at his best friend, he would gladly set Brad's hair ablaze. As this idea was gaining momentum, Brad braked the Jeep into a clearing of full sunlight. Jerking to a halt, Josh marveled at the beauty of the hardwood forest and the eager waters of an Allegheny tributary. They had arrived at their morning's put-in point.

Expedition kayaks and broken twigs removed from the 4 x 4's roof rack, the camping gear was stowed with military precision. Each piece of lightweight equipment had a place and a specific purpose or it would have been left behind. Overnight kayak camping is economy and roughing it at its most basic. The fresh bottle of Jim Beam and bundle of Punch Gran Puro Santa Ritas, double-secured in zip-lock baggies, were among the most important necessities packed.

The plan was to kayak half-way to Josh's car; camp, drink, smoke cigars, shoot the bull, and get Brad home Sunday night in time for sobriety to return before his first patrol Monday morning. As Josh folded the Allegheny National Forest map, he again realized that he didn't need to be sober Monday morning. He briefly visualized his resume that would need updating.

"Hey, dude," Brad cajoled, flipping his best buddy's bucket hat off his head and into the awaiting stream, "where'd ya go?"

"I'm right here, buddy."

"Ya drifted off."

"I've never been fired before," Josh lamented.

"We're gonna drink, smoke, and cuss that out of you this weekend. Let's go."

Josh nodded and leaked a brief grin as he knew why he and Brad had stuck together since high school. While different in many ways, they shared a bond. They had each other's backs. Butts secured in kayaks, they clicked paddles and shouted, "Numquam Mori Rah!"— roughly translated from their Freshman Latin dictionary as, *Never Say Die*—a lacrosse gladiator chant to curdle a foe's blood. "Numquam Mori Rah!" echoed from the narrow limestone gorge as the intrepid adventurers slipped into their first rapids of the day.

* * *

Brad set a torrid pace. He knew this section of the Allegheny tributary and was off to the races. Laughter, screams, cursing that would make a sailor blush, the two best friends challenged each other's kayak skills. The lead was passed back and forth like a well-rehearsed ballet – a pas de deux – with white-capped rocks forcing barre work to avoid a chilled dunk.

Brad initiated the lunchtime break. Rounding a sharp bend that settled into a calm eddy flanked by hardwood trees and moss-covered boulders, he beached his kayak among low-hanging willows. Wading mid-calf into the stream, he signaled Josh to the secluded beachhead. Kayaks secured on the craggy bank, legs were stretched and hamstrings relaxed.

"Love these kayaks," Brad said, "but, puts the legs in a God-awful, unnatural position."

"That's why wimps are in canoes and row boats," Josh laughed. "You spend too much time flattin'-out yer ass in a police cruiser, eatin' donuts."

Josh ducked to avoid the head-slap he knew would come as Brad rose to retrieve some power bars and beef jerky from his dry-pack. The mention of donuts triggered the need for a carbo load. Josh deftly snagged the guaranteed-too-dry grub hurled at his forehead.

"Always better at defense," Josh bragged.

"That's offensive," Brad punned.

A double groan shared, the two teammates laughed, tossed smooth stones into the water, and planned their next segment. The best of the rapids behind them, Brad found their position on the map and predicted their end of day target point.

Josh rose and walked up the bank behind a hickory tree, "Lighten the load," he said.

Brad proceeded to pelt the hickory tree with stones. "You got the bladder of a fairy princess," he yelled.

"Can't a guy get some peace?" Josh begged.

"You can't remember the last time you got a piece," Brad laughed, satisfied that a college degree wasn't required to master the English language.

"Very funny, you couldn't spell homonym if your life depended on it."

"I know I ain't one."

Josh acknowledged the play on words as he knelt to splash his hands in the stream. As he flung a handful of water toward his buddy, he lost his balance and almost fell into the stream. Recovering to his knees, he flicked a sunning frog off a rock. That's when he saw it; a Zip-lock bag, bobbing in the shallow water near the bank. He retrieved the heavier than expected polluting trash and moved to sit beside Brad.

Disgusted at the plastic bag dropped at his feet, Brad kicked it aside toward Josh with, "Some jerk upstream needs to manage his trash."

Leaning forward, Josh picked up the soggy bag. Puzzled at its heft, he ripped it open. While not totally waterproof, the bag had protected the singular contents from Mother Nature's ravages pretty well. Josh pulled the leather-bound book free of its damp prison. A quick thumb through the half-filled journal revealed inked sketches—birds, flowers, animals—free verse musings, and short diary entries. Each entry dated and signed with a stylized, cursive *"MB,"* Josh surmised that *MB* was female.

Brad grabbed the journal and surveyed it quickly. "What, no treasure map?" Dismissing any further interest, he tossed it back into Josh's lap with, "Looks like you found some bedtime reading."

Josh rose and giving it no more thought, stuffed the journal into his backpack. "Let's go."

Kayaks launched, they proceeded downstream. Save deer, skunks, and the occasional water snake, the float to their planned evening campsite was uneventful. If any time on a national preserve waterway could be uneventful, they settled into a rhythm of swapping leads and shooting through minor rapids. The gentle current encouraged shooting the breeze and reminiscing about old high school flames. Brad was a good listener when Josh vented about being fired. Josh understood the economic realities of changes in markets and product launch strategies, yet it proved therapeutic to voice his frustrations. Brad's major contribution to Josh's improved mood was his presence. Brad got it: a shut mouth sometimes communicated more understanding than proffered advice that wasn't solicited.

Having arrived at a promising beachhead to set up camp, it didn't take long to pitch tents, gather firewood, and prepare for a night of booze and cigars. It was easy to unpack as kayak camping dictated minimalism and economy. Tuna packets and power bars consumed; it was time to light a cigar. In rummaging through his backpack, Josh retrieved the journal that had been all but forgotten.

* * *

Dusk settled into a darkness compromised by the Milky Way and a flickering campfire. March 21: "Oh, the butterfly flutters atop the purple lavender. I take in the fragrance, yet it diminishes not," Josh flipped ahead a few pages, hoping to find something a bit less syrupy.

"With the devil himself as my witness," Brad pleaded as he pointed the stub of his second cigar of the night at Josh, "read one more passage from that silly girl's journal and, and, I'll gut and field dress you with my belt buckle and piss on your rotting carcass."

March 27: "Oh, the passion.... [*** *illegible* *** *water damage*] My heart paces, races, traces the arc of my existence," finger down his throat, Josh choked on his own laughter.

Brad rose, threw his spent cigar into the fire, removed his belt, and stumbled toward his doubled-over buddy. His zipper was half-down to fulfill the urination promise of his threat when he tripped and tumbled onto a defenseless Josh.

Feigning how a lavender-loving MB might react, Josh summoned his best high-pitched falsetto in proclaiming, "Oh, you brute. Spare my virginity. Oh, dear mother of all that's sacred. No! No!"

Brad rolled off, saying, "You are sick."

"No! No! Yes? If you are gentle. Oh, yes."

"Sick, sick, sick."

"Don't you like MB's sensitivity?" Josh laughed.

Relieving himself onto the hot rocks surrounding the campfire, Brad winced at the steaming stench of boiling piss.

"Now who's sick?" Josh proclaimed as he inched away from the pungent steam.

"MB is sick," Brad opined. "Who writes that kind of garbage?"

Solo cup bottoms once again hidden by Jim Beam and fresh Santa Rita's lit, the two literary critics poked the campfire with sticks. Josh tossed his flashlight, then the journal to Brad, with, "Here, you read something sweet. Might improve your social skills."

"Screw you," Brad fumbled as he maneuvered whiskey, cigar, flashlight, and journal. He flipped a few pages forward and read, April 2: "The majesty ..." Skipping forward again, April 7: "It hurts ..." Skipping to the last entry, May 15: "Help! I might as well...." Brad stopped, gulped some Jim Beam, looked at Josh and said, "Oh, my God!"

"Oh, my God, what?" as Josh pulled a full drag on his cigar.

Brad tossed the journal, hitting Josh in the chest.

Juggling to right the upside-down journal, Josh turned his back to the campfire to find the last entry. The dancing campfire light a challenge, he read, "Help, I might as well kill myself."

The two kayakers made eye contact and fell silent. Josh scrolled a few pages back, then forward. Skipping back and forth, he lingered on an entry, reading to himself.

"Okay, asshole," Brad blurted.

Squeezing his place in the journal between thumb and index finger, Josh handed MB's scribbles back to Brad. "Here's where it switches."

"Switches?"

"Yeah. Before this entry it's all puppy dogs and daffodils."

Brad scanned the post-puppy entries with a case-file diligence learned at the sheriff's academy. "And, after?" he checked entries involving pleas for help – abject despair. "Your journal girl has been kidnapped!"

"Kidnapped? When?"

The best friends spent the next hour shoulder-to-shoulder, draining a single, shared flashlight, hunched over MB's plea for help. *River bank not visible... its sound provides some comfort...*

rustic cabin... chickens... mangy dog... bib overalls... the honey is sweet... shack ... camouflage pickup... kill myself... it's over.

"Lots of clues, but... nothing precise," as Brad closed the journal.

"MB might be," Josh paused, "dead."

"Days, weeks ago," Brad guessed. "Or, she might still be held captive." Barely audible, Brad continued to himself, "Upstream."

"What?"

Deputy sheriff mode had kicked in. "I wonder how far upstream?"

"The journal's in fairly good shape," Josh observed as he examined the leather binding more carefully.

"Her last entry was only three weeks ago – she's alive," Brad suggested.

"So, tomorrow?"

"We hustle downstream, check the map. Guess how far to put in upstream," the law enforcement expert pronounced.

"And spend Sunday afternoon looking for a mangy dog chasing chickens not entirely visible from the bank?"

"It's a start."

* * *

At the crack of dawn, it was a downstream sprint to Josh's Subaru. No banter, no idle chatter. Only focused kayaking as though an Olympic time trial for the last podium spot was on the line. No water snakes flung down a shirt collar. By mid-Sunday morning, they had a map of the Allegheny National Forest spread across the Subaru's hood. Brad fingered his way upstream until he honed in on a put-in spot a half-day's float above the location of his Jeep.

"Here," Brad tapped the map, "let's start here."

"That gets us upstream of yesterday?"

"Yep, definitely upstream of where you found the journal."

"Wonder if it's far enough?" Josh asked.

"We ain't startin' in Canada. I gotta get back to work Monday morning," Brad added.

Josh wasn't sure if unemployment felt depressing or liberating. In one sense, he had a new mission – find MB.

* * *

While Sunday morning's speed trek was a record breaker, the afternoon's float was more of a saunter; a relaxed stroll through the park. Josh searched the left bank, Brad the right. They switched sides, paddling upstream to change their perspective, double-back, and beach in an inlet or river bend cove to take a leak or stretch their legs. Conversation was nil to none, except to complain about needles in haystacks. No chickens. No mangy dogs. Not even downwind of a smelly dude in bib overalls.

After four fruitless hours, they had searched a winding ten miles of National Forest riverbank. Beautiful, yet haunting, as MB might be buried beneath its splendor. Or by some slim chance, imprisoned in a dilapidated shack around the next bend. Failure at hand, Brad's Jeep was around the next bend.

Kayaks strapped atop the Jeep, they reviewed the map one last time. Brad folded the map and started to secure it in his vest.

"I'll take that," Josh said.

"What?"

"I'm staying."

"Alone, on the river?" Brad admonished. "You know better than that."

"MB's alone. I'm going to find her."

"She's dead, Josh. All my law enforcement training says, she's D-E-A-D."

"I'm unemployed. Two more days. Then I'll come home."

Brad could tell from his years of coming in second to about everything Josh did, that his logic was falling on deaf ears. Shaking his head, he handed Josh the map. Brad then dug into his locked console and retrieved his sheriff department issued satellite radio. "Check in twice a day."

"Oh—"

"-Oh, nothin'. Twice a day, or I'll gut and field dress you with my belt buckle and—"

"-piss on my rotting carcass."

Rules established, Brad deposited Josh a half-day's float upstream of where they had already searched. This would explore new territory and provide another check of areas downstream to where the Subaru was parked. Josh would camp Sunday night and begin his MB rescue at first light, Monday.

"You know you won't find her."

"Maybe."

"Check in."

Waving the satellite radio pouch, "Yep, twice a day."

With the remaining daylight, Josh read and re-read MB's plea for help. He thumbed back and forth between the last lavender puppy dog entry and her first, frightened plea, searching for a clue. It would be a sleepless night.

* * *

Still sleepless at the crack of dawn, the tossing and turning came to a merciful end. Josh had spent the entire night thinking of MB. *How long has she been held captive? How would he ever*

167

find her? Even if he found her, who is the smelly bib overalls guy?
Would he kill her? Kill him?

Camp broken, kayak loaded, Josh sat cross-legged on the river bank, MB's journal in his lap. Deep in thought, he alternated between piecing together MB's clues and flinging stones into the gentle current before him. No more cigars. No more whiskey. He was singular in focus. Quiet. Yes, he would slink silently downstream, be as one with the river. The rush of the rapids would mask his passage. His arrival at MB's prison would be unannounced. Knife. Call in coordinates on the satellite radio. Knife. Could he actually use a handheld weapon on a foe? Another human being? This would not be a lacrosse stick body check against a nationally ranked Johns Hopkins opponent. This would be real, close quarters combat. No referee to call a foul. Wait for backup. Lacrosse stick – short stick. That's what he needed. An All-American with a weapon he knew. He could feel his heartbeat in his ears; an adrenaline rush like no other. The Native Americans who first played lacrosse didn't stop by Dick's Sporting Goods – they made their own sticks. First break on the river, he would fashion a short stick weapon. It was time. Josh eased the kayak into the eddy and mounted his steed. His pulse quickened with the first paddle stroke downstream.

Three hours of nothing. Almost mid-morning with no results. Plenty of deer taking their first drink of a new day, pondering, *what's this dude doin' in my river on a Monday morning?* An abundance of water snakes that would have enjoyed being air mailed at Brad's head. Such a waste. Josh paused, listened, hid beneath low-hanging branches to concentrate on sounds. Out of character sounds. Sounds that didn't belong in the early morn of a national forest.

The satellite radio chirped. An unexpected sound that startled Josh. He gasped and fumbled the radio. Had Mr. Bib Overalls been close at hand, Josh's position would have been revealed. Breathless, he pressed "receive."

"Josh?" came the familiar voice through the scratch of static.

"Yeah, it's me," Josh responded.

"You, okay?" Brad asked.

"Yeah."

"Listen up, buddy. Can you hear me?"

"Yep. Some static, but it's okay," Josh was glad to hear another voice.

"Her name is Mary Beth."

"What?" shocked that it was real. A real person. This was no game.

"Mary Beth Tolliver. Missing person report filed two months ago, Scranton area."

"Shit!"

"Ya gotta stand down, Josh," Brad ordered.

"What 'cha mean, stand down?" Josh responded.

"Allegheny National Forest Rangers and local sheriff team comin' on site tomorrow mornin'."

"How about today?" Josh asked.

"It's dangerous. Get to your car and stay put," Brad ordered.

"I'm here. I'm searching today."

"Damn it, Josh. Don't be a hero."

"I'll camp at Subaru spot tonight. Promise. Meet you there."

"Check in if anything happens. We can track your coordinates from your satellite radio."

"Got it."

"Dead head to camp. Shoot the river. No searching," Brad was emphatic.

"Bad connection," Josh lied. "Gotta go."

"Asshole! Stand down," followed by static and nothingness.

Josh had no intention of standing down. He would be methodical, searching his way to his base camp. It was mid-morning. Six, maybe eight hours to his Subaru. He was smart. He would be careful. One more hour and he would take a power bar lunch break.

* * *

Josh had it memorized, but he kept reading MB's clues – Mary Beth's clues. *River bank not visible... its sound provides some comfort... rustic cabin... chickens... mangy dog... bib overalls... the honey is sweet... shack... camouflage pickup... kill myself... it's over.* Mary Beth. Flesh. Blood.

Lunch break over. A six-foot sapling at river's edge surrendered its future. Only an inch in diameter, the deep serrated back of his knife felled the wannabe hickory in short order. Another five minutes and Josh was swinging a four-foot, homemade lacrosse stick. Not exactly straight, the green sapling sported great whipping action. The slingshot-like "Y" formed by the first spread of young branches would support a makeshift basket. Josh ripped tender bark strips from another small tree and wove a jock strap-like doohickey in the "Y" of his new weapon. Unsure if he remembered this skill from the kindergarten hot-pot holder he made his mother or his Eagle Scout survival camp lashing training, he felt as if any Iroquois or Shawnee Indian ghosts lurking in the national forest would be proud. Not as strong as deer hide or rear leg tendons, he was still confident of his design.

His bark strip, tight-mesh weave would not assist in catching anything – his design didn't anticipate any catching. Squatting at river's edge, Josh selected a dozen, golf ball-sized stones. Penn State's top scorer his senior year, he netted a stone and took aim at a stately sycamore on the opposite bank. From only thirty feet, the stone hit square on – square on the boulder beside the sycamore. At this rate, Goliath would have had his way with Bathsheba, and devoured David for dinner.

His second fling lobbed its way to graze the sycamore, but a stellar jay on a nearby branch mocked him. *Ha. Ha. Caw. Caw. That's all you got?* Looking up and downstream to confirm that no one witnessed his shame, Josh reloaded. Taking aim at the smaller, feathered target, he rifled. Summoning his NCAA finals skills, he owned it. Total commitment. The branch hosting the sassy jay splintered, spraying bark on the now-humbled bird. Flying to safety, the jay hurled language that would make a turkey vulture blush. Four more shots and Josh's confidence grew. He gathered only a few replacement stones as ammunition appeared in abundance. He need not weigh himself down.

It was 2 p.m., Monday afternoon. Lacrosse weapon secured in his cramped kayak, ammunition stones at the ready, Josh decided to paddle upstream for five or ten minutes. Not that it would make any difference in his needle haystack venture, he wanted to stick to a plan. Structure – less chance for error, less random. He maneuvered sideways and let the current turn him back downstream. Slow. Methodical. He slid from shadows to dappled sunlight. He tacked as if sailing in a regatta from one bank to the other. Silent. He added no sound to that already provided by the stage-two rapids in their millennial-long taming of jagged river rocks.

Three o'clock. Josh beached at a bend in the river. Map in lap, power bar half consumed, he guessed he would arrive at his Subaru put-in camp in three or four hours. Folding the map, he marveled at an industrious spider spinning its dinner-snagging web. The web had already captured a moth and a newly imprisoned honey bee. Downing the final bite of power bar, Josh eased into the current.

Noting what appeared to be a stage-two rapid ahead, Josh felt a tickle on the back of his neck. As he reached to rub his neck, the tickle changed to a full-fledged *OUCH*! Swatting his neck, he smashed the varmint. Inspecting his hand, a squashed honey bee wiggled its last twitch. *Damn,* he thought as he rubbed the back of his neck. Pinching the already-swollen spot, he succeeded in removing most of the bee poison sac. *Interesting how a worker bee sting results in the bee's demise. Like a suicide bomber sacrificing himself for the good of the hive.*

Almost into the rapids, it hit him... *mangy dog... bib overalls... the honey is sweet... shack.* "Shit!" he yelled. "The honey is sweet."

How many billions of insects are in the forest? His brain raced – raced almost as fast as his kayak approaching the rapids. *Back! Back! Stay out of the rapids!* He paddled in reverse. Less of an athlete would be shot to the base of this stage-two. Josh succeeded in banking at the head of the rapids. *How far have I traveled from the spider web?* He decided to check in with Brad and then return upstream.

Retrieving the satellite radio, he initiated the call, "Brad, Brad, can you hear me?

Nothing but static.

"Brad, Brad!"

"Yeah, I'm here," Brad answered.

"Can you satellite track my position?"

"It'll take a bit, describe where you are."

"Probably three hours upstream of my Subaru camp."

"Asshole, you're not deadheading," Brad scolded.

"Listen, I'm just shy of what looks like a stage-two rapids."

"Shoot downstream, now!" Brad insisted.

In the middle of communicating, "I think I found a clue," Josh's radio went dead. Not even static. He wasn't sure how much, if any of his last message was received. He also didn't receive confirmation that Brad had succeeded in tracking his location. Josh tried again, "I'm heading back upstream, 'bout a half-mile." He was sure that this message was swallowed into the nothingness of the churning river beside him.

Filling his pockets with stones, Josh stowed the dead radio in his backpack in the kayak hatch and proceeded upstream. The paddle was not difficult, aided by the rush of adrenalin as he pondered his next move. The spider-web bend in the river returned quickly. The spider had been diligent. His web was mostly complete and now had trapped a butterfly and another honey bee. He exclaimed to himself, *Damn, what's the odds of that? This is more than a coincidence.*

Josh retrieved his backpack. Confirming his supply of stones, power bars, map, compass, binoculars, and tent, he secured anything not essential to a two or three-day woods survival in his kayak. He tested his lacrosse weapon with another dead-on shot at an oak tree across the river. Hiding his kayak under some low-hanging branches, he worked his way deeper into the forest.

* * *

With each break on his trek into the forest, Josh reviewed Mary Beth's journal hints. She referenced a *rustic cabin.* She wrote that *the river was not visible,* but she could hear it... *provided some comfort.* Rather than hike deeper into the forest, with the river at his back, he settled on a zig zag pattern; up and downstream from the spider web where he left his kayak.

After an hour of twisted ankle, low-hanging limbs swatting him in the head, and detours around briar brambles, he paused to take a compass reading. Peaceful. Quiet, except for his labored breathing. Too quiet. Too peaceful. If he couldn't hear the river, neither could Mary Beth. He concluded he was too far into the forest. While not placing too much credence on honey bee evidence, he hadn't seen one; other than the ones stuck in the spider web. He headed back to the river.

Backpack secured in the kayak; he took stock of what he'd learned. The zig zag pattern with the river at his back made sense. Very similar to how lifeguards organize search parties when a swimmer slips beneath the surface in murky water. Organized. Methodical. He would stick with that approach. Honey bees are everywhere. Based on how much territory a flying insect can cover away from a hive, Josh decided this might be the least reliable of Mary Beth's clues. The sound of the river. River not *visible* from her *rustic cabin* prison. But she could hear it. The river provided *some comfort.*

Josh decided to search further downstream. As he pushed the kayak away from the bank, it dawned on him that he'd only searched one side of the river. Paddle straight-armed above his head, he screamed, "Stupid jerk!" Slapping the water with his paddle, "No wonder you got fired. Ya gotta search both banks."

His task doubled in scope, frustration, and despair. Bending forward to rest his forehead on the kayak, he drifted. The river was quiet. So quiet. He was dealing with too many variables. Floating downstream, he decided that Mr. Captor tended a bee hive near his cabin. Like the *mangy dog*, Josh wouldn't see *bib overalls, honey bees*, or the *rustic cabin* until he actually found Mary Beth. The river was dead quiet. He raised his head, "That's it. She couldn't hear this river, not here."

Josh was invigorated. The rapids. Mary Beth could hear the river because of the rapids. He was returning to the stage-two rapids ahead. He decided he would start his zig-zag search pattern when he first heard rapids and end his search—both sides of the bank, yuck—when the river eddied. It was settled, he had a new search strategy. He may not have a new career plan. Not yet. That would come after Mary Beth.

* * *

It was dusk, Monday. He was tired, having double-searched two rapids, Josh had to stop for the day. He chose a gentle section of the river and made camp. There would be no campfire, he didn't want to announce his presence or get ambushed. He had provisioned for only a weekend jaunt. He rationed his remaining power bars through Tuesday night – one more day. Surely, Brad and local authorities would show up by then. He felt like a pioneer, that Eagle Scout with the survivalist merit badge. Except this was real. No pretend capture the flag games. If Mr. Captor's mangy dog sniffed him out, Josh would be dead.

Pleasant dreams.

* * *

Tuesday, dawn. Josh was so tired he slept through the night; he had no nightmares about Mr. Captor. Monday's adrenaline-filled forest traipsing had sapped every ounce of energy. He failed in his first attempt of the day in contacting Brad, even though his satellite radio had remaining battery juice, along with abundant static. Josh swore under his breath that he hadn't mastered this hi-tech radio transmitter. He would try again later. He had mastered orienteering; he could read a map. After confirming his location, he hurled a few stones across the river, disturbing a raccoon's washing of her morning breakfast. When it came to lacrosse, he still had it.

He turned into the slow current and listened for the rapids he expected around the next bend. It dawned on him that he wasn't at work. No coffee mug in hand. Tuesday morning and he wasn't on the phone with Shanghai, no conference rooms, no team meetings. He had been relieved of those. Fired. His mind drifted to his resume that at this moment was like him – adrift – a blank page. Hard to write a resume without having a goal, visualizing a future. He was rocked, literally, out of his daydream as a boulder and the nose of his kayak occupied the same space. The boulder almost won. At the headwaters of a stage-two, Josh beached and repeated his Monday routine. Kayak hidden, backpack donned, compass in hand, Josh tacked into the forest.

When splashing water sounds grew faint, Josh checked his compass and wove his way parallel to the river. Not wanting to stumble upon Mary Beth's cabin prison to his own surprise, he was cautious at the placement of every step. He felt like a Native Indian, stalking a young buck; a snapped twig would echo a warning and his family would go hungry another day.

Back resting against a towering tree, map in his lap, Josh tried to raise Brad on his satellite radio. Failure, only static. *Static. River. Bark – Bark. Static. Bark?* The satellite radio squawked. Josh got goosebumps as he silenced a squealing radio that might betray his position. *Mangy dog!? Bees. River sounds.* Was he close? Becoming as one with the pine-needled forest floor, he surveyed a half-circle perimeter around his position. He saw no cabin. Keeping the river sound in range, he changed his vantage point by 50 feet and repeated his 180-degree scan. Repeat. Again—for half-an-hour—repeat, again. Nothing. Lying flat on his back, steadying his breathing, he listened. *Thunk... thunk.* Unidentifiable. *Thunk.* He Army-crawled toward the sound. *What is it? A state park campground? Chopping wood?* On his stomach, he parted low-level bushes. It was the sound of wood chopping, but there was no campground. Josh had Mary Beth's journal memorized; all the puzzle pieces fit: mangy dog, chickens, camouflage pickup beside a rustic cabin, and the wood-chopper was wearing bib overalls.

Confirming it was in the "off" position, Josh buried his satellite radio in his backpack. Guessing the distance to the cabin was less than 100 yards, the last thing he needed was a check-in call from Brad. It was almost noon. Mr. Captor wiped his brow, gathered some split firewood, and kicked his cabin door open with his foot. He followed his mangy mutt into the cabin.

Josh decided to improve his position. Doubting that a free-range chicken would announce his presence, he maneuvered to within 50 feet. He considered reporting his position to Brad, but determined it too risky. He surveyed the primitive homestead: one- or two-room cabin, smaller shed or root cellar. *Would Mary Beth be in the cabin or the root cellar? Is she even alive?*

Turning options in his head, many of his questions were answered when Mr. Captor exited the cabin, carrying a tin pail, covered by an old dish towel. At the root cellar door, digging into his pant pocket for something, he fumbled with what Josh determined was a key. Josh's pulse quickened as he realized, *Mary Beth is alive! She just received lunch.* Mr. Captor re-emerged from the shed after only five minutes. He had left the lunch pail. Padlock secured, key in pocket, he ambled back to his cabin.

Josh had a plan. Step one was to take a risk; he turned on his radio. Volume killed, he assumed, or more appropriately hoped, that his position could be tracked by Brad. Radio stashed in his backpack; he again hoped any wayward sound would be muffled.

Step two: take a rest. Stay put for four to five hours. He'd wait for dinnertime, another tin pail.

* * *

Doing nothing for the entire afternoon was excruciating. Josh worked the plan over and over, making only minor adjustments from his initial brainstorm. Makeshift lacrosse stick checked and rechecked, stones counted and recounted, pulse controlled; about the time he figured he had another two hours of waiting, the cabin door opened. So much for the controlled pulse. Mr. Captor, ax in hand, headed for his wood pile. *Thunk. Thunk.*

Josh considered a change in plans. Mr. Captor was focused on his wood chopping. *I'll bull rush him while his back is turned. Hit him with a close-in shot aside his head. No! That mangy dog will bark.* As Josh was mulling over Plan B, Plan C, and ready to return to his original plan, the wood chopping stopped. A plaintive whimper seeped through the gapped boards of the shed.

"Shut up!" Mr. Captor yelled.

The whimper escalated into a sob.

Ax buried in disgust in the chopping stump, Mr. Captor kicked the mangy dog aside and started toward the shed. "You asked for it sweetheart, I said shut up!"

Josh felt the surge of adrenaline communicating that it was show time. The game clock was ticking and his team was behind. He needed a quick score; no time for an assist, it was up to him. Hickory stick loaded, he rose and noted his adversary, at the shed door—padlock in left-hand palm shaking—anger out of control.

"Shut up, bitch!" He was so upset, he had trouble inserting the key.

Josh whirled and visualized scoring the tying goal. The makeshift hickory stick flexed as expected. A stone whizzed toward his foe's head. At the very moment Josh anticipated impact, the target lowered; in his fit of rage, Mr. Captor had dropped the key. The target stooping in the weeds, the stone missile intended for Mr. Captor's right ear thundered with a thud off the shed door.

In the burst of the ensuing seconds, Josh jumped into the clearing with his reloaded weapon. A surprised Mr. Captor spun around, shark-like dead-cold eyes pierced through Josh. Now free of any bushes or low-hanging branches, the All-American lacrosse player side-armed a rock that connected with the grizzly man's kneecap. In college, Jugs radar guns had clocked Josh at close to 100 miles per hour. The sound of shattering bone sent a chill up Josh's spine. The blood-curdling howl hurled his way by the wounded man in bib overhauls flashed chills that almost burst with electricity. Mr. Captor collapsed to his knees, but he gathered himself, limping toward his cabin. Dragging a worthless right leg, he made slow progress toward safety.

Josh flung another rock, striking the man in the hip. An average high school goalie would have blocked this shot. *Damn,* Josh thought, *striking a wounded animal in fleshy, meaty body parts just pisses them off.* His reaction was proven correct; Mr. Captor yelped like a crippled dog as he stumbled to the cabin door. Rock number three hit the wounded animal square in the middle of his back, between his shoulder blades. Josh knew this shot wouldn't win the game as it wasn't one of his better deliveries. It did tumble his foe to the ground, away from the cabin door. Reaching to steady himself, Mr. Captor leaned against the side of the cabin and fell again. Drawing his good leg beneath him, he raised enough to see Josh reloading his hickory stick. His eyes communicated that he would kill Josh; the man grabbed the ax handle and pulled himself up. He forced the ax free of the chopping block stump and faced Josh, dead on.

"Ya snot-nosed asshole," he slobbered, blood stains visible through his bibs, his right kneecap blown to smithereens. He stood erect, ax handle across his chest. Like a gladiator, knowing it was kill or be killed, he lumbered toward Josh.

Separated by only 35 or 40 feet, Josh knew the clock was ticking down. He feigned left, right and released another shot. He knew the errant result before he heard the ringing plink of stone on ax steel. Not that the fiftyish forest hermit was nimble, he got a lucky block. Josh was nimble, he knew he could run away. But he could not abandon Mary Beth. He deemed it wise to distance himself from the crippled animal. He jockeyed between his foe and the prison shed. Hand in pocket, he hoped his face didn't provide a poker tell that he had retrieved his last rock. Were he at the river bank, he could re-stock. A quick glance at the ground at his feet revealed only dirt and weeds. To get to overtime, he would have to score now.

Limping like a reincarnated movie monster, dragging his busted leg, Mr. Captor's eyes projected terror. He was going for it all with one shot. He raised the ax, both arms above his head, emptying his lungs with a blood-curdling roar as he hurled the ax tumbling at Josh. Josh's last stone struck flat sternum bone at the instant the ax was released. The whirling ax arched past Josh's head but sliced a deep cut in his right forearm before embedding deep in the shed door. Josh whirled and grabbed this right arm. He collapsed to his knees.

Mr. Captor slumped to the ground. He didn't move.

"Ah, shit!" Josh screamed. He labored to get to his feet. The cut was deep in Josh's arm, but not a mortal wound. Looking at the weeds beneath his feet, Josh decided it fruitless to search for the key. He liberated the ax from the shed door and chopped at the padlock with his left hand. On the third swing, he liberated the lock from its hinge, as rotted, aged wood splintered. The afternoon sun bathed the shed floor with sunlight.

"Mary Beth?" he called.

Hearing only a faint whimper, he stepped into the dank prison. His eyes not yet adjusted to the darkness, he called her name again, "Mary Beth."

Curled in the corner, knees gathered in a fetal position, a feeble reply cried, "Go away."

Josh cautioned his way to kneel beside the defeated young girl. A hand to her shoulder, he felt her tremble, turn away.

"You're safe, now," he whispered.

Through unkempt, matted hair, her tear-filled brown eyes met his. Smelling like an unwashed basset hound, she was disheveled. What had probably been khaki slacks now were dirty, smudged, stained. Tennis shoes muddied. The "Penn" on her university sweatshirt could barely be read. A faded purple scarf was knotted around her neck; the only thing that looked, and smelled like an effort had been made to keep it clean. She shook, cried and accepted Josh's hand. As he started to assist Mary Beth rise to her feet, Josh heard the mangy dog bark. He released Mary Beth's hand and ran to the door.

"Don't leave me!" Mary Beth screamed. "Don't leave me!"

Uncertain of Mr. Captor's condition, Josh grabbed the ax and approached the mangy dog that was standing over its master. Keeping the ax between himself and the dog that continued its incessant barking, Josh observed the slow, yet steady rise and fall of Mr. Captor's chest. He was unconscious. He thought about locking him in the shed, but he had busted the padlock. The best alternative was to escape to the river. Mr. Captor was crippled and couldn't pursue them very well. Josh decided to get as far away as he could. He gave the ax a random heave into the dense forest and rushed back to Mary Beth.

"You left me!" she cried. "How could you leave me?"

As Josh steadied Mary Beth to her feet, she pounded her fists into his chest. "You left me!"

"Trust me. You're safe." Josh reassured.

Josh assisted Mary Beth into the daylight. She squinted and covered her eyes, saying, "I haven't seen the sun in weeks."

Josh implored, "We gotta go."

Josh couldn't go; he slowly sank to the ground. Now seated, he felt the rhythmic throbbing of his ax wound. His adrenalin rush had waned. This was real pain.

Mary Beth sat beside Josh. She winced as blood pulsed from Josh's wound. She turned his arm and examined his forearm underside. "This looks bad," Mary Beth sobbed, thinking she was not yet free.

"I've felt better," Josh forced a laugh.

Josh surveyed the surroundings and fumbled through his backpack, slamming it to the ground. "Damn!"

"Damn what?" Mary Beth pleaded.

"My first aid kit is in the kayak"

"River's not far... I can hear it," Mary Beth reassured.

Josh admonished, "Tourniquet. We have to stop the bleeding."

Mary Beth rose and looked around. Neither of them wore a belt. She fingered her lavender neck scarf and took a half-step back. Reluctant to surrender her scarf.

Josh was silent, but his eyes communicated, *what?*

Untying her scarf, she knelt beside Josh. "Here," as she tied the scarf below Josh's elbow.

The boy scout in Josh instructed, "Do a double knot."

"Like this?"

"Yes," as Josh pointed to a small sapling. "Break off a small twig."

Josh inserted the pencil-sized twig between the double-knot and twisted. The pulsing blood flow stopped.

Mary Beth, in a voice of praise, blurted, "Boy Scout?"

"Just a little."

"Tenderfoot?"

"Maybe a bit more," Josh smirked. "Let's put some distance behind us."

It was slow going, having been held captive in the shed for two months, Mary Beth was frail and weak. Josh retrieved his backpack and transferred his last two stones to his pant pocket. He would replenish his bullets first thing upon returning to the river. He half-supported and half-carried Mary Beth; she used his hickory lacrosse stick as a crutch. It was the helpless helping the wounded.

Josh's orienteering experience told him they were leaving a drunken bull moose trail through the forest; even a blind city slicker would be able to track them. With a broken knee cap, he doubted that Mr. Captor would be able to catch them. While they had to press on, they both pleaded for a brief respite.

Josh had failed to include his own injury in calculating success in reaching the river. Dizzied and weak, Josh stumbled and caught a foot on a tree root. He was in pain.

As they sat on a fallen log, the river sounded closer. Josh unzipped his backpack and grabbed his radio. He tried to call Brad, but got only static. He felt it was now safe to leave the radio on, hoping their location might be tracked.

"How did you find me?" Mary Beth whimpered.

"Your journal."

"Thank God."

"How did you sneak it out?" Josh queried.

"Caleb, that's his name, took me out for some exercise."

"How often?" Josh asked.

"Time stopped for me... didn't have any meaning. Maybe once a week. I rehearsed, did a dry run, twice. About a month ago, I slipped it into the river."

"I found it Saturday."

Realizing how lost and disconnected she was, tears returned as she asked, "What is today?

"Tuesday, July 19," Josh rose and offered his hand. "We gotta go."

Needing more rest, but fearing a return to brutal captivity, Mary Beth didn't hesitate as she took his hand. There was something firm, yet gentle about his hand. For the first time in months, she felt comfort, a confidence, safety. Her eyes met his and didn't flinch away.

"We gotta go," Josh repeated.

* * *

The sounds of the river got louder. It couldn't be far. Each step pained both Josh and Mary Beth. Josh reminded himself that the cabin was within earshot of the river and they had left an obvious trail behind them. They assisted each other and began a slow slog to find the kayak. Mary Beth was slow from her recent captivity and Josh slower yet from his blood loss. It took only 15 minutes for Josh to find his beached kayak.

It was Mary Beth who retrieved the first aid kit from the kayak. "We're not moving another step until we fix that arm."

Knowing she was right, Josh sat, propped against a tree trunk. He figured he might as well be a good patient and get this over with.

Mary Beth arranged a selection of weapons beside Josh and started by pouring half the bottle of hydrogen peroxide on Josh's wound. She encouraged Josh to loosen the pressure of the tourniquet. His own survival training knew this a good idea; he didn't squabble. The blood oozed a little but the pulsing had abated. Mary Beth spent the balance of the hydrogen peroxide on the wound.

Josh giggled at the bubbling fizz, "My mom used to convince me this was little angels dancing the germs away."

"She's right." Mary Beth agreed as she diverted Josh's attention away from the impending doom of the rubbing alcohol in her hand.

Josh jerked as he screamed, "God damn you witch."

"Now, now Joshie, be a good little patient."

"You snuck up on me."

She dressed his wound with gauze and replaced the tourniquet with a small rope. Glad to have her lavender scarf back, she rinsed it clean in the river.

"Time to rest now, Josh," as she covered him with branches and boughs. Mary Beth chose a large tree separate from Josh so she could stand watch. As night settled over the forest, it didn't take long until Josh's snores joined the chorus of crickets and frogs. He needed this.

Mary Beth collapsed where she stood, and sobbed. She had been through hell, and now a stranger was forcing his will on her. Would she ever be free? Mary Beth had not had a peaceful sleep since her capture. Now was no different. She tossed and turned and twitched into a recurring flashback of Caleb. "No," she pleaded. Like previous nightmares that recalled every detail and horror, it was as though she had to relive the terror. She begged and pleaded, let me wake up. If only I could wake up, it would be over.

But she didn't wake up; the nightmare persisted.

Caleb left the shack. The shack goes pitch dark as the door is closed – then the sound of the padlock being locked. Maybe she would get some peace. Her flashbacks never answered that prayer. *The shack interior was dim with limited light entering through cracks in boards and shingles. A single ray of light illuminated a fork on the floor. A weapon? Would she have the courage to plunge it into Mr. Bib's neck?*

Mary Beth explores the shack floor. Her face is bruised, blood streams from the corner of her mouth. She crawls forward. She touches the fork – caresses it to her chest. It's not a weapon, it's a tool. She pries a splintered floorboard loose. The board creaks as she wiggles it free.

The board is loose in her hand. Why can't I be free? Wake up! You know what happens next. Wake up! Make it stop.

She removes a second floorboard. Below the floor is lightly packed dirt. Mary Beth uses the fork to dig. Dig. Dig. Dig.

The mangy dog barks. Mary Beth holds her breath. Wake up! No more.

Mary Beth has removed six inches of dirt. She hits something. She digs frantically with her hands. On her knees, straddling the hole in the floor, she pulls on the object. A decomposing, bony arm and hand in a blood-stained white blouse falls from her grasp and sticks half out of the floor.

The mangy dog barks. Caleb fumbles with the lock.

Mary Beth lets loose a blood-culturing scream, "AHHH!"

Josh woke Mary Beth with a touch on her shoulder and she looked at him with wild eyes. She battered Josh as she flailed with both hands.

Josh yelled, "Wake up. You're having a nightmare."

Mary Beth collapsed and fell asleep, again.

* * *

It's always an early rise when sleeping under the stars. They gathered themselves as Mary Beth quizzed, "Which way?"

Josh realized they hadn't put many miles behind them. He would have liked to kayak down river to his Subaru, but a one-person kayak could not accommodate two people — particularly when one was as frail and dependent as Mary Beth and he only had one good arm. Hands on hips, he looked up, then down the river; he figured that his Subaru was three or four miles down-stream. Decision made, he pulled his life jacket from the kayak and handed it to Mary Beth.

"No way," came the immediate refusal.

"Thirty feet," he motioned to the opposite bank. "We're only going thirty feet."

"I'm too weak to swim!" Mary Beth shouted.

"You won't even get wet," Josh promised, with a hint of a concealed lie. "Trust me."

As Josh assisted with the life jacket, he clued Mary Beth to his plan; they were crossing to the other bank to conceal their trail. They would hide the kayak and hike to safety. Josh confirmed he had no intention of shooting any rapids.

"With that bum arm?" Mary Beth challenged.

"River isn't deep – my legs work just fine." Josh admonished.

Casting a wary eye his way, Mary Beth donned the life jacket. Kayak loaded, including Josh's backpack, Josh entered the water to steady the kayak. To her surprise, Mary Beth was able to wiggle into the correct cockpit position.

Handing Mary Beth the paddle, Josh instructed, "Use this to help with your balance."

"How?"

"Don't worry, pretend you're walking a tightrope."

Looking at their goal across the ripples, Mary Beth frowned and sighed, "Right."

Josh planned to steady the kayak's stern with his good arm, using the floating torpedo as a kickboard to guide Mary Beth across the fledgling river. Halfway to their destination, all was well until Mary Beth wobbled and over-compensated. With a mind of its own, the kayak twisted free of Josh's grip and rolled upside down. Josh was trained and skilled at righting an inverted kayak, Mary Beth was not. Ten feet from the target bank, Josh regained his grip, moved mid-kayak, starboard, and dove under water. He pushed Mary Beth toward the bank. Popping to the surface, Josh was eye-to-eye with a frantic Mary Beth who flailed at him with the paddle.

With two kicks and a shove, the kayak struck the bank. Josh crawled to safety and banked the kayak.

Able to stand in the slow-moving water, Mary Beth wiggled onto the bank. Spitting snot and vomit, she screamed, "Trust you!?"

Josh accepted her screams. He deserved it. Still coughing and choking, Mary Beth collapsed on her stomach. Josh tried to blank out her dry heaves as he dragged the kayak into the underbrush away from the bank. Convinced it would not be easily found, be stripped the kayak of his backpack and lacrosse stick weapon.

Seated beside Mary Beth, he issued a not-so-convincing, "I'm sorry."

"Sorry? I've feared for my life for months and you almost drown me in one afternoon."

"I think you'll survive."

Through the last of her gasps, she asked, "Now what?"

Map in his lap, Josh showed Mary Beth his best guess of their current position. "And here's my car," he tapped the map.

"How far?"

"About three miles."

"Through this dense forest?" she lamented. "I can't walk that far, and I don't think you can either. You need medical attention."

"Only about thirty minutes by kayak," he said.

"I'm never getting in another kayak, as long as I live," she pronounced.

"I could go—" Josh started.

"-No, you don't, you can't leave me! And with only one arm?" Tears formed to solidify her resolve.

Josh patted the back of her hand and confirmed, "I'll never leave you."

For the first time in months, Mary Beth forced a smile. She looked back across the river and the source of her pain. "What if we?" she paused.

"What if we, what?"

She looked upstream, downstream. Pointing to the hidden kayak, she offered, "What if the kayak goes down-river, but we hike up-river?"

Puzzled, Josh started, "Why dump the...?" Stopping, it dawned on him. "A decoy, just like a pick-'n-roll..."

"A pickle roll?"

"A basketball or lacrosse play. The kayak will crash somewhere downstream. Caleb will search, if he looks at all, might find the kayak downstream. We go upstream."

The sound of the name Caleb made Mary Beth tremble.

"A decent diversion," Josh admitted. "He'll find the kayak and assume we're dead." He unfolded the map and fingered to a position upstream. "There's a service road here," he tapped the map with authority.

"We only need civilization," she added. "Let's look at your wound."

Mary Beth gently removed the twig from the tourniquet and unknotted the rope. The ax cut no longer oozed blood – maybe a seep of a drop or two. Just enough to keep the wound clean. The rope tourniquet was no longer needed. Mary Beth leaned into the river's edge and rinsed her scarf, tying it back around her neck.

Josh had retrieved the first-aid kit from the kayak and fumbled, one-handed, trying to apply treatment to his wound. Mary Beth stopped the embarrassing display of medical malpractice and applied ointment and a clean gauze bandage. Josh offered a tortured smile.

They sat in silence for only ten minutes when Josh was ready to move. He slipped the kayak from its hiding place. He confirmed that he had salvaged only what he needed and stashed the paddle in the kayak. Staring at his old friend, something seemed missing. He looked up at Mary Beth and said, "Give me your scarf."

This is the second time Mary Beth was being forced to part with her scarf. Tears formed as she clutched her scarf behind her back. "My Dad gave me this scarf. It's the only thing that helped me survive."

"It will continue to help you."

"How?" she whimpered.

"If Caleb finds it, it might convince him we both went down with the ship." Kneeling beside his kayak, he appealed with an outstretched hand.

Mary Beth shuffled her feet, looked up and down river, and stared at Josh. She slowly produced the scarf from behind her back, wadded it in a ball and brought it to her cheek. Their hands touched as she surrendered her scarf.

"And how about this goofy bucket fishing hat?" she challenged.

Josh grabbed it from her and slopped it back onto his head. Hands on hips, he took on a blustered pose with, "Bite your tongue."

"You're dead, right?"

"So?" he retorted.

"Something like a Viking funeral," she emphasized with drama.

"Without the fire."

Mary Beth hit him hard, with, "A GOOD Viking dies with his hat on." Mary Beth extended her hand, one last demand. "Give me the damn hat."

Josh limped to the kayak and shoved in his hat. "Happy now?"

As he placed it in the hatch with the same reverence he would bury a kitten, he gave it a final pat. Easing the decoy into the river, he gave it a push, trying not to think about three-thousand dollars floating out of sight. Stone bullet supply replenished, backpack shouldered, warrior stick in hand, they agreed to walk 20 feet away from the river to conceal their position.

Another try to alert Brad on his satellite radio proved fruitless. Josh reported his strategy and position in case his transmission might be received. Leaving the radio in the "on" position, he secured it in the backpack.

Turning to Mary Beth, Josh encouraged, "Ready?"

"I feel like Sacajawea," she almost laughed.

"Good, we shouldn't get lost."

* * *

Ranger Clark leaned over the hood of his Forest Service truck, studying a well-worn map, "Show me again."

Brad pointed to a spot not labeled on the Ranger's map, "About here."

"About? About?"

"Yeah, I know."

"The reason it's 'about' is because it's not an authorized put-in spot," the ranger scolded. "That's a fire control road. Sometimes you weekenders drive me nuts."

"Ya gotta admit, it's a good spot," as Brad tried some not-so-well-received humor.

The ranger's glare burned a hole clean through Brad. As a fellow officer of the law, Brad had expected a tad more professional courtesy. When tempers cooled, the search team understood where Josh's Subaru was "illegally" parked. It was clear from their actions; Josh's radio transmissions had not been received. They had no idea about his location or his strategy.

Any remaining tension was broken when Ranger Clark's radio squealed, "Johnson calling Clark."

Pulling the radio mic from his truck dashboard, Ranger Clark responded, "Johnson, what 'cha got?"

"Better come to Logan's Bend," came the matter-of-fact response. "Got a dead kayak."

"Ten minutes, on our way, Johnson. Out," Ranger Clark replied.

"Let's go, Deputy, we got a lead."

Brad held on for dear life as Ranger Clark drove the narrow forest fire roads like Brad drove the back alleys of Pittsburgh. It took only twelve minutes to arrive at the bank the locals knew as Logan's Bend; a hairpin turn at the midway point of a stage-three rapids.

Ranger Johnson directed the new arrivals to his find — a busted and splintered expedition kayak.

Brad kicked the ground and swore, "Shit!"

"Your friend's?" Ranger Clark asked.

"Yep," Brad admitted.

"Not good," Ranger Clark said.

Pants wet to mid-thigh; Ranger Johnson dragged the mostly-destroyed kayak out of the river. Deposited at Brad's feet, upside down, it looked hopeless. Sharp boulders had gouged huge holes.

Brad knelt beside his best friend's splintered kayak. He rolled it over and examined the cockpit, removing the paddle, he held it like a memory of Josh.

"I'm sorry, Deputy, let's go," Ranger Clark said.

Brad rose, paddle still in hand, and turned his back to the kayak, the river. In disgust, he spun and threw the paddle at the mutilated kayak, striking the cockpit dead-center. He let out a defeated war whoop and doubled over, hands on knees. He ran to the kayak and kicked it with such force that it rocked with the paddle disappearing into the knee-well.

"Ranger!" he screamed, as he retrieved the paddle from the kayak. "Ranger Clark!"

"Yes?"

Holding the unbroken paddle with both hands, Brad faced Ranger Clark and asked, "In a canoe or kayak accident, where would you find a paddle?"

"We rarely find them," Clark said.

"And if you do?"

"Well, they're usually beat up, and..."

"And?" Brad couldn't contain his excitement.

"And," the conclusion dawned on the forest ranger, "and, they're rarely—"

"Rarely, as in... never? Brad tossed the paddle to Clark.

Catching the paddle like a major league shortstop, he commented, "Never in the same spot as the kayak. Usually downstream." He inspected the paddle that had nary a scratch.

"Never!" Brad laughed.

"Damn... never snugly secured in the cockpit," Ranger Clark grinned, again inspecting the paddle. "Your buddy shoved this in the kayak."

"He's trying to set someone on the wrong trail," Brad offered. "I know his every move." Brad proceeded to inspect the kayak. The main section of the kayak contained no other clues. Ranger Clark was unloading the front storage hatch item by item; all the usual camping gear was confirmed as Josh's: tent, sleeping bag, rain slicker. The inventory was proving worthless until Clark held up a tattered scarf.

"Shit. What's that?" Brad was puzzled.

Holding it outstretched between thumb and index finger the way one might handle a dead skunk, Clark winced, as he grimaced, "Whatever it is, it's ugly purple and smells like garbage."

Brad handled it as delicately as its odor deserved and said, "Lavender... not purple." Examining it in more detail, he handed it back to Clark, suggesting, "Check out the monogram."

Not appreciative of the second opportunity to handle the offending scarf, Clark confirmed, "MB."

"Mary Beth Tolliver. Josh found her!" Brad was ecstatic.

"Holy crap! Now, where are they?"

"The Subaru is upstream from here, right?" Brad asked.

"About half-a-mile," Ranger Johnson confirmed.

Clark and Brad agreed it made sense to check out the illegally parked Subaru.

* * *

The hike up river delivered Josh and MB to a service road within half-an-hour. Overgrown and rutted, the going was tough, but easier than traipsing through virgin forest. Their objective of heading up river wasn't successful as the service road in that direction ended at the river. The other direction angled away from the river, but appeared to head downstream. They agreed that dead-ends were rarely productive, leaving only one choice.

Rest stops were frequent due to Mary Beth's and Josh's weakened conditions. Josh was as forceful in encouraging progress as he dared, considering what Mary Beth must have experienced in the last two months. They stopped at a junction of two service roads. Josh, compass in hand, tried to find their position on his map. Mary Beth capitalized on the opportunity to rest. After ten minutes of unsuccessful *this way, no that way* indecision, Josh put it to a vote. Mary Beth agreed with his recommendation that a service road closer to the river was better than going deeper into the forest.

They both needed more than just a nap. Josh was awakened when a squirrel thought his hiking boots tasted liken an acorn. It wasn't clear whether he or the squirrel were more frightened when Josh started kicking and yelling.

The sight of the frightened squirrel scampering away almost brought a smile to Mary Beth. She hadn't smiled in months.

"Mary Beth, we need to move on, before the sun sets."

Mary Beth did not protest. She rose to her feet and dusted herself off.

Mary Beth was the first to notice, "The river. We're nearing the river again. I hear it."

They stopped and quieted their breathing; the forest was silent, except for the faint gurgle of the river. "We should be cautious, go slower," Josh suggested.

"I'm all in favor of slower," Mary Beth agreed.

They made eye contact and shared a relieved laugh.

"Yes, slower, and quieter," Josh offered a more subdued laugh.

After two more twists and one turn, Josh pushed a low-hanging branch aside to reveal a setting sun reflecting off a shiny object. Five more steps revealed the object to be the passenger-side rearview mirror of his Subaru.

Josh was overcome. Not only had he gotten the game into overtime, he scored the winning goal. While Mary Beth sat on the ground behind the car sobbing, celebrating with a much-deserved rest, Josh circled to the front and pounded his fists on the hood with his own celebration.

The crack sounded like a tree branch breaking from a direct lightning strike. It's not clear whether Josh jerked in the direction of the sound because he heard it, or due to the sharp pain in his right shoulder. He hit the ground as the second rifle shot destroyed the passenger's-side headlight.

"Lay flat!" He screamed to Mary Beth. "Behind the car!"

It had to be Caleb. Josh pressed his stomach into the ground as he wiggled under the Subaru. Each movement sent pained nails through his shoulder and right arm. He was frantic in his search in his backpack for his binoculars. Perched on his left elbow, binoculars focused on the far bank, he didn't find the camouflaged truck until the third shot rang out. His Subaru windshield and rear tailgate window seemed to shatter simultaneously as a single bullet blasted through the car. Caleb was standing on his truck bed, leaning on the pickup truck cab to steady his aim. Josh's hickory lacrosse stick was useless at this range and against this foe. His only advantage was distance and the river separating them from Caleb.

Josh wormed the length of his Subaru, dragging his backpack and throbbing right arm, until he reached Mary Beth's position. The measure of safety he now felt with the shield of a ton-and-a-half of steel guarding him was not shared by Mary Beth. She was close to a full-fledged panic attack. Josh, now burdened with two serious injuries, nestled close to Mary Beth providing security near her shaking body.

As bullets continued to pepper his car, a new sound pierced the air. It was his satellite radio. He retrieved the radio from his backpack and hit receive. For the first time in days, he and this new-fangled technology were on the same wave length.

"On your wing, right. Forty feet."

Josh pressed transmit, "Brad!"

"Got your back, pardner," Brad assured.

"Do you see him?" Josh begged.

"No, where is he?" Brad asked.

"Opposite bank. Camouflage pickup truck. Ten feet in."

"Directly across from you?"

"No, off center, 30 degrees, right."

"Stay put, Josh. I gotta shift a bit."

Mary Beth interjected, "What's happening?"

Josh rolled toward Mary Beth and placed his index finger to his lips communicating, *shhh*. He placed his good arm around her shoulder providing reassurance.

"Josh?"

"Yeah."

"Got a clear shot, but only when he takes aim to shoot."

There was a pause. The length of no response seemed eternal.

"Josh, you there?"

Another shot rang out resulting in the smell of leaking antifreeze.

"Yeah, I'll pop up for a split second," Josh whispered.

"Stand down. No way."

"Get set. I'll give you a 3-2-1."

"No!"

"Set your sights, Brad. Here goes, 3... 2... 1" Josh maneuvered to his knees and jumped to his feet for what to Mary Beth seemed like forever. For an agonized second, Josh was visible beside the Subaru. The shot from across the river spun him around as blood and tissue splattered on the Subaru side window. He hit the ground with a yelp of pain in his shoulder as Caleb pulled off two more rounds.

Mary Beth let out a blood-curdling scream, "NO!"

Caleb's shots hit car windows and were accompanied by rapid fire retorts from rifles to Josh's right. The angle and proximity to Josh and Mary Beth made it sound like they were in a World War I foxhole. Mary Beth gasped. Echoes of rolling thunder faded as quiet fell over the forest, except for the constancy of the river. An eerie kind of quiet.

Brad and Rangers Clark and Johnson walked into the clearing and approached a shivering Josh and Mary Beth. Brad knelt, a hand on Josh's good shoulder, and announced, "It's over, buddy."

Moving beside the still-terrified young lady, Brad offered a hand that was accepted, although with a noticeable degree of caution. He assisted Mary Beth to her feet and liberated a dead leaf and a twig from hair that needed serious attention. He reached into his shirt pocket and placed a lavender scarf in her still-trembling hand, "I believe this is yours."

Mary Beth made eye contact with Brad and released tears she had harbored for two months. She buried her face in her lavender scarf. Her long ordeal had come to an end.

Her moment of deserved peace was shattered by the blare of an ambulance siren and realization that Josh was in serious condition. The blue/red flashing lights danced an evil jig off the peace of the river rapids. Josh, now strapped to a gurney, unconscious as his head falls to the side. Mary Beth, beside the gurney, placed a hand on Josh's chest as she sobbed, "Thanks, tenderfoot." She tousled his hair as the gurney was loaded and doors closed in Mary Beth's face.

Brad, standing at the river's edge, looked back at the ambulance. Josh's tatty bucket hat in his hands, buried his face in the hat. In one motion, he flung the hat into the river and watched it float downstream. He bowed his head and cried.

Josh's bucket hat floated parallel to the ambulance as it sped down the service road, lights flashing. The ambulance crossed the river on a bridge as Josh's hat continued under the bridge and downstream, out of sight.

The ambulance lights faded into the distance as a painful silence surrendered to increasing sounds of crickets, birds, and a gentle stream that built to a crescendo of roaring river rapids.

* * *

Though unconscious, Josh somehow sensed the difference between gentle tumbles, roaring rapids, and the BEEP, BEEP, BEEP of life support equipment. Josh, motionless in a hospital ICU bed, surrounded with hi-tech medical equipment, he was tubed from head-to-toe, in an induced coma.

His father, James Whitlock, was seated beside the bed, holding his son's hand. Mother, Sara, seated in a corner, read from her well-worn King James Bible.

Sara continued with, "And they shall beat their swords into plowshares..." as Brad entered with coffees and Danish. She smiled at Brad as she finished with, "...and their spears into pruning hooks."

Brad returned the smile. Sara closed her Bible, rose, and gave Brad a quick peck on his cheek.

"How's my buddy, today?" Brad chirped.

As Josh's lifelong friend, Brad was like another son to the Whitlocks. "No change. We should know more this afternoon," James offered.

Brad confessed, "I don't know much about induced comas... it's been a long 30 days."

"You've been a trooper, Brad," Sara cheered.

"The doctors started the exit coma protocol two hours ago," James said, without any tone of emotion.

"He'll make it," Brad encouraged.

"It's touch and go," James replied.

The starkness and cool delivery of Mr. Whitlock's words disturbed Brad, as though the father knew more about the cold truth than Brad wanted to accept. Brad looked at his almost-parents and offered to stand watch. "You two look bedraggled. Take a break. I'll tell him dirty jokes I heard at work today."

James was quick on the trigger, with "So much for the plowshares and pruning hooks."

Sara smiled as she agreed, "Let's take a walk, Jimmie."

The Whitlocks left, giving Brad a pat on the shoulder as they threw exhausted glances back at their son.

Brad paced around the room, studying the dials and gauges. He picked up the Bible, giving it a quick thumb-through, and put it down. Brad sat in the chair beside the bed and messed up Josh's hair. He held Josh's hand and lowered his forehead to the clasped hands. He stared at the ceiling as he started, "A rabbi, a priest, and a penguin go into a bar..." Brad sobbed as he looked out the window, forgetting the punchline.

"Ya took too many bullets, buddy," Brad whispered.

Brad put his forehead back on the clasped hands, and prayed, "Come on buddy, give me a sign. I'll pull the plug. What 'cha want, buddy?"

* * *

It was the middle of the night. Two dreary parents stood vigil over an unresponsive son. Sara, Bible in her lap, Sara begged her silent husband to talk with her.

"It's been two days, Sara," Jim finally broke the silence.

"I'll pray another three, or 30, she responded in a determined tone.

James knelt at his wife's feet and held her hands in his, "What would Josh want honey? Maybe it's time to let him go."

James laid his head in Sara's lap. She stroked his hair. They cried together as Sara stared off into the nothingness of the night.

Sara whispered to God, "My boy's got more goals to score."

* * *

Brad lost count of the hours. The days. He knew the nursing staff by their first names. He entered Josh's room. Nurse Alice was checking dials, gauges, gizmos. Brad stood by the windows, out of the way. As Nurse Alice left the room, she shook her head "no" to the doctor who had just entered the room. They whispered, inaudible to Brad. The body language, the vibe was cold, as Nurse Alice left the room.

Sara and James, in each other's arms, tearful, entered the room. James approached Brad, grasping him by the shoulders, as he stammered, "B-Brad, I'm... sorry." James broke down and returned to Sara.

Brad, shaken, paced... with a frantic zeal he got in the doctor's face. Staccato finger in the doctor's chest, he accentuated each word: "Get to overtime. He always wins in overtime."

With all the sympathy he could muster, the doctor told Brad, "Sorry, son. It's time to let him go."

Seeking support, comfort from anyone, Brad failed. Others in the room averted eye contact. Brad stormed out of room in a huff of rage.

The doctor turned to the Whitlocks saying, "I'll leave you to say your goodbyes." Quietly, he left the family and stood beside Brad. The silence in the corridor was deafening. The doctor broke the silence educating Brad on a truth of medical science, "Son, it hurts when we fail... the field of medicine can only do so much."

With reddened eyes, Brad told the doctor, "He's the brother I never had."

James exited the ICU and embraced Brad and walked slowly toward the waiting area.

The awkward silence was broken by a scream from Josh's room. Brad's first reaction was that Josh had died. It was Sara yelling for the doctor. "Ah! Doctor! Doctor!," Sara wailed.

The doctor and Brad rushed into the room to find Sara seated on the edge of Josh's bed, holding his hand. His little finger had an erratic twitch. A tear welled in Josh's eye and rolled down his cheek.

Sara stood and clutched her Bible to her heart. "Come back, baby."

The doctor stood over Josh, shinning a light in each eye. "Nurse! Call Dr. Fredericks, STAT!"

Sara, eyes toward the heavens, shouted, "My boy's got more goals to score. Praise the Lord."

Brad fist-pumped the air as the jumped, "It's overtime, pardner."

* * *

The next six months passed as a blur. Brad was learning new first names in a Pittsburgh physical therapy facility; he worked with Josh every day. The gym blared Rocky-like music alternating with *Flashdance* – it was Pittsburgh, after all. While Josh gained weight and muscle mass, Brad lost weight.

Brad gave up competing with Josh on the mind task portion of therapy. In the six months Brad worked with Josh, he never beat him in: checkers, chess, Rubik's cube, and picture puzzles.

For Mary Beth, the time went by in a flash. Reunions with family, friends. Photographers. Press conferences. Lawyers. Psychiatrists. She had trouble sleeping. Her appetite had not yet returned. Her hair did look better. The lavender scarf barely survived its re-introduction to a washing machine; though in shreds, she vowed to keep it.

Brad's routine as a deputy sheriff would not become routine for another month. Having killed someone in the line of duty, while a hero in all circles, bureaucracy had him assigned to desk duty until internal affairs completed its investigation. He rejected all inquiries from reporters and lawyers. Other than sheriff department-required psychiatric evaluations, he had no interest in spilling his guts to a shrink. He relished his time working as Josh's rehab challenge partner.

Josh spent most of his time with medical professionals. His shoulder and arm would mend with 75% functionality. When he challenged an orthopedic surgeon's use of *75%*, he didn't like what he heard: *Son, lacrosse is in your past. No more 100 mile-per-hour goals for you.*

With physical therapy completed, Josh sat at his laptop, blank page staring back at him. He saved the document as "*Resume*" and closed his computer.

* * *

THREE YEARS LATER

Mary Beth was enjoying the afternoon sun, bouncing her six-month-old son, on her knee. Not understanding lacrosse nuances didn't inhibit her yells and screams from the stands as Pittsburgh Central Catholic staged a comeback in the high school state finals. Score tied, clock running down, Central Catholic's All-State goalie was under intense pressure; they were a man short for the final 30 seconds of the game due to an overly aggressive cross-check.

"You just made it, honey," Mary Beth said to her frazzled husband. "Thanks for the Coke." It was hot and her Sir Galahad had made a quick run to the concession stand.

"Any change?" Brad asked.

"Cross-check penalty."

"Damn," Brad swore.

Elbow to his ribs, Mary Beth scolded, "Not around the baby." Continuing to bounce her son, she instructed, "Don't you listen to Daddy, Joshua."

"Darn," came Brad's sheepish correction.

Mary Beth stood and screamed, "Watch out! Pickle roll! Pickle roll!"

James Whitlock winked at wife Sara, "I don't recall we had pickle rolls back in the day."

With a gentle pat on his knee, Sara dead-panned, "Showing your age again, Jimmie."

Giving his wife that "spare me" look, Brad yelled, "Numquam Mori Rah! Numquam Mori Rah!"

Being short-handed, Central Catholic High could have used divine intervention — it didn't come. Only five seconds remaining, the goalie made a noble attempt as the thigh-high shot glanced off a teammate, diverting the winning score into the net. As time expired, defeat burdened heavy. Coach Josh lowered his chin to his chest for only a second. A brisk walk to mid-field and a "great game" handshake with the opposing team's head coach, he didn't feel defeated. His team had played well.

His All-State goalie did feel defeated. A senior, it was his last chance at a state championship. Josh met his dejected goalie just as he lowered his helmet to his side. Coach and team leader embraced; an embrace that confirmed to Josh he had chosen the right career.

With his one good arm around the teenager's shoulder, Josh exhorted, "Chin up, son. You're a winner." A second embrace was interrupted as Josh saw a man walking up behind his goalie. Stepping aside, Josh shook the man's hand and said, "Thanks for coming, Dave." Turning to his goalie, Josh said, "Bobby, I'd like you to meet Mr. Pietramala, head lacrosse coach at Johns Hopkins."

Coach Pietramala congratulated Bobby saying, "Great game, Bobby."

"Thank you, sir," Bobby beamed as they shook hands.

Sensing something strong about Bobby's character had just been communicated, Coach Pietramala said, "Let's talk next week."

Another firm handshake with Josh, Coach Pietramala pulled Josh closer as he said, "We should talk soon, too."

"Yes, sir."

Josh raised his new, soon to be ratty bucket hat, as he acknowledged the fans and pointed to his best friend, Brad.

Coach Josh had a spring in his step as he made the rounds to parents and underclassmen who needed some encouragement.

THE END

* * *

ZIPPO

C aptain Henson curled in his usual fetal position on the tattered straw mat embedded into the dank mud floor of his solitary confinement prison cell. He took some comfort in hiding some personal effects and a glass picture frame in a hole under his straw mat. Sunrise dappled his cramped bamboo space that had become home for the past ten months. His tiger cage shook as Japanese shouts interrupted a not-so-peaceful sleep. *Is it Tuesday? Day for a 30-minute walk-around? Had it been almost a year since I ditched The Zippo Gang—his B-29 Superfortress bomber—in the Sea of Japan after a successful bombing raid over Japan's homeland?*

While Kojo Island harbored makeshift POW holding cells, its primary mission supported a battery of anti-aircraft guns protecting Japan's west coast. Captain Henson hadn't actually seen the defensive emplacements, but he heard their nightly barrage. He also hadn't made eye contact with his surviving flight crew. Secret Morse code communications confirmed that three of his eleven-man team were held as prisoners near his bamboo cage.

The scramble out of a crippled and sinking B-29 left little opportunity for Henson to save lives or salvage personal effects. Each day as the light faded and shadows lengthened in Kojo's jungle, Henson sorted through the knapsack buried beneath his straw mat in the corner. He stroked his fingers across the cracked glass of a framed photo and lock of hair from his yet-to-be-held newborn daughter. He didn't mind that his King James Old Testament was missing a begat or two as the Psalms and most of Isaiah survived intact. Flicking the top of his father's Zippo lighter open/closed produced a grimace that melted into a smile as he pondered his luck in hiding this family treasure up his rectum the first week of his captivity.

Captain Henson had no access to a mirror. However, from the bleeding sores on his arms and legs, the blistered feet, the loss of two teeth and at least forty pounds, he figured he was no longer a handsome high school quarterback.

The four surviving Army Air Corpsmen communicated nightly using a delayed, fractured form of Morse code. They tapped stones together, adding a two to six second gap between each letter. The more random the gap, the better. While as slow as frozen molasses, getting "stoned" each night maintained sanity and kept spirits hopeful. They also coordinated plans that might be used to escape or sabotage Kojo Island's defensive mission.

Navigator Staff Sergeant Polansky connected the dots between the 2 am island blackouts and the dull roar heard over the mountainous horizon. "Dash-dot-dot-dot," Polansky paused. "Dot-dot-dash-dash-dash," he continued. And with an encouraging conclusion, he rocked, "Dash, dash, dash, dash, dot."

Henson smiled as he imagined his flight crew mouthing, *B-29*.

While the four fly-boys could see each other's tiger cages, they hadn't talked directly since ditching in the Sea of Japan. It took months to hatch their plan. They collected organic material on their weekly walk-arounds: coconut grass, leaves, scrap paper. They deposited their contraband in a designated location for Henson to consolidate in his prison cell. Day-by-day, Captain Henson converted his bamboo cell into a tinder box. He quoted Psalms and Isaiah by heart as he tore the final pages of King James into freedom fuel. He used the broken glass shards from his daughter's picture frame to weaken bamboo lashes in the corners of his cell. He rocked, "Dash, dash, dash," and, "dash, dot, dash." *(OK)* Henson waited.

In the pitch black of the next new moon, at precisely 2 am, Kojo Island went dark. A distant rumble settled over the Sea of Japan. Henson tucked his daughter's picture and lock of hair in a tattered shirt pocket. He caressed his father's Zippo lighter to his chest and said goodbye. With a flip of the top and flick of the steel wheel on flint, Henson propped the mischievous lighter in the corner of his cell. A tongue of fire kissed its way up the bamboo wall setting Psalms, Isaiah, and nature's trash ablaze. Henson's tiger cage exploded in a fireball.

Henson bum-rushed the weakened corner of his cell, shielding his face with the remnants of his bomber jacket. The cage collapsed, spreading a conflagration throughout the dense jungle floor. Henson fought his way through the underbrush, freeing his flight crew from their bamboo cells.

The four Air Corpsmen ran to the hoped-for safety of the water's edge. Flaming target at their backs, roaring thunder approaching over the black horizon, The Zippo Gang linked arms as they reached two friendly fire realities: Kojo Island would shoot down no more American fliers and the crew of The Zippo Gang had successfully completed its final mission.

* * *

THE SOUNDS OF SILENCE

"How did it go, doctor?" the elderly Mrs. Jones asked. "He won't be paralyzed," the short answer came. "Removing a brain tumor this robust has a high probability of stroke-like results. Your husband isn't currently exhibiting any of those symptoms. But, don't get your hopes up on his hearing ever returning."

Stan Jones had been completely deaf for the past five years. The fast-growing tumor had taken its toll. Too much pressure on the auditory nerve. Cantankerous doesn't come close to describing life with bricks-for-ears Stan.

Ethel tried to walk a mile in his shoes. Sounds were everywhere. Defining each day, each moment. At her sister's recent funeral, the music touched her soul. The horse hair bow drawn across the taut strings meowed its way into her heart. At the end of the service, all was quiet as the funeral director closed the casket. The metal-on-metal locking of the eternal clasp arched a raucous ricochet off the cathedral ceiling and down her spine.

Grandchildren fought over who got the biggest piece of pumpkin pie. Doorbells rang raising expectations that Publisher's Clearinghouse might be parked in the driveway. Rain pinged the corrugated tin roof of the reunion picnic shelter. Ethel's husband had missed five years' of Lawrence Welk re-runs. He skipped social events, church; even Reds games because he couldn't hear the crack of the bat.

Ethel held her breath as she entered the recovery room. The surgery threatened a seventy-five percent chance of paralysis. She already knew that bullet had been dodged. The prospect that her beloved Stan would hear the orchestra at Coney's Moonlight Gardens on their sixtieth anniversary next year was only five percent. Her heart pounded in her ears.

She heard her snoring husband and pulled the curtain aside. A gentle touch to his shoulder, she whispered, "Love you, Stanley."

Stan opened his eyes and said, "Ethel, why are you shouting?"

* * *

TEN-MINUTE DRAMA

Writer's note: Ten-Minute Dramas are becoming more popular in academic circles, regional theatres, and amateur writing groups. The genre sharpens writer dialogue and gives actors a chance to dive into a role, many times with little or no notice. Whether performed in a small club setting, a local tavern, or on the stage, these short productions help writers and actors hone their craft.

Here's a quick key to abbreviations used in this section:

EXT = Exterior
INT = Interior
CONT. = Continued
SL = Stage Left
SR = Stage Right

The writing format follows that traditionally used in stage plays and movie screenplays.

I wrote "Stuck" in a University of Cincinnati College Conservatory of Music Drama Writers' Workshop. It was fun seeing my work produced by future Broadway and Hollywood talent.

"Woody" is a quick write, just for the fun of it.

* * *

STUCK

FADE IN:

EXT. CARNIVAL BROKEN FERRIS WHEEL – DUSK –
PRESENT DAY

Ferris Wheel shakes and jerks, lights flicker, it is stuck.

CHAIR ONE (lower, forward-most chair)

TRISH, twenty-five, spaghetti-strap summer dress, cute,
caresses 12-oz cup, from which she periodically sips a straw.

Trish scoots away from JAKE, twenty-eight, country-western,
Levi's jeans, cowboy hat. Jake is cocky, drunk, and keeps rocking
the chair.

                    TRISH
     Please, stop!

                    JAKE
     Sour puss.

Trish glares at Jake, as if "really?" Jake stops rocking.

                    TRISH
     Thanks.

JAKE

Must be my ADHD. Skipped a pill this morning.

TRISH

First blind date. Stuck atop a Ferris Wheel with a chemically dependent hillbilly.

JAKE

Remember? You pinged me on the internet first. We've only been stuck up here ten minutes.

TRISH

Seems like hours. My internet post was honest.

JAKE

You didn't ask about any attention deficit disorder.

Jake waves cowboy hat wildly at someone on the ground.

JAKE (CONT.)

Hey, bitch!

Trish grabs safety bar as chair rocks wildly.

TRISH

What's wrong with you?

JAKE

Ex-wife.

TRISH

Since when?

                        JAKE

That one? Last year.

                        TRISH

That one? How many ex's do you have?

                        JAKE

Only two.

                        TRISH

I see you're still on speaking terms.

                        JAKE

Can't.

                        TRISH

Can't speak to her?

                        JAKE

Nope. Violates restraining order.

Trish gives look of despair, places forehead on safety bar.

EXT. CARNIVAL BROKEN FERRIS WHEEL –
PROGRESSIVELY DARKER

Ferris Wheel quivers, lights flicker.

CHAIR TWO (highest chair)

PETE and MAGGIE, thirty-something married couple gently
rock chair. Space between them.

PETE

Oh, fifteen minutes I suppose.

MAGGIE

'Member that ski lift at Vail?

Both laugh and lean in, shoulders touch, briefly.

MAGGIE (CONT.)

Trapped right in front of that snow making gizmo. Now, that was stuck.

PETE

You looked like the Abominable Snow Man.

MAGGIE

Yer pecker didn't thaw 'til 1 am.

PETE

You were very helpful. Happy anniversary, Maggie. Five great years.

MAGGIE

There have been some good years. You proposed on a Ferris Wheel. State Fair.

Pete wiggles, shuffles feet nervously. Starts to speak, retreats then eases into an awkward tone.

PETE

Since we're stuck up here, something on my mind.

MAGGIE

Me too.

PETE

Really? You first.

MAGGIE

No, you.

PETE

On the count of three. Blurt it out. One.

MAGGIE

Two.

PETE/MAGGIE (Together)
PETE: Three. MAGGIE: Three

PETE/MAGGIE (Together)
PETE: I want a baby. MAGGIE: I want a divorce.

PETE/MAGGIE (Together)
PETE: A divorce?! MAGGIE: A baby?!

MAGGIE

A baby?

PETE

A divorce?

EXT. CARNIVAL BROKEN FERRIS WHEEL –
ALMOST DARK

CHAIR THREE (back-most chair)

LOUIS and FRED, handsome, high school seniors, spaced apart on chair.

FRED

You what?

LOUIS

He's my priest. He won't tell any-

FRED

—any of his fag priest bros? I'm not...

LOUIS

Not what?

FRED

Ready. I'm not ready.

Louis places arm over the back of the chair.

FRED (CONT.)

I know I'm, I'm gay. I just can't... can't. I'm not ready to come out of the closet.

LOUIS

What's it like in there?

FRED

In where?

LOUIS

Your closet.

FRED

Dark. Lonely. Aren't all closets?

LOUIS

My closet was lonely. But not all that dark. It was a hell I needed to escape.

FRED

Crap. Out of closet looks like hell to me.

LOUIS

Hells are personal. Imagine a gay guy, out in the world faking it as straight. What's his hell like?

FRED

That's me. A fake. That's my hell.

LOUIS

Take your time, there's no rush. You're not alone.

Louis closes a small portion of the space between them.

EXT. CARNIVAL BROKEN FERRIS WHEEL – NOW FULLY DARK

CHAIR ONE

Trish gurgle-slurps the last of her drink from her cup.

                    JAKE
              (reaches for the cup)
I'll take that.

                    TRISH

It's empty.

                    JAKE

Good. I gotta piss.

Jake turns his back, kneels on chair, unzips pants, pees in cup.
Trish glances once in disgust, turns, faces away.

EXT. CARNIVAL BROKEN FERRIS WHEEL – DARK

CHAIR TWO

                    MAGGIE
You think a child will fix us?

                    PETE
I didn't know we were broken.

                    MAGGIE
                   (halting)
Kinda like this Ferris Wheel.

                    PETE
Temporary. Just a little bump.

                    MAGGIE
I don't mean, broken, like this Ferris Wheel.

PETE

It's those damn yoga classes. Pilats. Meditation.

MAGGIE

Last two years—

PETE

—years? Two months? I get that. But, two years?

MAGGIE

We talk past each other. Never to each other.

PETE

Aren't we on the same track?

MAGGIE

Like a train track, maybe.

PETE

A train? I like trains.

MAGGIE

The rails are in sync, but never intersect. Always at a safe distance... parallel. Apart.

PETE

Apart? Apart doesn't sound safe. Aren't you safe with me?

MAGGIE

Too safe, like this Ferris Wheel. 'Round and 'round. I get more forward motion from my yoga.

PETE

And your pirates.

MAGGIE

It's Pilates.

PETE

Pirates. Pilats. Pilates. Who gives a shit?

MAGGIE

I do.

EXT. CARNIVAL BROKEN FERRIS WHEEL – DARK

CHAIR ONE

Trish bangs forehead on safety bar.

Jake zips up pants, balances cup of piss, clumsily twists back into his seat. Trish slides to extreme end of chair, hands extended, holds Jake at bay.

TRISH

Stay.

JAKE

Like a dog?

TRISH

Fido, sit.

Trish tries to scoot further away, draws imaginary line down center of chair. Secures hands on safety bar, defensive.

Arms folded over bar, Jake balances cup. Shakes bar as if it's the back of the front seat of his parent's car.

JAKE
(juvenile whine voice)

Mommy, sissy's buggin' me. She's lookin' at me.

Jake cocks head as if listening to Mommy's response.

JAKE (CONT.)

No way, it's mine.

Jake stomps feet like a frustrated child.

JAKE (CONT.)

It's my juice. I'm not sharing.

Trish looks around, as if "who is this nut talking to"?

JAKE (CONT.)
(resigned)

Okay. If I have to.

Jake scoots a little closer to Trish, offers her the cup.

JAKE (CONT.)

Here.

TRISH

That's it. This date is over.

Trish rises to knees on chair, turns back to camera.

JAKE

Where the hell ya think yer goin'?

Trish stands, balances on wobbling chair. Jake reaches for her, unsuccessful. Trish climbs into the superstructure.

Focus widens from a single car to entire Ferris Wheel structure.

Jakes stumbles dangerously as he grabs for Trish's ankle.

JAKE (CONT.)

Holy shit!

All on Ferris Wheel reach for Trish, chairs rock wildly.

Louis sits on floor of his chair, legs dangle precariously.

All panic. Ferris Wheel jerks, lights flicker.

ENTIRE CAST (except Trish)
(chaotic lines on top of each other)

She's gonna fall.
Grab 'er.
Crap.
She's nuts.

PETE

Damn.

MAGGIE

What the f...?

Trish at Pete's side of topmost chair, places her foot on the seat between Pete's legs. Pete reacts as though his crotch was just violated. He grabs her around the waist as she spins, crash-sits between Pete and Maggie.

PETE
(octave higher)

What the f...?

MAGGIE

And you are?

TRISH
(gasps for breath)
Huh... Scared. I'm... scared.

Jake kneels on chair, balanced, points cowboy hat at Trish.

JAKE

Hey, bitch!

Trish removes a sandal, flings it at Jake. Jake ducks, cup of piss falls from his hand. Jake watches it tumble, winces to connote it hit someone.

JAKE (CONT.)
(shouts up at Trish)
Restraining order! Now, I'm the one needin' a restraining order.

EXT. CARNIVAL BROKEN FERRIS WHEEL – DARK

CHAIR THREE

Louis and Fred settle back into their chair, sit closer.

FRED
I know I'm gay. I wonder if she knows she's insane.

LOUIS
Probably only temporary.

FRED
Me, or her?

LOUIS
That's for you to figure out.

FRED
Tough choice.

LOUIS
I didn't say "choice".

FRED
Why would anyone choose to be abused? Discriminated against. I was born this way. I didn't choose.

LOUIS

That sounded sincere. Not rehearsed.

FRED

It's the real choice that I have to rehearse?

LOUIS

Real choice?

FRED

Telling my Dad. When? How? How will I introduce the real me to my family? My friends?

LOUIS

Don't your friends already know? Know the real you?

Fred stares off in space, then nods "yes".

LOUIS (CONT.)

And if they know... might your dad know, too?

Fred stares straight ahead. Louis looks at Fred.

EXT. CARNIVAL BROKEN FERRIS WHEEL – DARK

CHAIR ONE

Jake abandoned, raises gaze and addresses camera directly.

JAKE

I've had them sneak out of my apartment before I wake up. I've been dumped every which way possible. But! I've never, ever been left stuck atop a Ferris Wheel. Who the hell climbs...?

Jake stands on chair, extends arms, hat in hand, shouts below.

JAKE (CONT.)
Hey, ex-wife bitch number two! Ya happy now?

FADE OUT.

THE END

* * *

WOODY

EMPTY STAGE – TWO CHAIRS

VENTRILOQUIST enters, carrying old suitcase. Places suitcase on floor, in front of chairs. Arranges chairs, adjusts, confirms setup. Satisfied, sits on chair.

Looks around, as if waiting for someone. Looks at watch. Exasperated. Rises, opens suitcase flat on floor. Returns to his chair, checks watch, looks left/right.

WOODY (wooden dummy puppet) limps in stiffly, SL. Glances at audience. Steps into open suitcase, sits yoga-style, flops limply. Beat. Rises slowly, twirls forearms around elbow joint. Deep knee bends. Sits on chair next to Ventriloquist.

Ventriloquist and Woody make eye contact. Ventriloquist stares at Woody, exasperated. Woody ignores, unfazed.

> ### VENTRILOQUIST
> So?

> ### WOODY
> So... what?

> ### VENTRILOQUIST
> Yer late, Woody.

WOODY

Not my fault.

VENTRILOQUIST

Whose fault is it?

WOODY

This is your gig. I'm just the dummy.

VENTRILOQUIST

That's a poor excuse, stupid thing to say.

WOODY

Not my words. You're the ventriloquist.

VENTRILOQUIST

I'm under a lot of pressure. Do you think it's easy? Always in charge? Thinking for two?

WOODY

Thinking. Is that what it's called?

VENTRILOQUIST

Asshole.

WOODY

Don't have one.

VENTRILOQUIST

Very clever. Think yer funny?

WOODY

I don't write the dialogue.

VENTRILOQUIST

We've got a show to do. Woody, for once, try to be funny.

WOODY

I don't write the dialogue.

VENTRILOQUIST

Come on, hop up. On the lap.

WOODY

Nope. Going for the thigh tonight. Gonna perch close to the knee.

VENTRILOQUIST

What's yer problem?

WOODY

I'm not the problem.

VENTRILOQUIST

I suppose I am?

WOODY

Every time I sit in your lap, you wiggle me around until you get all ...

VENTRILOQUIST

All what?

WOODY

I'm embarrassed. All... worked up.

VENTRILOQUIST

Worked... up?

WOODY

Yes... up. Okay, make me say it. Does it turn you on when I say it? Wiggle me around, you get an election. Hard...

VENTRILOQUIST

Election?

WOODY

Hey, yer the one with the speech defect.

VENTRILOQUIST

E-rrre-ction.

WOODY

E-llle-ction.

VENTRILOQUIST

It's hard for a ventriloquist to differentiate between an "l" and an "r".

WOODY

Hard, huh? There ya go again, hard.

VENTRILOQUIST

And I suppose you don't... ever?

WOODY

I'm knotty pine and spruce. I always have a woodie. ..
I AM Woody.

VENTRILOQUIST

Now that's funny. We're gonna have a good show tonight.

WOODY

I'm sittin' on your knee.

Ventriloquist places hand on Woody's back, as if lifting him
to his lap. Woody slides forward onto knee. They look at each
other, then stare at audience.

VENTRILOQUIST

Aren't you going to say hello?

WOODY

Hello.

VENTRILOQUIST

That's it?

WOODY

I'll say whatever ya want, boss.

Ventriloquist slides Woody back onto his lap. They make eye
contact. Woody scoots forward onto knee.

WOODY (CONT.)

Slide me back up there again, you'll get a splinter where
it's gonna hurt.

VENTRILOQUIST

I should've gotten the plastic model.

WOODY

Now who's the dummy?

VENTRILOQUIST

Let's show 'em the cigarette, beer chug gag.

Ventriloquist puts cigarette in Woody's mouth. Woody bounces cigarette wildly as he talks.

WOODY

Gag is right. Isn't it 'bout my turn for the beer? Let's switch places. You smoke... I'll chug.

VENTRILOQUIST

I can't condone underage drinking.

WOODY

Underage?

VENTRILOQUIST

I've only had you five years.

WOODY

Had? So impersonal. Had? Other things are "had." You "had" a cold. You "had" syphilis.

VENTRILOQUIST

That's a lie.

WOODY

I was there. She was u-g-l-y. The stuff I put up with. Expected to keep my mouth shut.

VENTRILOQUIST

Next time, I'm cramming you in the suitcase.

Woody slowly applauds.

VENTRILOQUIST (CONT.)

What's that for?

WOODY

I might be in the suitcase, but yer still gettin' the clap.

VENTRILOQUIST

This gig is over. Back into the suitcase you go.

Ventriloquist and Woody rise. Woody stands in suit case and applauds.

WOODY

OK, we're done. Let's all give him the clap.

Woody continues to clap as BLACK OUT.

THE END

* * *

NON-FICTION (TRUE)

Writer's note: While these stories are true, some names have been changed to protect the innocent or the stupid. The writer's name has not been changed. First person "I" is "me" – as in autobiographical.

CONTAINED

My Hollywood agent tells me to contain my enthusiasm. Stifle, restrict, kill; pick a boxed-in word, or words that apply. Let me explain. I have this imagination that creates stories that I think are movie-worthy. However, as an un-optioned, un-produced screenwriter, I have to think small – small budgets, small sets, small casts. I've been admonished to never send my agent anything big. Only produced writers are allowed to think, and write, BIG.

What in the heck does "contained" mean? The entire movie needs to take place in one location, preferably one room. Think about the production company setting up lights, camera, and a director yelling, "Action!" Two actors in a psychiatrist's office: the psychiatrist, one chair, and the patient, spilling his/her guts on one couch. No flashbacks; the camera can't leave the psychiatrist's office. Before I hear admonitions, "It can't be done," recall that Hitchcock did it in *Rear Window* with Jimmy Stewart seated in a wheel chair. But I'm not Hitchcock.

Here's a few of my ideas that are high on the non-contained list:

- *Barnstorm:* An afraid-of-heights loser wants to be a pilot. We have dive-bombing biplanes, World War II dogfight flashbacks, a county fair rodeo, hundreds of spectators at a climactic airshow, and ten-plus locations. Just imagine the production insurance required.
- *The Ghosts of Serpent Mound:* A midnight murder of two young lovers desecrating a 1,000-year-old Indian

mound stymies an archaeologist's dig. Extras, crowd scenes, outdoor shoots at half-a-dozen locations (think rain delays).

- *Up the River:* Kayak scenes on river rapids. Mostly outdoor forest filming in remote locations. (The novella is in this anthology.)
- *Grandpa's Trunk:* Teenage time travel to Nazi-occupied France. This one sent my agent over the edge, "Don't you ever send me anything like that again." Gotta love the gentle rejection. (The short story is in this anthology.)
- *Infant King Kong:* I just dreamed this one last night. A mad scientist exhumes King Kong's brain from the last rendition of this classic movie and extracts DNA. In a truly mad moment, the scientist breaks into the Columbus Zoo and implants (yep, impregnates – wow, this will be fun to film) Fifi, the local silverback gorilla. In 8½ months, Fifi gives birth to a perfect clone of King Kong. The infant gorilla is stolen by someone other than the mad scientist. Monkey business ensues. I can hear my agent screaming, "What is it about 'contained' that you don't get?"

I think I'll stick to flash, short stories. Four-hundred-word limit? Are you kidding? I'll try to contain myself.

* * *

THE FARMALL F-20

N ot my favorite tractor, but my most memorable. As the Model T was to Ford, so was the F-20 to International Harvester. Basic. No frills. A whopping twenty horsepower of generic, red paint that could pull a two-bottom plow across a farmer's field. Hard to steal. Hand crank that broke many an arm of the unsuspecting. Manufactured from 1932 to 1939, cost a thousand bucks. My adventure occurred in 1958, twenty years of rust, grease, and dirt exuded an "I'm the Boss" patina. The F-20 won.

Father farmers make mistakes. Some mistakes result in the loss of fingers. Arms. Sometimes death. Most mistakes are just close calls, teaching moments that prompt dads to say, "Don't tell Mom. Let this be our little secret." Driving a tractor into a ditch is one such moment. No damage. Nothing flipped over. Might have taken an hour to extricate. That's another story involving the green John Deere 720 diesel tractor.

Ten-year-old boys constantly harangue and beg, "Come on Dad, let me _____." Fill in the blank. Independence is taught and learned in the delicate balance between Dad saying "yes" too soon or too late. My Dad said "yes" too soon at the end of one hot July day. I lived to tell the tale, so there goes the spoiler alert. I still have two arms and ten fingers.

Dusk threatened. The F-20, still purring, sat in the corn crib lot closest to the barn lot. Work day done. A short jaunt of one hundred yards. Maybe less. Maneuver through two gates, one ninety degree left turn, park, engine off. Easy.

"Let me, let me," I pleaded. "I'll drive it up here. Oh, please."

A scratch of the chin. Rub of the bald head. And then, the answer, "Aw, OK. But, no monkey business."

I was off in a flash. Up on the draw bar. Clutch depressed, gears grinding. Legs too short to sit on the seat and hit the clutch or brake. Accelerate. Superman wasn't this cool. *Hum, wonder what this lever does?* Hang on, here comes the teachable moment.

The lever on the left of the steering column operated the after-market hydraulic gizmo. Sometimes the F-20 had a front loader bucket or snow blade attached. The hydraulic lever would raise or lower whatever was attached. The current attachment was a ten-foot boom, like a flagpole sticking horizontally out the front of the tractor. Booms are very handy in lifting stuff into a wagon or truck. Always a lot of "stuff" on the farm.

As I'm driving through gate number one, I should be executing the required ninety-degree left turn to enter the barn yard. Instead, my ADHD, and the F-20 are in high gear. I'm focused on the hydraulic boom going higher and higher. As it rises over the main electric power line delivering electricity to the barn, I correct—more correctly, over-correct—my error. I lower the boom. Snap goes the electric line. Sparks dance on the gravel lane. A quick recovery would have resulted had I steered left through the barn yard gate. Lady luck was preoccupied. No time for me.

The flag pole boom, now at a perfect forty-five-degree angle, was ready to pierce the metal skin of the above-ground fuel tank. Remember that broken, dancing, sparking electric line? Yep. Panic time. Diesel fuel doesn't explode. Not true for the five-hundred gallons of gasoline buried under the dancing electrical lines.

Enter Walter, our deux ex machina hired hand. More nimble and just as timely as James Bond's disabling of the nuclear bomb in *Goldfinger*, the day is saved. I lived through another teachable moment.

Crap, here comes Dad. A scratch of the chin. Rub of the bald head. A kick in the seat of my pants, as he says, "Let's not tell Mom."

* * *

BULL'S EYE

I wouldn't learn the precise mathematical name for it until six years later in my first college calculus class at Ohio State: linear transformation. A multitude of algebraic equations could be solved simultaneously, thus outlining the parameters, or range of possible solutions to a complex problem. For example, a manufacturing operations manager could plot the factors of production: labor, raw materials, delivery time, customer demand, competitor price sensitivity, all on vectors that could reveal the most profitable mix of variables to aid production decision making. Each vector reduced to a simple equation that a ninth-grade high-schooler could solve. Solve all the equations simultaneously? Now we're talking college calculus. That wouldn't come for me until 1968.

October, 1962. I was a freshman at Simon Kenton High School. Lees Creek, Ohio–population 110. I know, because I did the 1960 door-to-door census. I also knew where the popcorn-ball lady lived. Had to get there early on Halloween before she ran out.

October, 1962 is also when the world held its collective breath during the Cuban missile crisis. Khrushchev had taken the measure of Kennedy after his humiliation 18 months earlier in the Bay of Pigs and found the youngster to be weak and naïve. The cold war was about to heat up.

At Simon Kenton High School, as with every other school in America, we practiced duck-and-cover. Lot of good that would do. Particularly in Lees Creek, Ohio. We knew we had a big bull's eye painted on our chest. We wouldn't have to wait for senior year physics to learn about nuclear fusion. We might experience it firsthand. Really? Lees Creek, Ohio? Why would little Lees Creek be of any interest to the Russians?

Linear transformation. Vectors. Pull up Google Maps and find Lees Creek. Obviously, we didn't have Google Maps in 1962. But my sleepy farm village was the solution to a Russian missile calculus targeting problem. From greater downtown Lees Creek, it was a crow-fly 43.09 miles to Wright-Patterson Air Force Base in Fairborn, Ohio. B-52's. Nuclear bombs. At the first alarm, all the B-52's would be airborne. Some on their way to Russia, others would scatter.

Clinton County Air Force Base was a Strategic Air Command scatter base in Wilmington, Ohio, 13.62 miles from Lees Creek. It was a poorly kept secret that some of Wright-Patt's B-52's would be deployed, or scattered to within spitting distance of my high school. The 302nd Wing of the Strategic Air Command, another vector.

The Air Force had also located a Nike facility 20.06 miles from Lees Creek. Nike anti-bomber, MIM-3 Ajax surface-to-air missiles were designed to protect Wright-Patt, the Clinton County AFB, and the popcorn-ball lady in Lees Creek.

One last point on the map and our weird-shaped, four-sided equation had its final vector, one last equation. Our very tired crow, that never attended college, could easily fly to the Melvin stone quarry that was only 6.47 miles northeast from Lees Creek. Most of the gravel for road construction and concrete came from this huge layer of limestone that was only about thirty feet below the rich farm land surface.

We practiced fire drills and duck-and-cover bunches during October, 1962. I don't remember precisely when the "Event" that prompted this chronicle occurred, but it was definitely before Halloween. One has to appreciate a high-schoolers' mindset at the time. Kennedy and Khrushchev were playing nuclear chess. B-52's were airborne, constantly. Some were probably already scattered within 13.62 miles of my second story Social Studies classroom.

Then it happened. Right on schedule. Every Tuesday afternoon at 2:00 p.m., the Melvin stone quarry would dynamite a new chunk of limestone off its rim. The sound waves hit the side of Simon Kenton High School in Lees Creek, Ohio, 30.29 seconds later. The windows rattled and shook, like clockwork.

Not one to let this event go unappreciated, I started bouncing my legs up and down like every other ADHD kid knew would be appropriate under similar circumstances. Other guys in our second-floor classroom joined in the chorus – teachers had previously admonished us not to do that.

The vectors were now all perfectly aligned. The windows rattled. B-52's flew over Turkish air space, at the edges of the Soviet Union. The teacher yelled, "Duck-and-cover!" We all hit the deck.

The rhythmic ADHD leg bouncing on the second floor caused the ranks of florescent ceiling lights on the first floor beneath us to sway back-and-forth. A rather-light-in-the-loafers teacher below panicked, ran out of the classroom, jazz hands flailing. He pulled the fire alarm.

We evacuated the building and looked toward the northeast horizon, fully expecting to see a mushroom cloud. The girls cried. The boys laughed, particularly those of us who knew how to spell ADHD. Khrushchev blinked. It was probably Kennedy's finest hour. The United States promised to remove some obsolete missiles from Turkey.

In 1968, I got a strong B in my first college calculus class because I understood vectors and linear transformation. The popcorn-ball lady died of natural causes at the glorious age of ninety-two. Truth be known, she probably passed out in a bowl of caramel corn on a Tuesday afternoon October, 1962. At precisely 30.29 seconds after 2:00 p.m. She's buried in Lees Creek Cemetery, under a limestone grave marker blasted from the Melvin stone quarry.

* * *

EUGENE

B eing born and raised on an Ohio farm doesn't initiate many Blacks into a close circle of friends with a young White boy like me. Two of my childhood heroes were older Black men: Oscar Robertson and Frank Robinson. I doubt that they remember me. Even after a four-year relationship, I doubt that Eugene remembers me either.

I first met Eugene on a shadowy, moonlit night in 1960. This older Black man was dead and buried four short years later. With the evening news full of Selma, Montgomery, and Martin Luther King, I was full of questions. Eugene was the blackest man I'd ever seen. His gap-toothed grin seemed frozen in time as the moonlight glistened off his gold caps. Try as I might, he ignored my frequent visits to his vine covered, one-room red brick house nestled at the intersection of Elm and Jackson streets in Sabina, Ohio. Is it too much for a twelve-year-old boy to expect one answer? One answer in four years?

It's not like the questions were tough, meaning of life inquiries. I never tried to stump him with the legal nuances of *Plessy v. Ferguson* or *Brown v. Board of Education*. I probably pissed him off when I asked if it hurt his feelings when Mark Twain referred to Huck Finn's friend Jim, as that N-word. I guess it was presumptuous to think that an old, wrinkled Black man who looked like 1929 death warmed over would honor such a question from a White brat like me.

Most of the urban legend Eugene stories were true. Yes, he got a new suit of clothes on his birthday; the day he was found north of town, dead near the 3-C highway. Yes, he was stolen, kidnapped, hi-jacked and taken on a tour of Ohio State – where he was found abandoned on a park bench. The "maybe" or "maybe not" ending to that last adventure involved a rush trip to University Hospital. I choose not to believe that exaggeration.

The one-room red brick spring house still stands at the corner of Jackson and Elm in Sabina. From his death in 1929, one-and-a-half million visitors, gawkers, pranksters, and I peered through the wrought iron bars at the old Black man. Had he not been buried in 1964, I'll bet Eugene would be dying to share his wisdom with new generations of White wise guys like me.

* * *

YEAST

I have two childhood memories of yeast, one fabulous, the other, not so great. Born and raised on an Ohio farm, I've spent a fair amount of time around fermentation. Now, don't get ahead of me. This recollection has no still or any illegal brewing or distillation. Wet hay rots, gets hot, and emits a rather foul alcoholic vapor. Yuck. Corn silage ferments and provides a daily happy hour for dairy cows and the farm boy serving it up. Corn squeezins. Some farmers were known to have lined the bottom of their silos with crock jugs plugged with a corn cob. Tons of pulverized corn filtered into an angelic, and legal cocktail.

A first pleasant memory was the brewer's bi-product mash delivered in wooden-stave, yellow barrels. Fifty-five gallons of heavenly delight. A five-year-old's eyes actually cross in wonder standing downwind of this cattle feed supplement. This gives yeast a good name.

A second memory advances my life-calendar another five years. I'm now ten. Dad took me to Cincinnati Gardens to see the Cincinnati Royals NBA team. Or more appropriately, to see my idol, Oscar Robertson. Not sure how my farmer father scored floor tickets in the second row, but we sat close. It was winter. Snow outside. Much too hot in the then-aged arena— long since demolished—let us pause for a moment of silence. Toward the end of the game, the arena was even hotter. The beer vendors had their rhythmic patter down pat, *get moody with Hudy*, with eager patrons around us spilling as much beer on the hardwood floor as they guzzled down their gullets.

Decades of spilled beer never actually drying, created swollen wood boards very similar to the bowed staves of the wood barrels in which the brewer's mash was delivered to our beef and dairy cows on the farm. In short, it smelled dank. A blend of Grandma's yeast rolls and Grandpa's socks.

Ever the one with never-ending questions, I asked, "What's beer taste like, Dad?"

Always telling the truth, never missing a beat, Dad's dry response came, "Horse piss." We had a team of Belgian work horses, a tad smaller than the more familiar Clydesdales. If anyone knew what horse piss tasted like, it would be Dad.

Drinking in moderation resulted. I never actually tested the hypothesis as the draft horses were replaced by an International Harvester "M" tractor. I accepted my father's theorem, untested, unconfirmed. Had to be true — why would Budweiser use all those Clydesdales in their beer commercials?

Gotta love yeast.

* * *

THE PORK FACTORY

F armers manufacture stuff. They plant seeds that grow into ears of corn, kernels of wheat, and oats for horses and little round-faced Quakers who look like the old round-faced Quakers on round cereal boxes. Guernsey cows produce milk and little cows called calves. I was raised on a hog farm that produced bacon.

A pig is a factory. Corn and water goes in one end. Manure with little embedded bits of undigested crackles of corn come out the other end. What's left between the two ends is called pork. Hams are closest to the end furthest away from the factory inputs. It's often said that the butcher uses everything except the pig's squeal. This is a story about the undigested crackles of corn in the... you get the picture.

The feed supplement salesman is basically a factory production efficiency consultant. He promises to convert this oink of a factory into a more efficient machine. By changing the chemistry of the inputs, the pig factory produces better pork chops.

"Really?" my dad challenged.

"Yep," the salesman confirmed. "Tweak the magnesium, adjust the phosphorus, and add a touch of iron. Bingo, bango. Your pigs produce more bacon."

"Prove it," Dad demanded.

"Can do."

"How?"

"We send a sample to the university and you'll get a full computer printout with recommendations."

"That's nuts. I'm saving up to send my kids to college. I'll be darned if I'm sending one of my pigs to Ohio State."

"Come on, Ben," the salesman laughed. "We ain't gonna send the whole pig. Just a sample of some pig poop. Pigs are like a factory. OSU will evaluate the tailings, the waste. If the waste has fewer nutrients in it, that means the factory, ya know, the pig, kept that good stuff inside it. More efficient. Better bacon. More profits for you."

"That's crap," Ben smirked.

"Exactly. That's the point."

Two weeks later, the mailman delivered a package from Ohio State. There it was. A computer, green bar printout of Ben's pig factory efficiency ratio, including recommendations. I was most interested in the cellophane-wrapped contents that accompanied the computerized pig crap report. It contained, and this is no bull: freeze-dried pig manure. The university returned the manure sample. Sanitized, but still, I was now in possession of two pounds of flaky, university-processed pig manure. Because it had attended college, this wasn't your average dumb pig shit. This stuff had been to college. Now, what would an ornery 14-year-old boy do with this treasure?

Ole Floyd had been our hired hand forever. He lived in the tenant house down the road. He kept his Mail Pouch chewing tobacco stash on the workbench in the barn. He bought this stuff by the case. I can't type these words as fast as your brain processes them, so let's cut to the chase. I settled on a 75/25 mixture. A half-and-half blend would have been too obvious. Being a chewing tobacco connoisseur, Floyd would come looking for me. Ten percent university-approved would hardly be worth the effort. Twenty-five percent seemed about right. Mix, mix.

I kept this secret for thirty years. Floyd attended my Grandma's wake at the First Baptist Church. Old, but he looked great. New blue suit. He was probably buried in that suit years later. Surrounded by my siblings and cousins, I confessed. I've never seen Floyd laugh so hard. I think Grandma even had one last grin in her.

* * *

WHISTLE-STOP CARNATION

Senator Goldwater stood on the back platform of the same train car that Truman used in his Presidential whistle-stop tour in that historic Dewey electoral contest. Playing hooky from school, I strangled the handrail inches away from my hero. To this day, I remember his wisecracks about the TVA and left-wingers.

Too young to vote or drink 3.2 beer, but old enough to go to Vietnam, I was enthralled as Goldwater spoke to my heart. His campaign stop in Blanchester, Ohio lasted all of 15 minutes. Our county Republican Party chair presented Mrs. Goldwater an armload of red carnations that she proceeded to toss to the adoring crowd. Elbows flying like the lead jamming queen from the Bay Area Bomber roller derby team, I held my position as the train chugged off to its next stop. Eye contact riveted on Mrs. Goldwater, my arm outstretched, she answered my prayer. A long-stemmed carnation left her hand and arched its skyward path toward me. I snatched it in mid-air.

Over the next 25 years, I treasured my Goldwater carnation. Initially dried and pressed between the pages of my grandparents' over-sized family Bible, a single laminated petal held an honored position in my wallet. Get a new wallet? Tough decisions, transfer the contents—driver's license, credit cards, Goldwater laminated carnation petal—to my new wallet.

Cycle forward 25 years to the late eighties. I lived in Los Angeles. Attending a business conference in Baltimore, I convinced a group to take a side trip to Washington, DC. At 1 am, it's beyond time to head back to Baltimore. We stayed, standing at the bottom of the U.S. Capitol Senate steps. Bam! The Senate adjourned with senators ambling down the Senate steps. I buttonholed my California senator, Pete Wilson.

It's as though the heavens opened and an archangel directed my attention to the top of the Senate steps. It's HIM! I stopped mid-sentence and gently maneuvered Senator Wilson aside. On a diagonal, I leapt, ran full tilt up the Senate steps. Later my friends would tell me that the Capitol police were closing in fast. When I reached Senator Goldwater, I grabbed my wallet. That's when the Capitol police reached for their weapons.

Short of breath, I told my idol my story. Just as I hope God will hear my plea (and excuses) at the pearly gates, Senator Goldwater was gracious and attentive. On reflection, I now realize he had no choice. I blocked his path down the Senate steps and he was hobbled, cane in hand, from recent hip replacement surgery. In short, he was trapped.

Now aware of the Capitol police presence, I saw them peel away as they overheard my story. While Senator Goldwater might have given them a nod, I suspect they became bored with my excruciating details.

I opened my new wallet, timing the dramatic extraction of "IT" with the inflection of my voice with all the emotion of the past 25 years. I fumbled. Stammered. It was gone. Chin on my chest, I was speechless. Under my breath I damned the day I became an adult and had cleaned out my wallet. Tough choices indeed.

Senator Goldwater transferred his cane from his right hand to his left. He placed his hand on my shoulder and said, "Son, it's alright. It's alright."

Take me now, Lord.

I escorted him down the Senate steps, small talk of which I have no recollection. Senator Goldwater got in his car—Chrysler LeBaron—rolled down his window and waved goodbye. TO ME. He honked his horn. AT ME.

His horn played "Dixie."

* * *

THE BIRDS AND THE BEES

It's the most dreaded day in any father's life. A man would rather sit naked on a block of ice at a church committee meeting than cover the facts of life with his daughter. I was prepared—at least with the paraphernalia—if not for the emotional gauntlet through which I was about to venture.

Seated in the family room, hormone-enhanced daughter at my side, I emptied the bag of stuff from the local pharmacy on the coffee table: creams, suppositories, foams, condoms. I had it all.

"Oh, Dad," she begged. "Make it stop."

"Okay," I agreed. I wanted it to end too. Like a broken record, I repeated it again and again. "Guys are after one thing. Only one thing."

"Oh, Dad."

"Hey! I'm a guy. I know. Guys are after only one thing."

"Oh, Dad. Please stop."

"I'll stop when you say it."

"Okay, if you promise to stop. Guys are pigs. Guy-pigs are after only one thing."

Whew! It was over. An embarrassed daughter ran to the driveway to shoot some hoops. I crawled to the bathroom to splash some cold water on my face. Exhausted—physically and emotionally—I peered into the mirror and pondered wrestling my younger daughter down to the family room and ruining three lives in one day. Lucky for all, she was not home.

As I exited the garage to join the hoop shooting, I dropped the birth control paper sack in the trash can. I doubted that

Goodwill Industries would have accepted the donation. The basketball had been abandoned in the side yard. Beside it rested Chase Warner's Moped. It was 1986; who rides a motorized bicycle in 1986? The cutest guy in my daughter's seventh grade class, that's who. But where was he? And my newly educated, yet still hormonerized daughter?

The question didn't dawdle long. From the woods flanking our side yard they emerged.

"Hey, Mr. Page. Can I have this?" young Chase asked.

Turning around, I was relieved that he was referring to the orange and white road construction barrier he and my daughter had freed from its Georgia-kudzu prison.

"Sure, fine with me," I said.

It was when he started to jerry-rig the metal sawhorse on the back of his Moped that I intervened. "No, no," I insisted. "Come back with your dad. You need a car for that thing."

Off he puttered. I was pleased that Mopeds didn't have a back seat. Drive-in movies were a thing of the past. Once in a while the old man wins.

About an hour later, I was losing a spirited game of basketball horse to both daughters. The senior Warner pulled his Mercedes into my driveway. The trunk lid popped open as the younger, twelve-year-old sperm machine jumped out and ran toward his orange-and-white, traffic-barrier treasure.

Whereupon I yelled across the lawn and into the woods, "Hey, I know what you're after."

It's been thirty years and my daughter has yet to forgive me.

* * *

259

THE GRAPH

It was an upper-level economics class—micro, I believe—I'd have to pull out my college transcript to be sure. I don't remember the course number. Transcript would answer that question too, but I'm too lazy to rise from my laptop right now to ascertain such micro details.

Economics was half of my double major. Except for a bait-and-switch Econ 442—really a master class in statistics with its over-indulgence on F-Distributions and Chi Squares—I was a pretty good student. I still hate statistics, but I'm over that. I needed an "A" in Micro Econ to compensate for the crappy Econ 442 professor's inability... oh, I'm over that.

A senior, I had figured out the ropes of success at a university as large as Ohio State. I knew how to sign up for 22 quarter hours and then drop the one class with the weirdest professor. I bought used books when possible, gravitating toward those previously owned by females, as they made more legible markings in the margins. In the late sixties, there were very few female business majors, and they were smart. Might as well take note of their used book markings.

It was winter quarter, 1970. I was graduating early and on my way to the U.S. Air Force Officer Candidate School. Things like that happen with a lottery number of... oh, my... I can't remember that number; I think it was 41. It was the first draft lottery and my number was so low, that pigs would fly before I could avoid military service. I wasn't about to hop on the 1970's Underground Railroad to Canada. A quick leap forward to close a loop, the officer training I received in the Air Force was top notch. I achieved "distinguished graduate" status.

The point of that last digression is simply to point out the importance of graduating on my early schedule and getting to San Antonio and Lackland Air Force Base to grab my 2nd lieutenant slot before some other dude flew over the horizon and nabbed it.

Back to the point at hand. Econ. I needed this class to graduate. I also wanted an "A." I was a great note taker. I used a cheap, spiral-bound notebook, a separate notebook for each class. There were only about three weeks left in my college career. I remember it like it was yesterday. I had just filled the last page in my Micro Econ spiral notebook when the professor sketched a complex graph on the chalkboard. I'm not talking about some rudimentary demand/supply curve or marginal revenue product formula. This was my streetcar to heaven. In one graph, all of micro-economics was at my fingertips. The fountain of all economics knowledge was elucidated in this one x/y axis square of lines and parabolic honey. The Forum of Rome was not built on a foundation as solid as this one graph.

I was out of paper. A student today would whip out an iPhone and take a picture of the best graph ever. In 1970, I'm up the river without a paddle. I'm sinking fast, not even a boat. Necessity created panic, then invention. I drew the graph on my right thigh. Bic pen on Levi's. It was perfect. Later that day I transcribed the most perfect micro economics graph ever to a new spiral notebook.

The next two weeks on campus were a blur. Meeting with advisors to confirm I had the requisite credits to graduate early. Rent cap and gown. Pass the final Air Force physical for Officer Candidate School. College graduation assured, I focused on the unknown; my head would be buzzed and I would become an

Air Force officer. I don't remember many final exams. But I'll never forget Micro Economics.

It was an essay exam. Only three or four questions. Sure enough, the last question required total recall of "the graph". I hadn't memorized it—didn't need to—I understood it. I could draw it and explain it in my sleep. My blue book had it perfectly sketched, by me, turn it in, get an "A". Then I saw it, indelibly inked, on my right thigh. OH SHIT! My mother had told me to do laundry. Would the professor see it? I turned pale, then blushed one of the reddest reds possible. Maybe if I pissed my pants, the professor might be distracted by the wet spot and not conclude that my alleged cheating had earned me an "F" and expulsion. OH, DOUBLE SHIT!

I took a long, slow walk of death to turn in my blue book, positioned against the top of my right thigh. In one motion, I tossed the blue book on the professor's desk and dropped my pen on the floor. Kneeling to pick up my pen, I made eye contact with the good professor as he wished me well.

To this day, I can still see the graph, burned into my retina. Off I went, into the wild blue yonder.

* * *

MOM ATTENDED MY
DRAFT PHYSICAL

Writer's note: this was a prompt in a Cincinnati writing group. What follows is a perfect match for that prompt. It is 100% true except (1) the "Mom" part is a total fabrication, and (2) this happened to a close friend of mine, not me, so the first person "I" has him, not me, telling the story. Got that?

* * *

It was March 27, 1968. My *Alice's Restaurant* day of fame. "Take the X-rays sweet pea," my mother cajoled, "the Army will never take someone with a right leg one inch shorter than his left leg. You can't even march in a straight line."

With a large manila envelope tucked under my arm and Mom hovering like a queen bee ready to sting, I showed up at the Pasadena Armory where the two-hour humiliation would be conducted. As I recall, I was the only draftee with his mommy in attendance. As I peed in the cup, she implored, "Wash your hands, Honey."

Eighty-seven draftees paraded around the cold armory in their boxers or briefs. From station-to-station I pleaded, "Hey, won't someone look at these X-rays?" If nothing else, the Army is consistent. Each answer came back, *"Later, show the doctor."*

When ten pairs of feet were ordered to toe the line, and "drop-trou", some of my compatriots thought the woman should have left the room. Nope. Mommy stood her ground. Latex gloves in place, the tight-gripped fulltime lumberjack and weekend Reserve Army torture artist snaked his way down the line. In turn, we each dutifully turned our heads and coughed. Thinking that a periodic change of gloves should have been employed in this task, I glanced down the line to discern how much penicillin would be in my future.

It was finally showtime, my personal, one-on-one with the Army doctor. Dr. Maj. Cold Hands sat at an Army gray desk in a small cubicle just off the Armory gym floor. Row upon row of freezing, splintered wooden benches creaked on the perimeter of the pine gym floor under the nervous twitching of 87 potential soldiers and one determined woman. Mom shared a bench with a skinny Black kid, all of eighteen. He was beyond embarrassed by his predicament and hoped this woman would not be his future drill sergeant.

Dr. Maj. Cold Hands yelled, "Walker, front and center." I cinched up my underwear, clutched my X-rays, and shied into the cubicle.

"Sir," I pleaded. "My family doctor thought you should see my X-rays. My right leg is a full inch shorter than my left leg."

"Toss 'em here son, let's have a look." The doctor eased the film from the envelope and held the foil up to the light. Squinting, he said, "Back up." I complied and took one step back from his desk. "Back up," he repeated. I might actually be good in the Army, as I followed each set of orders without pause. Dr. Maj. Cold Hands took one last look at my X-rays, and ordered, "Back up more, son."

By now I'm standing completely outside the good doctor's cubicle, on the Armory gym floor, surrounded by future soldiers cheeking wooden benches. All eyes were on me as I cocked my hip to exaggerate my deformed leg to highlight my hoped-for unfitness for Army service.

To my shock and dismay, Dr. Maj. Cold Hands yelled, "Drop 'em, boy." With feared compliance, I dropped my shorts to the floor. There I am. Buck naked, shorts draped around my ankles, and colder than an icicle clinging to a frozen gutter.

Then those glorious words that would get me out of the Army, but stunt my ego for decades, "You're right son, it's short. You're deferred."

Mom rose, patted her bench mate on the shoulder and lamented, "You're screwed, dude."

* * *

ELVIS HAS LEFT THE BUILDING

June 25, 1977. Riverfront Coliseum, now U.S. Bank Arena. I was there. I saw Elvis leave the building. Little did I know it would be his next-to-last concert due to his donut-induced death on August 17, 1977.

My brother-in-law, Tim, a student at UC, snagged me the tickets. For safe keeping, he secured them in his father's back porch insurance agency office safe. Smart move? Not so much. "Secured" is an understatement. This safe was a relic from a previous century, the kind of safe that Wiley Coyote would rig with ropes and pulleys hovering over his Road Runner nemesis.

This safe had a five number combination that got a mind of its own if the dial were spun too briskly. In short, the numbers would change. Yikes! A distraught Tim sat, cross-legged in front of this safe for every spare moment of three weeks. No luck.

Laura and I drove the 2 1/2 hours on the morning of the concert from Van Wert, Ohio to my in-laws' house. 1977 – no cell phones. No updates. As we pulled into the drive-way, there was a triumphant UC college student greeting us, waving two precious tickets in the air.

It was a fabulous concert. It was fat Elvis, split pants and all. I remember it like it were yesterday.

Cycle forward to August 17, 1997, the twentieth anniversary of Elvis' death. I'm stuck on an Atlanta freeway. A radio talk show about the anniversary of Elvis' death caught my interest. A caller had tickets for a cancelled concert – scheduled after his death – tickets that he decided to keep rather than get his money back. He asked how much this souvenir was worth. I almost choked at the $500 answer.

I double-choked and turned pale as the repartee continued. The radio host asked the caller what an unused ticket for a concert that took place might be worth. The caller pondered why an Elvis ticket would go unused.

I screamed at the radio, "Because my brother-in-law spun the dial on the damn safe!"

Before revealing the collector value, the radio announcer qualified that the ticket had to be in mint condition. No frayed edges. I screamed again when he said, "Five-thousand dollars. EACH."

Imagine if those tickets had come out of the safe AFTER the concert. I would have ripped them to shreds in frustration. That would have cost me ten-thousand dollars. What an idiot. In retrospect, seeing Elvis two months before his death might have been worth the ten-thousand dollars. Uh, maybe not.

Elvis has left the building.

* * *

NEVER AGAIN

I was one of one-hundred in the darkened auditorium. Tough guys. Four ladies; they were tough too. In a few weeks we would be 2nd Lieutenants in the U.S. Air Force. The tough guys would all go on to pilot school. They couldn't wait to fly jets over Vietnam. Air Force officer candidate school was life changing.

Appropriate warnings issued; the black-and-white newsreel started. It was stuff never seen on T.V. The Allies were liberating concentration camps, death factories in Germany and Eastern Poland. Huge pits. Bulldozers pushed emaciated bodies around like abandoned, splintered fence posts on a construction site. Except fence posts don't have arms and legs that flop around. Allied Army officers forced prim and proper German housewives and grandmothers out of Sunday morning church services. *"But we didn't know"* denials didn't excuse them from carrying bodies to the mass graves, soiling their best Sunday-go-to-meeting dresses. Tough guy, future Air Force officers watched in stunned silence. Most wiped away tears.

Decades later it was Yad Vashem in Jerusalem. I saw lamp shades fashioned from human skin. Mounds of eyewear wire frames, shoes, buttons. Then the Holocaust Museum in Washington D.C. It was all so macro. Huge. Hard to take in. Assuming the identity of a specific person with her passport made the Washington D.C. experience more personal. But it was easy, or should I say, convenient to stay detached. Swallow hard and move to the next exhibit. Wanted to get to the Smithsonian Air and Space Museum before it closed and see the Wright Brothers' plane. So very detached. Convenient.

The Center for Holocaust & Humanity Education OLLI offering might have been convenient, but it was not detached. The testimonials were personal. Real time. No scratchy black-and-white newsreel in a darkened auditorium. No large open pits with bulldozers. A real person. A survivor, with a real story.

I applaud the curriculum with its personal involvement, the exercises, and level of class participation. The words "Never Again" take on new meaning as these survivors will not be with us much longer.

"Never Again" is personal.

* * *

REVENGE

Office lunch klatches are part of our culture. Hundreds of thousands of them all over the country. Four, six, seven co-workers go to lunch together, every day, every week, year-in-year-out. They know each other better than they know their own spouses. Being a human resources guy, I avoided them – no full-time membership – but I would periodically wander by and be waved over to fill an empty chair.

Sarcasm, biting humor, tongue-in-cheek; all raised to an art form in these groups. I was summoned to a table to settle an argument in our company cafeteria. Tray down, I heard the arguments: "What's with this new 'after hours, walk me to my car service'?" Mary Alice asked.

While not responsible for this area, I was aware of its origin. "Well, with the start of Daylight Savings Time, it gets dark earlier. With our downtown office location, some ladies are uncomfortable walking to their car alone."

Mary Alice quickly responded, "So, I'm supposed to ask a security guard to escort me to my car?"

"That's the idea," I confirmed.

"Have you seen these security guards?" she asked.

Steve jumps in with, "Ask one of the female guards to escort you."

"What good would that do?" Mary Alice argued.

"Well," Steve paused for effect, "don't you think a rapist would choose the pretty one?"

All hell broke loose. As the HR guy, I almost choked on my corn muffin.

Cycle forward to the next day. Once again, I was summoned to an open chair – same lunch klatch. I should have gotten a poison dog from the street vendor wiener wagon. I guess I'm a slow learner.

The group was deep into a discussion of the latest product recall that hit the news. Evidently, defective condoms were breaking all over Los Angeles. A specific brand had been recalled, but only a limited batch.

Steve quizzed, "How am I supposed to know if I got one from a bad batch?"

Ralph commented, "The serial number."

"What serial number?" Steve asked.

"Stamped on the rolled-up end of the, you know..." Ralph added, embarrassed.

"Really? Where?" Steve continued, to his chagrin.

"Oh," Mary Alice said, waiting for Steve to take a drink of iced tea, "I guess you've never had to unroll yours that far."

Oh, sweet revenge.

* * *

FIREWORKS

Valentine's Day

My 20th floor Los Angeles office had a drop-dead view of The Griffith Park Observatory, Hollywood Sign, and, on a clear day, Catalina Island. Except in summer when the smog was so thick I couldn't see squat. That's when I closed my drapes to mask the depression, knowing it was there but couldn't see it. Crap.

It was the second Saturday of February. Drapes open. I was working on a special project in an office that was suffocating. I had forgotten that, in a moment of abject futility, the company shut down the air conditioning over the weekend to save forty-seven cents. Outside, I could see snow-draped mountains, the Pacific Ocean, and almost touch Catalina while sweating like a farm-fresh pig at my desk. The contrast prompted a drape closing.

Air circulation restored on Monday, February 10, I opened my drapes. Sarah, our receptionist, didn't have much of a view. People entering from our elevator lobby had the view of Sarah; she was a knockout. As the Chief HR Officer, I never used terms like that . . . then. Now? I'm retired. I confess. Sarah was hot. She was so sizzling, she had two boyfriends on the hook at the same time. The office banter and teasing started on Tuesday. Flowers? Chocolates? Which stud would win her heart on Valentine's Day?

Not to be outdone, each dude had two dozen long-stem roses delivered early on Wednesday, February 12. The same florist. The same vases. Same, same, same. Except, one had baby's breath – nice touch of white, purity caressing the red-hot roses. Did I mention that Sarah was hot? Not as sure about the purity.

The office staff was brutal. Two guys at the same time? Ever the mediator and calming influence, I offered Sarah a solution.

"Solution?" she queried. "That assumes I have a problem."

"Major league, sweetheart," I wouldn't dare utter that in an office today.

"Oh?"

"You have dates this weekend?"

"Naturally."

"With both?"

"Not at the same time," she grinned, thinking that might be worth the exhaustion.

Knowing it a low blow, but flinging it all the same, I pondered, "What will you do with the roses?"

Feigning circus juggling skills, Sarah retorted, "Rotate them."

"In the heat of passion, you'll remember baby's breath or sans purity? Sounds death defying to me."

"What would you suggest?"

"You can't take either set of roses home," I mused.

"Then both Brad and Bart *perfect names for our intrigue –* would be upset."

"Leave them here in the office Friday. Tell them you forgot. Simple. Problem solved."

Not completely sold on the strategy, Sarah returned to her business duties. The flower predicament continued into Thursday.

Thursday the 13th Sarah hadn't resolved her dilemma. That's when I dropped the unrefuted choice on the table, "You know, you'll have to leave them both here all weekend."

"That does make some sense," Sarah admitted.

"Except," long pause for emphasis, I offered, "they'll look like crap on Monday. It'll be hotter than you—*in my dreams I said that*—hotter than hell in here over the weekend."

"Such a waste," she admitted.

I offered an alternative on Thursday afternoon and again 87 times on Friday, Valentine's Day, "I'll take one off your hands for five dollars."

My entire staff begged Sarah to pocket the five bucks, just to shut me up.

I rarely, as in never, buy my wife flowers. She cried that Valentine's Day. I remember she liked the baby's breath.

Independence Day

Sarah's manager, Kat, graciously invited the entire HR staff to her lovely Glendale home for a July 4th pool party. Hot dogs, beer, all the usual. Seventy-five percent of my staff and guests were/are 15 years my junior. Attendance was high as Kat was an excellent host, the staff collegial, and everyone knew Sarah would be there. Did I mention it was a pool party?

I don't remember whether Sarah brought Brad or Bart. Maybe Brian or Bret. I don't even recall her pink and yellow bikini. I do remember the fireworks that night, as Sarah approached my wife and asked, "Did you like your Valentine's Day flowers?"

Busted.

* * *

NUGGET

I buried a friend tonight.

The pick of the litter. Pick might be a stretch, as his pup siblings had already been picked. Didn't know that when I phoned the golden retriever breeder. Drove an hour plus with two daughters and wife Laura to get the only one left. When we left I didn't fully appreciate that Nugget would be a perfect match, the only one for our family. Nugget threw up as we pulled into our driveway — evidently his first car ride. It took four attempts to find our family dog.

First attempt: a rescue puppy with long legs and webbed feet, returned to the rescue lady when we realized that fully grown black labs average 130 pounds. Second attempt: another rescue dog that bolted and ran away because I opened the car door before attaching a leash — this farm boy was ill-trained in use of hi-tech dog paraphernalia. Farm dogs? Never on a leash.

Third attempt: Peanut gets his own paragraph. A pet store purchase. Okay, give forth, a major-league error. Peanut, a beagle-like cross between Norman Bates and The Unabomber, turned on my pre-K daughters. A bark here, a nip there. He scared all of us. Matt Margolis, a self-described dog whisperer—*"We Treat Your Dog With Love"*—ran TV ads in Los Angeles promising he could train any dog. Imagine what this must cost, a dog psychologist in LA with a TV advertising budget.

I lied. Peanut gets more than one paragraph. Laura and Peanut (leashed Peanut) showed up for their dog psychoanalysis appointment. The miracle worker Matt Margolis who can "save" any dog, took one look at Peanut and exclaimed, "Fear biter! Fear biter!"

Laura called me at the office, distraught, "The miracle worker wants to kill Peanut."

"What?"

"You heard me. The world's most famous dog psychologist advises, demands, that Peanut be put down."

That brings us to Nugget. What a great dog. He followed Laura around like the lovable puppy he remained for 13 years. Never any privacy. While she read a magazine in the powder room, he rested his head on her thigh.

Little did Nugget know Laura would insist on his neutering when he spent too much time roaming the woods behind our Atlanta home. Payback came with the best practical joke ever. One day after the fateful surgery, one of my co-workers called Laura, "Are you the owner of the golden retriever I see fetching the morning paper on Misty Oaks Drive?"

"Yes, who are you?" she inquired.

"John Brownfield, I live around the corner on Spaulding Road. I got your number from the Edwards, your neighbor."

"How can I help you, John?"

"I have a registered female golden and I'm looking for a stud match. Is your golden registered?"

"I think so," an innocent Laura responded.

"Great. What say we team up; I'll give you pick of the litter and $500."

"I'm sorry, John. We just had Nugget fixed this morning."

"Oh, no! He's such a magnificent animal. I'm sorry to have bothered you."

My entire department, hovering in my office around the speaker phone, about exploded. A hesitant and somewhat evasive Laura related the phone call to me that evening. I let her flap in the wind for an eternity of 15 minutes. Terrible husband.

Years later, she called the office and told me Nugget died. Boom. Sudden. This magnificent animal headed down the driveway to fetch the morning paper when a chipmunk darted across his path. Nugget changed direction on a dime—leapt in the air—collapsed dead before his paws returned to the ground.

The drive to our cabin on Lake Lanier was long and quiet. A torrential rain masked my tears as I dug a hole beside the path that led to the lake; a path Nugget had raced down for ten years. With each shovel of muddied earth, I thought of pioneer families crossing the Kansas/Nebraska prairies who buried grandma or a child. I worked myself into a funk royale. I was a wreck. Soaked.

I buried a friend tonight.

* * *

THE STREETS OF PHILADELPHIA

I won a second term on the Van Wert City Council, November, 1977. Population 12,000–typical Midwestern Ohio small town. Great place to raise a family; I had a two-year-old and another one in the hopper. After six years at a small company, it became clear that career opportunities would be limited unless this little minnow found a larger pond.

That larger pond was Philadelphia. Instead of walking two blocks to work, I became a South Jersey train commuter, long enough to read the paper or catch a short catnap. Followed by a five-minute walk up Broad Street to wake up and get the juices flowing. Everyone's walk to work was brisk, focused. No window-shopping. Get a cup of coffee from the same street vendor – same route, same people.

The walk to the train station after work was less focused. More of a saunter, an exploration of zigs and zags. I would later learn that the New York City Manhattan walks were much the same. Window-shopping, new faces. In my first month, January, 1978, this naïve minnow swam upstream to Rittenhouse Square, one of the original urban green spaces planned by William Penn. Standing at the corner of 19th and Walnut streets, the pay phone behind me rang. I was only one month removed from Van Wert, Ohio. Thirty miles to the west of Van Wert, in Ft. Wayne, Indiana, radio station WOWO beamed its 50,000-watt signal into Ohio. Its annual Christmas promotion had Pavlov's dog's saliva still coursing through my brain. WOWO would randomly call pay phones throughout its listening area. If someone answered with a Santa-induced, "Ho Ho, WOWO", a fifty-dollar prize was the reward and entry into the Christmas Day drawing for a trip to Hawaii.

Waiting for the light at the southeast corner of Rittenhouse Square were a number of normal Philadelphians. And me. The pay phone rang. Ring ring, Pavlov. Salivate. Hand on the receiver, I answered, "Ho Ho, WOWO."

It wasn't a Christmas promotion. WOWO's 50,000 watts had not followed me to the City of Brotherly Love. There was love in the air, and it was more brotherly than this farm boy had expected. It was a solicitor. And he wasn't selling Reader's Digest or Columbia Records or vacation property in Florida. He solicited me. Welcome to the big pond, minnow. I was being invited for a drink at the Sheraton on Market Street. I played along; this was fun. Free entertainment. As newfound tomcat friend played with this little mouse, it suddenly hit me. I was the mouse. As I eyed the apartments, condos, hotels, and other skyscrapers that encircled Rittenhouse Square, I felt trapped. It dawned on me that this was not a random radio station call. The solicitor with whom I was toying was toying with me. He could see me, but I couldn't see him. I hung up the phone and took a hurried, circuitous route to my train station. I was late for dinner and haven't answered a pay phone since. It took me three months to amble by Rittenhouse Square again.

Other than losing twenty dollars to a street hustler in an ill-fated game of Three-card Monte, only one other life lesson came from my short twenty months on the streets of Philadelphia. Life's ladder has many rungs. People climb up, people slip down. It's rare that the climbing and slipping can be experienced at the same time.

It was the first real day of spring, April whenever. Monday, after a weekend of freshening rain. Jonquils were stretching to soak up the early-morning sun. I had just bounded up the steps from the train tunnel to greet an enthusiastic Broad Street. "The Guy" in front of me exuded positive energy. Tan suit, pastel blue shirt, pink polka dot tie. There was something unique about the spring in his step. Final job interview? First day on a new job? New girlfriend? Gonna get laid in a broom closet with the janitress after work? Whatever it was, "The Guy" climbed another rung on life's ladder with every step he took.

The City of Brotherly Love had a population of 1.5 million. Total for Southeast Pennsylvania was probably closer to 3 million. No need to conjecture how many witnessed "The Guy" climbing the Broad Street ladder of success at 8:05 on that beautiful spring morning. The commuters in front of "The Guy" saw the bus coming up Broad Street and quickened their pace. The commuters behind "The Guy", including me, saw the bus and slowed our pace. "The Guy" was all alone. Bounce, bounce. Springy step. Higher rungs – up he climbed. The city fell silent. We could hear him whistle.

Wait for it. Wait. Just as the quickened- and slowed-commuters had expected, the bus hit the only remaining puddle of water left within a five-mile radius of downtown Philadelphia. The tsunami arched over the sidewalk and cascaded half-way up the second floor of the building shading the sidewalk. "The Guy" disappeared. A collective gasp-laugh-ouch echoed from the Rocky steps at the art museum to Independence Hall. An "I'm-so-embarrassed-I-laughed-when-the-overly-obese-aunt-crashed-through-a-rickety-chair-laughs" at a family reunion. You know the kind of laugh. Admit it. You've all laughed it. All the oxygen was sucked out of the air. Broad Street gasped. Hyperventilated. Business productivity didn't return to normal until mid-morning. The Philadelphia Stock Exchange considered closing until noon.

Naval midshipmen can do it. Firemen can do it; slide down a ladder with hands and feet on the outside vertical supports, feet never touch the rungs. Top-to-bottom in one, smooth motion. "The Guy"?

He did it. Bottom rung of life, in one fell swoop.

Excuse me, I think I hear a pay phone ringing.

* * *

THE DAY A CO-WORKER MET
REGGIE JACKSON – AGAIN

F rank Bloom had a silver tongue. He could talk his way out of any jam. It was fun hanging around him, as long as you didn't mind being second, in everything. Frank would jump into someone else's story and steal the punchline. He was always the center of attention. When he gets to heaven, he will one-up God.

We never quite knew what to believe. If someone was all a 'twitter because they'd met a United States Senator, Frank would butt in and relate his most recent meeting in the Oval Office. Really? Truth be known, his stories were mostly true. It's relevant to my story that Frank had previously bragged about having met Reggie Jackson, the baseball player.

I don't recall the exact date—it's irrelevant to my story—but, let's assume it's the mid-eighties. That works, as Reggie Jackson wasn't inducted into Cooperstown until 1993. We were attending a meeting at the Hyatt Regency Embarcadero in San Francisco. Mid-morning break and off went Frank to the gift shop to buy something.

There he was, thumbing through a magazine: Reggie Jackson. Frank walked right up to him, extended his hand and said, "You're Reggie Jackson."

Not missing a beat, Reggie pumped Frank's hand, smiled and said, "And, you are Frank Bloom."

Rushing back to our meeting, breathless, Frank held court with every detail. "He remembered me. Reggie Jackson remembered, me!"

"Damn," a nameless skeptic retorted, in disbelief.

"H-he shook my hand, and called out my name," Frank continued with an uncustomary stammer.

That's when I acknowledged, "And, you're Frank Bloom," as I tapped my forefinger on Frank's name tag.

* * *

THE INTERVIEW

P rior to the days of Skype, GoToMeeting, Zoom, quality video conferencing wasn't readily available to the great unwashed. As a gig consultant, I had to find a Kinkos and schedule screen time to keep in touch with clients.

While on a six-month assignment in Warren, PA, I had an interview scheduled with a potential client in Seattle, WA. This future gig piqued my interest; the Mercedes company car prompted the wearing of a freshly starched white shirt. As was my custom, I donned coat and tie and looked professional from the waist up; khaki shorts and loafers wouldn't be on camera.

The nearest Kinkos was in Erie, PA. Ouch. A local suggested I use a facility on the outskirts of town. It was a retired, Pennsylvania State Government, red-brick campus large enough to house 5,000 people. Now underused, it housed not-for-profits and government agencies.

The interview went well. I was somewhat distracted by the "crawl" at the bottom of my big screen monitor. The top "crawl" depicted the Seattle company name and location. All good. Usually, the bottom "crawl" would display my current location to my hoped-for client in Seattle. Terror.

At the conclusion of the interview, I couldn't let it pass, I asked, "Does my current location appear on your screen?"

"Yes, it says Warren, PA," came the comforting response.

My actual screen crawl said: Pennsylvania Institute for the Criminally Insane. I didn't get the Seattle gig.

* * *

SIMPLE TRUTHS

J ust say it. Simply. Clearly. Only once. No pomp or circumstance needed, even though a wedding is at the core.

Sandy Springs United Methodist Church is only three miles from Dunwoody United Methodist Church in the upper class, Northern suburbs of Atlanta. The churches are separated by light years on the basics.

As a choir member at Sandy Springs, I was dumbfounded when our director announced at the end of rehearsal, "I've been fired." Then the bombshell, "Because I'm gay. The Administrative Board can't stomach this sinner cohabitating with the altar every Sunday morning."

The tearful discussion with the choir centered around "choice". Gary simply and clearly said, "Anyone who thinks being gay is a choice needs to walk a day in my shoes. Who would ever choose the road of hell a Southern gay man travels every day?"

Made sense to me. I quit the choir. It took me another six months to switch churches and join Dunwoody UMC. Gay marriage became the hot issue in Atlanta, and throughout the entire country. It was starting to sweep through my new church home.

Out of the blue, one Sunday, Wiley Stephens, the senior pastor deviated from the rigid order of worship. This good ole Georgia bulldog stepped from behind the pulpit and directly addressed five-hundred Southern parishioners with eyes that could pierce steel. With unquestioned resolve he said, "Listen up, 'cause I'm only gonna say this once. Whether two gay people decide to get married has absolutely nothing to do with the sanctity of my marriage or relationship with Linda. 'Nough said."

Gary Arnold and Wiley Stephens. Simple truths, simply stated.

'Nough said.

* * *

TIME ZONES

Her hand shook. Phone number dialed. Busy. "That's not possible," Linda pondered. Her mother was never on the phone at this hour. She re-dialed.

Awakened at 6:00 am Sunday, California time, the elderly Mrs. Miller fumbled the bedside phone, mumbling, "Hello."

"Oh, Mom," Linda Baker said, relieved. "I must have mis-dialed your number twice."

"What time is it, Sweetie?" Mrs. Miller asked, as she settled her head back onto her pillow.

"Mom, you better sit down."

"Sit down? Hell, I'm lying down. What time is it? Am I late for church?"

"I'm sorry, Mom. It's 9:00 am here in Pennsylvania."

"And you wake me at 6:00? Oh, my. Are the kids alright?"

"Kids are fine, Mom."

"Is it Chuck? Oh, no. There's been an accident," the tension in the old widow's voice rose.

"Mom, we're all fine. Just listen."

"Ya wake me at six in the morning to tell me ya'll are fine? Is this one of yer pranks?"

Linda still made time zone errors in keeping in touch with her California roots. Husband Chuck had accepted a promotion to the Philadelphia company headquarters and moved grand-kids and dog 3,000 miles away from Los Angeles Grandma. Linda did her best to keep her mother in the loop about soccer teams, scouts, and other goings-on. Last year's Philadelphia midnight call to wish Mom Happy New Year was laughed off as a 9:00 pm California mistake. It was the early morning California calls that lacked a sense of humor. This morning's 6:00 am announcement that *we are all fine* fell in the *where's the humor in this?* category.

Only half awake, Grandma Miller rolled to confirm the time on her clock radio. 6:05 am. Exasperated, she hung up the phone and pulled the covers over her head.

At precisely 6:06 am, as expected, Grandma's phone rang again. "No, I don't need a car warranty and I've already enrolled in Medicare," she blurted as she hung the phone up again.

At 6:07 am, Mrs. Miller let the phone ring seven times before answering, "Yes, dear. This better be important."

"Damnit, Mom. I won the lottery. Four-hundred million dollars!" she exclaimed, and hung up on her mother.

At 9:08 am, Linda let her Philadelphia phone ring ten times before answering. "No, I'm not eligible for Medicare, goodbye."

"Listen here, you sassy bitch. Who raised you?" the now awake gray-hair implored.

"Are we done with the pleasantries now?" the daughter asked.

Both women were breathing, panting, as if they'd experienced their first Chippendale's night out. Time zone differences aside, it was a straightforward event. A young woman in Philadelphia calls her mother in Los Angeles—hand and voice quivering—to share news that her fist clenched Saturday night's winning lottery ticket worth $400 million. As is was April 1, it took a good half-hour for Linda to convince her now wide-awake mother this was no prank. It's all so simple. Straightforward. Until.

Husband Chuck had not yet been advised of wife Linda's good fortune. A bass in his church choir, Chuck had an early Sunday morning routine. He always sang for the first service and was out and about on his usual - Seven-Eleven stop for a cup of coffee and the Sunday Philadelphia Inquirer. Straight to church. Sing at first service. Peruse the paper between services. Not an early riser, wife Linda, an above average soprano, would join the choir for the second service. She wouldn't see Chuck until 10:30 am. She'd share the good news right before second service choir warm-up rehearsal.

Chuck listened, bored. He seemed detached. Altos and sopranos hovered, pushed, tried to get a glimpse of Linda's winning ticket. The choir director dreamt of a new Steinway.

"You're not hearing me," Linda insisted, as she waived the lottery ticket in her husband's face.

Hubby grabbed the ticket from her hand, saying, "You can't sucker me on April Fools," as he tore the ticket to shreds and walked away.

On her hands and knees, an ashen, frantic Linda gathered remnants of her millionaire status. The entire soprano section looked like a flock of chickens, pecking at scattered seed corn in the barnyard.

Even the raucous laughter from the huddle of basses and tenors didn't interrupt the lady's jig saw puzzle assembly. "You what!?" a fellow bass bellowed.

"Wait 'til she discovers the drawing date on that ticket," Chuck whispered.

"It's next week's ticket?" a tenor queried.

"Yep. I saw the winning numbers at Seven-Eleven, bought a new ticket, snuck home and did the ole switcheroo in her purse."

Chuck is now in his third year of alimony payments and one-room apartment life.

* * *

ARE YOU LONESOME TONIGHT?

I've driven across the United States a number of times. It's a beautiful country—mountains, prairies, deserts, farmland—each route offering a unique, almost spiritual experience. Route 66 conjures images of George Maharis and Martin Milner Corvetting from town-to-town in pursuit of television adventures. Many episodes created angst whether the duo would be split as one pondered whether to stay put, usually at the behest of a charming young lady.

I divide my cross-country treks into two categories: with spouse and/or children and solo. Non-solo trips are lucky to average 300-miles daily. Issues of bladder control, McDonald's playlands, and driver need to scream at the horizon have a limiting influence on daily progress. The supervision of urchin passengers include head counting at each stop. If I've said it once, I've repeated it a thousand times, "It's now or never; this train is leaving the station." Let the record show, I've never knowingly left a child in a strange city. As an aside, I did forget my wife at church one evening; but, that's a story for another day.

The balance of this writing recounts a memorable solo drive from California to Atlanta, Georgia. I had left my BMW convertible with a friend in Los Angeles in an attempt to sell it. The 2000 dot.com crash had flooded the Silicon Valley market with a surplus of ego vehicles like mine. While everybody's somebody's fool, dumping my "baby" into this declining market didn't hold much promise. Gleaming in the California sun and fairly priced, no car screamed, *hey, I want to be wanted,* like my black-on-black yuppie machine. This car should sell in a week.

I wasn't left with many options when my friend called, after two months' of declining asking price, with an, "I'm sorry, there are no buyers for your car in this market." As I struggled with the decision, it became clear that I needed to get my convertible to Atlanta.

This solo drive would be different: quick, no McDonald's playlands, no 300-mile days. My goal was an 800-mile daily average. Interstate 10 lacks the romance of Route 66. Rarely did I pop the convertible top. I didn't need 80 mile-per-hour wind drowning out my CD's or a terminal sunburn on my forehead and balding head.

Dead-heading cross country can be boring. Early rise, strong coffee, drive, stop to gas and rid system of coffee, switch to Diet Coke, rest stop to rid system of Diet Coke, drive-thru sandwich on-the-fly, more Diet Coke. Blah, blah, blah.

There must be something to differentiate this trip from any other dude's solo drive from Los Angeles to Atlanta. Well, the day, or 24-hour period to be exact, I logged 1,200-miles was somewhat memorable. I recall it was 2 am. I had just passed through El Paso, Texas, proud of my 900-mile day. Exhausted, I decided to stop at the next flea bag motel that didn't look like it was owned by Norman Bates.

Pleased that I scored double queen beds at only $57, I unlocked the door and tossed my backpack beside the bed nearest the door. One final release of the day's coffee and Diet Coke, I removed my shoes, dropped my Levi's to the floor and slid between the sheets. I was zonked by 2:15 am.

At about 4 am, I was roused by a flushing toilet and a cough. Woozy, tired, I rolled over. Snoring started. Was I home? Damn, I'm not alone. Someone is in the other bed. I'm sharing a $57 motel room with a total stranger. At least Norman Bates might have given me my own room. I don't recall every detail, but I was back on the road within minutes, maybe seconds.

Eyes wide open, the balance of my 1,200-mile day went by in a flash.

* * *

WELL, SON

S mith Enterprises was an international corporation with a
long history of innovation and high margins. Family owned,
founder Smith was the hands-on Chairman of the Board, still
involved in day-to-day decisions. Old-man Smith was hanging
on to a company that was losing its edge – market value falling
from $1 billion to $750 million in the last five years. As a private
company, no stockholders, Smith was the boss; he controlled
the Board of Directors and his voice ruled the day.

I was retained as an executive compensation consultant to
develop a new incentive plan that would reward top execs for
returning the company to its previous days of glory. Working
closely with the Compensation Committee Chair, a set of goals
for the new plan was established: back-of-envelope simplicity
and fair to all stakeholders. The "fair" goal took on the tag line:
everyone should laugh all the way to the bank. The self-funding
plan would pay execs only if Smith Enterprises market value
increased and revenue/profits returned to previous levels.

The Compensation Committee was unanimous in its
approval of the new plan as was the full Board of Directors.
Chairman Smith agreed—his signature graced the plan document—and the plan was implemented. As a private company
with no public stock, valuing the company was not as simple
as referencing stock price in the Wall Street Journal. The new
plan provided for an independent valuation to assess the market
value of Smith Enterprises.

Cycle forward two years and the first determination of
incentive payouts. I had moved to California, joining a dot-com

software company. Smith Enterprises was a distant memory; until I received a telephone call from Chairman Smith's executive assistant—at 5:00 am Pacific Coast time. "Mr. Page, please hold for Mr. Smith."

Groggy. No warning or scheduling that would have enabled a quick cup of coffee. Only saving grace was the absence of FaceTime or Zoom as I'm stuck in my flannel jammies and hair all askew. Smith Enterprises was one of many clients. Which design? What was that short, bald guy's name who chaired the Comp Committee? Yikes, I'll get blistered.

It seems that Smith Enterprises' two-year results blew the doors off. Smith's market value had skyrocketed to surpass its previous high and topped $1.25 billion. Self-funded incentive plan? Indeed! Old-Man Smith and his family were worth half-a-billion dollars more in two short years. The catch, from Mr. Smith's perspective: the plan payout cost him $5 million. Not a bad investment for his $500 million.

Life is full of lessons-learned. When on a 5:00 am telephone call in flannel jammies, it doesn't help to remind an eighty-year-old billionaire geezer that:

1. The simple plan was penned by the Comp Committee Chair on the back of an envelope. References to Lincoln and The Gettysburg Address seemed inappropriate at this juncture.

2. The plan was self-funded so; *all parties will laugh all the way to the bank.*

"Well, son..." Mr. Smith started.

Any conversation that starts with, "well, son," isn't going to end well.

"Well, son," he paused for emphasis, "I'm signing these checks, and I'm here to tell you... I'm not laughing."

I haven't used that phrase since and I removed Smith Enterprises from my client reference list.

CHURCH SHOPPING

My family could write a procedural manual on how to choose a new church, complete with Gannt Charts and Excel spreadsheets. The Page Family Methodology has been field and stress tested at least 30 times. We've made only one mistake; it was remedied by a rapid deployment of our proven approach.

This recollection is based on Project 4A; search number one – one of three – in Atlanta, Georgia. For context, of the 30 searches, we actually attended 13 churches: all were Methodist, Presbyterian, or Quaker.

As it would be sacrilegious to copyright our manual, the Seventh Commandment waived, you are free to steal or lift any or all of these ideas. No royalties or tithes required.

Here are the basics:

1. Park the car.
2. Family team cheer, confirm assignments.
3. Daughters Miranda and Allison scatter to youth Sunday School classes.
4. Laura and I find an age-appropriate adult Sunday School class.
5. Reunite for church service.
6. Hang around after church to assign friendliness index.
7. Back to car.
8. Debrief.

For purposes of our discernment now, we will only delve into steps three and eight above and use one of our few forays into the realm of Southern Baptist.

Step 3 Miranda was 13, Allison 11 when we moved from Los Angeles to Atlanta. Mostly unpacked, when Sunday arrived, we hit the hustings. Imagine the courage it took for our girls to jump head first into these new situations, without a life vest or a first aid kit. We only moved our kids once; I marvel at military "brats" who moved every other year. What troopers!

Step 8 Not to inhibit or apply undue influence, we always let our girls issue their evaluations and opinions first. To set the stage, today's sermon was a hell-fire and brimstone expanding Moses' tablets from two to double digits and enumeration of a bagful of sins.

Miranda started with, "Why is he mad at me? I never met the guy."

Allison followed with, "Dad, what is gluttony?"

Back and forth it went: "Are all Baptists like this?" "The kids in Sunday School seemed normal." "I want my California Methodist church family back."

Miranda closed the children's portion of Step 8 with, "We are going to check out other churches... aren't we?"

Mom was quick with her verdict, "I'M STILL EATING CHOCOLATE!"

* * *

LOVE AN ACTUARY

A circle of friends shouldn't be people just like you. First the obvious; someone should be dumber than you. I try not to be that person in the various groups I frequent. Besides, I compensate by associating with close relatives, like my brother. At least one, no more than two should be more liberal. The one terrible at poker should be first on a speed dial list, again, that's obvious. I could go on and on, but my point is clear.

I recommend that every circle of friends should include one actuary. Go figure – exactly. Often (about 53.7%), actuaries travel in packs—a quotient of actuaries—be careful of adding too many to your group. Two actuaries in the same circle of friends is okay, if of the same sex. Perish the thought if an opposite sex actuarial couple falls in love and... yikes, they might breed and produce baby actuaries. I need a short break here to evaluate re-writing that last sentence. Let's move on during this evaluation period.

If an actuary drifts too close to your current circle of friends and you're not at or above your quota, check out the shoes. You may want to establish a dress code. Here's why – they are actuaries. Let's review a true example: we'll call him Robert, or William, or anything but his real name _____. Robert it is. At about 9:00 am I noticed something strange about Robert's shoes. Both brown. Both loafers. BUT, the left shoe had tassels and the right shoe was traditional penny loafer – no penny, Robert was cheap.

By mid-morning, 10:07 am to be precise, Robert was fed up with my harassment. My interoffice email inviting all comers to stop by his cube to check out his shoes might have been over the top. At 10:08 am, Robert went home to change his shoes.

At 10:38 am, Robert returned to the office, wearing the other pair of mismatched right/left shoes.

Ya gotta love an actuary.

* * *

SPONTANEITY

Not everyone in my intimate or oh-so-casual circle agrees that spontaneity is part of my charm. It is a huge part of what makes me... me, but there is widespread disagreement with my view of charming. Let's recount two examples, separated by 20 years.

Second example first. It's a new century: 2000. We live in a Bay Area mountain slice of heaven. Five acres of 200 foot-tall redwood trees. Career was on a roll with a few million dollars of stock options that would never vest; that's a story for another, more depressing day. Over my wife's objection, I'd purchased a black-on-black BMW convertible. On a Saturday morning, with 45 minute's notice, I announced, "Pack up, we're driving to Eureka, the Oregon state line."

After the first example, celebrating our tenth wedding anniversary in 1980 (try to keep up – that's 20 years earlier and documented later), you'd think my wife would have put her foot down. She didn't.

No reservations. Google Maps wouldn't be created for another five years; top down, not a care in the world, we weave our way up the California Pacific Coast Highway. Sunset at Mendocino. A local deli provided the wine, French bread, and cheese. I provided the spontaneity. We could almost hear the "stszz" as the sun disappeared into the Pacific.

Did I mention "no reservations"? No vacancy. Drive on. No vacancy. North. Drive on. Sure, we have a room. Two night minimum, $500 a night. Paid cash for the convertible – can't muster $1,000 for a B&B.

We drive. And drive. The romance of wine and cheese wears thin. I see a rustic sign promising "Cabin Retreat" and pull into the forest.

"Sorry, sir. I just rented the last cabin," the campground owner advised. "You are welcome to camp." She was gracious in providing pillows and blankets.

Camp? Ever try sleeping in a BMW convertible? Parked under a mercury-vapor nightlight, near the campground restroom? One of our better decisions, as the next morning would reveal, we drove 50 more miles before reaching civilization. Seems there was the annual Reggae-on-the-River Festival with 70,000 unwashed music lovers in the area.

We proceeded to Eureka, crossed the Oregon state line and deadheaded home. My wife gave me the silent treatment; I suppose her failure recalling our tenth anniversary, 20 years earlier, encouraged her reticence.

Back to example #1. Our tenth anniversary: 1980. We live in the Los Angeles area and hit the Pacific Coast Highway, North. With hotel reservations in San Luis Obispo, I thought a water bed would be fun, but that's another story. My life is full of other stories. We took a spin through The Madonna Inn and agreed we might return when our bank balance improved.

Time to head home – now no reservations, see a pattern here? – drive, drive. No Google Maps. No iPhone. Santa Barbara looks promising.

Laura pleads, "Off, now, this exit?"

Missed it. "I need more advance notice," I retort.

"Take the next exit, Mr. Spontaneity," she demands.

It's not the typical commercial exit: no McDonalds, no gas stations, no Holiday Inn. Looks upscale residential.

"There," she points up the hill, "on the right, park here."

I scamper up the manicured entrance, knowing this is going to cost an arm and a leg. I'll get a room and lie, not tell my wife how much it cost. I open the front door to an expansive lobby. The receptionist, decked out in crisp, white uniform-like garb throws a welcoming smile my way.

"Good evening," I smile back. "Do you have a room?"

"Excuse me, sir."

"Do you have any availability?"

"Why, yes we do. We have two rooms overlooking the garden and koi pond."

Not overly coy myself, I ask, "How much is a room?"

"Well, depending on the level of service, it ranges from $3,000 to $5,000."

"You're kidding," I choke. "A night?"

"Oh, no. Per month," as the kind lady further explained the full range of services.

Profuse in my thanks, I returned to a confused wife.

"Are we staying?" she asked.

"Maybe in fifty years," I smirk.

"Fifty years?"

"It's an assisted living center."

Spontaneous retirement planning.

* * *

RAISED BY YOGI

I swear I was raised by Yogi Berra. My dad loved baseball, just like Yogi. Dad was a catcher, just like Yogi. I don't know if Yogi rehearsed or had a ghostwriter feeding him non-sequiturs. For example, out on the town with fellow Yankees, when asked by a waitress if he wanted his pizza cut into six or eight slices, Yogi responded, "Six. I'm not hungry enough to eat eight."

Two selections from the thousands of paternal utterances explain all you need to know about why I am me. Both involve driving. Dad rarely used his turn signal. When he did, he was tardy—hitting the blinker midway through the turn—never before initiating the turn. When challenged, he always said, "I know where I'm going. "In 1978, my wife and I moved to Philadelphia. Long story short, Grandma died and the family farm where Dad was born and raised was sold. Dad retired at age 55 and moved for the only time in his 93 years. I didn't return for a visit for a year after the emotional auction that liquidated a lifetime of farm equipment and memories.

On my first visit back to Ohio in 1979, Dad took me for a drive around our old Lees Creek farm community. Per his usual, Dad didn't fasten his seat belt. Per my usual, I proceeded to lecture him on the dangers of such brazen behavior. As we drove by our old farm he admonished, "It's a short trip."

I retorted, "Don't you know that 75 percent of all traffic accidents happen on short trips, within five miles of home?"

Nary missing a beat, Yogi Dad shot back, "I fixed that. I moved."

I miss Dad.

ONLY LOVE CAN FIX SOME THINGS

I 'm a typical guy, I admit it. When presented the opportunity to ask for directions, I drive right on. My beloved spreads the never-can-be-refolded road map across the dashboard—clearly this is a pre-GPS confession and suggests, "*Dear, perhaps we should look for a motel.*" I play dumb. Every female spouse reader can predict the ending of this story based on the above facts.

It was the blizzard of the century, 2 am, some frigid below zero temperature. One-year-old daughter between us in a car seat that today would have us hauled before a Child Services tribunal. Pressing through Indiana, thirty miles to our final destination of Van Wert, Ohio, fifty mile-per-hour winds toy with two feet of snow across a flatter-than-pancake terrain. Visibility beyond the front bumper near zero. The only thing colder than the air whistling from the non-functioning defroster is the deadeye stare and unspoken, "*I told you so,*" from my wife regarding the number of motels we'd passed.

Flash. Blink. Tap the brakes. Slow down, slower. Praise all that is pure and holy. If this doesn't silence my wife, nothing will. Once in a while the guy wins. Yes! Three cheers for miracles. Can it be? He's going maybe only 20 mph, but – guy readers, it's our turn to rejoice – it's a snow plow. Who cares about zero vision? He's right in front of me. I have found Dorothy's yellow brick road. Don't gloat. Keep cool, all the way to Kansas, actually Ohio.

I tailgate my guardian angel for at least 30 minutes. He veers left? Yep, I go left. He dodges a mail box? I'm right behind him. I hum. I whistle. I tap drum beats on the steering wheel with my fingers. Smug. Arrogant. Triumphant. Those stress muscles up the back of my skull relax.

Is he slowing down? Stopping? Okay, follow his sharp, right-hand turn. The snow plow stops, flashers off, the exhale blast of air brakes give up the ghost.

The driver trudges through knee-high snow and taps on my window. Snow cascades across the front seat as I roll down the window, waking my daughter from her sweet dreams. Father error is indisputable when innocent babies cry.

"Hey, buddy," the driver shouts above the gale-force wind. "I'm home. Shift's over."

My hands in the twelve o'clock position, I strangle the steering wheel with my forehead pressed against the backs of my hands. My wife chokes back that snort of a laugh that caused me to fall in love with her in high school.

Only love can fix some things.

* * *

THE SCHOOL BUS

When I started the first grade, there were 22 students in my class. Over a period of ten years, after four rival schools consolidated, my graduating class had a whopping 93 students – normal for a rural Ohio school.

I was a second-grader when my school, Wayne Township – named after Mad Anthony Wayne – consolidated with Reesville, forming a new school, Simon Kenton. New friends. Train tracks passed within a half-mile of our new school – it took weeks before we stopped standing up to marvel at this welcomed interruption.

It's the second consolidation with New Vienna that provides the intrigue and adventure for this memory. An adventure that continues to this day.

A sophomore in high school, I knew lots of folks in the New Vienna community: 4-H, I attended a local New Vienna church, and I stayed with Grandma Page and Great-Grandma Page in New Vienna and terrorized the town as a kid.

I lived about two miles from my Simon Kenton High School. The first days of school with the New Vienna kids promised a whole new batch of friends. Our schools were friendly rivals and the consolidation was expected to go smoothly.

My school bus route was unusual, 90 percent of the students on my bus were from New Vienna – bunches of strangers. I was the first Simon Kenton student to board the bus; I hopped aboard and noticed a few giggles and snickers as I looked for a seat. It wasn't the first day of school, but definitely in the first week. I glanced down and confirmed my fly wasn't open. *What gives?* Every seat was occupied until I got nearly to the back; there was an empty seat beside a cute girl I didn't know. Being a guy of above-average intelligence, I sat next to Weegie Hughes – as an adult, she returned to her given name, Laura.

I forget when I learned that this random event had been planned by my future wife of 51 years. She had arranged that the only available seat when I entered the bus was next to her.

To this day, I write a short phrase in her birthday and anniversary cards.

Thank you for saving me a seat in your life.

* * *

CPSIA information can be obtained
at www.ICGtesting.com
Printed in the USA
LVHW041919120322
713227LV00001B/9

9 781662 837968